Wattsville

By

Juneus F. Kendall

ISBN: 1439270333

ISBN-13: 9781439270332

Wattsville, WVA.

Chapter One

The smooth, winding dirt road descended sharply for about a half mile under the cover of a dense, hardwood forest canopy before entering Wattsville.

The town sat in a narrow hollow closely rimmed by steep mountains. Houses sprinkled the hillsides and lined both sides of the road that ran east along a flat strip of land beside the creek. The rail-yard with loaded gondolas parked on sidings spread out to the west. Flames licking out of air vents around the domes of coke ovens along the creek bank illuminated the dreary western sky, radiated heat waves into the cool morning air and rumbled steadily against the stillness.

Wattsville occupied the upper or eastern part of the valley with a few "habitated" hollows such as Duck and Dogtown down-stream from the coke ovens. Privies jutted out over the creek banks and hog pens were scattered here and there at the water's edge.

Buffalo Creek collected water from numerous smaller tributaries and rivulets wandering down the mountainsides, skirted the edge of the town, accompanied the rail line through a narrow opening in the hills to the west and descended into the Elk River below Clendenin thirteen miles away. Any place else the stream would have added to the ambiance of the community. In Wattsville it was "just a dadburn nuisance" as Beatrice Parker, the cook at the hotel, liked to say.

"It floods in the winter, some child drowns in it ever year or so, and everbody thinks it's a place to th'ow things. You never seen such a collection of trash and old car bodies in all your born days."

Doc had been up for the last thirty six hours and he was exhausted. He ran his fingers through his oily hair and rolled down his car window as he approached the town. The cool air refreshed him momentarily. The road narrowed and took a little jog between the two houses of worship.

Not long after the Buffalo Creek Interdenominational Temple building was completed, an argument ensued over whether Christ actually washed his disciples' feet, or if that passage in the Bible were merely symbolic. A group split off and built The Tabernacle of Zion. The Tabernacle of Zion imposed itself defiantly on the creek bank and on the road; and appeared to squeeze The Buffalo Creek Interdenominational Temple against the hillside.

Church services were just getting underway as Doc drove between the houses of God. The sounds of singing collided in the space between the buildings, filled the hollow, echoed off the hillsides, caromed past the coal tipple, and fizzled over the rumbling fires of the coke ovens. Which song drowned out the other mattered inordinately to those pious singers - their voices straining for attention.

Rock of ages, cleft for me,
Let me hide myself in Thee;

SHALL WE GATHER AT THE RIVER WHERE BRIGHT
ANGEL FEET HAVE TROD...

Let the water and the blood,
from Thy side, a healing flood,

WITH ITS CRYSTAL TIDE FOREVER FLOWING BY THE
THRONE OF GOD...

Be of sin a double cure,

YES, WE'LL GATHER AT THE RIVER...

Save from wrath, and make me pure.

THE BEAUTIFUL, BEAUTIFUL RIVER...

There were separate pews for males and for females, and rails up the middle of the stairs leading to doors set apart in the front of the buildings to accent the custom. The steps on the left, or the ladies side, were well worn and the pews on the right were sparsely occupied. A preacher could get a crick in his neck sermonizing to his lop-sided congregation.

The women of the town socialized depending on which church they attended, and the men mingled freely outside while waiting for their womenfolk to emerge from services.

The men congregated under a tree for shade in summer or stood with one foot on the back bumper of a car for the warmth of the sun in winter months. They talked primarily about the mines, union activities, or about hunting and local sports. If it were cold enough or if it rained, they might go inside and sit in the back. Occasionally, they even attended service on a mild day, but not any more often than they could help.

"First place, it ain't manly and ain't no woman 'a mine gonna' henpeck me and tell me I got to go to no church. Les' I decide it on my own," they agreed with each other as they passed the time.

"Wonder what Alf's woman has got on him?" they speculated when they saw one of their cronies marching up the stairs all scrubbed and stiff. "Must be som'thin' right serious to git Alf inta' the Lord's house like at'. Suppose she'll get him to testify?" They guffawed and slapped backs around the group at the thought of old Alf testifying. "Take a mighty sturdy church buildin' to withstand that," they agreed as they contemplated the consequences of such an unlikely event.

Several waved or touched their hat brims as Doc drove by; he smiled and extended his arm out the window.

Congregations fluctuated back and forth over the years as loyalties changed, marriages occurred and personal feuds erupted. They had long since lost their distinctions of *"Wet Foots"* or *"Dry Foots,"* as the local barflies once distinguished them when their wives were out of earshot; but they had not lost their sense of rivalry.

If the weather allowed, the preachers opened their windows and competed to see who could preach and sing the loudest. Members stood to *"testify"* before the congregation as to their spiritual activities. It was kind of like confession in the Catholic church, but testifying was public.

"That bull of mine knocked Merle Prowse's fence down and trampled his missus' lilacs. I paid the damage and never uttered a unkind remark towards that animal. I held my temper in that tryin' circumstance and refrained from blaspheming the Lord's name," Orville Connelly might testify in his sing-song delivery. Hallelujahs and amen's interrupted and punctuated his narrative, and on a warm day the cacophony would drift across the road into the pews of the Tabernacle of Zion.

Or Brother Whipple might start out by the window speaking softly about how a swarm of hornets had chased him out of his corn field but he had held his temper. As he warmed up he might pull off his coat, then his tie and pretty soon he would begin hopping around from one bench to another. "I tried runnin' into the corn crib and out the back," he might sing. "But them bees refused to be cornered." Then with his shirt awry, his hair out of place, his red face dripping with sweat, he would bellow at the top of his lungs as to how he maintained his decorum in the face of his painful ordeal.

Momentarily the sermon at the Buffalo Creek Interdenominational Temple might even be halted in the face of the power of Brother Whipple's testimonial issuing forth from the vestry across the way.

Testifying was a man thing, "Praise the Lord," women almost never indulged themselves publicly. Preachers were "called," served without pay and were usually better at *"Hell Fire and Brimstone Damnation"* than at spiritual support of their parishioners.

"There's a lot of judgin' to be done between now and Judgment Day," Preacher Samples was wont to say and Pastor Goad predicted the condemnation of most of his parishioners to *"Hell's Fire and Perdition."*

It was not unusual to have a sermon begin at the pulpit and bounce to the alter rail, the top of the old upright piano, then two or three rows into the congregation. When

Preacher Goad was disappointed in his congregation, which was frequent, he would sermonize to the wall and exhort his flock to "*Get thee behind me, Satan*". Sometimes the power of God would be mighty real in those tabernacles of "the Lord" and souls were saved regularly, some of them repeatedly. Backsliding was a local tradition.

The lyrics faded as Doc drove on, but the piano chords pulsated into his consciousness until he closed the front door at home. He lay down across the bed and when Shirley came in from church, she covered him with a quilt. He was still sleeping later that evening when she and the boys had their supper.

Shirley turned down the quilt to climb in beside him when there was a knock at the door. She slipped on her robe and went to the front of the house.

"Sorry to trouble you so late Missus, but Birdie needs the Doctor awful bad." It was a neighbor of the Blackwell's who lived up on the ridge above town.

"I'll get him up. You wait here," Shirley said.

Doc came padding into the living room yawning and rubbing his eyes. "What's going on?" he asked.

"I guess Birdie Blackwell's about to hatch," the man answered. "Her Maw said you best hurry up. She's hurtin' real bad and the midwife cain't help her a'tall."

"You go on ahead and tell them I'll be there as soon as I can." After he got dressed, Doc kissed Shirley and drove out of town.

After his military service, Earl Sizemore had brought his new wife, Shirley, to Wattsville where he had grown up with mountain people, many of whom lived up isolated hollows hemmed in by mountains and side-stepped by progress. Their buildings were in disrepair; their farm and mining equipment lay rusting in neglected fields; privies settled unevenly in back yards; and barn walls rotting at their bases looked like old men in need of dental care. Doc understood mountaineers. He respected them. He was comfortable with them, but there were times...

The little shack was dark except for a couple of oil lamps and Birdie was writhing around in the bed moaning with pain. Doc drew up a chair and sat down beside her and put his hand on her abdomen.

"I'm here to help you, Birdie."

"Lordy Jesus, God A'mighty, Doc! Ooooh, Christ have mercy, Doctor Sizemore!"

"I need to check the baby's position, Birdie. Just hold still for a minute." He hastily slid his hand into a rubber glove from his delivery pack and reached up inside Birdie's vagina.

"Don't shove sa' hard, you're killin' me!"

"Hold still, Birdie! Hold still, now! I'm trying to help you, Birdie. Let go of my hand! Damn, Birdie, let go! I'm about to get it Birdie. Hold still now! It's turning Birdie! It's turning!" Suddenly, water gushed out between Birdie's legs and her abdomen collapsed. "Damn, Birdie! Damn it all. Now I'll have to deliver this baby rump first."

"Lordy Jesus! Doctor Sizemore. I couldn't`a stood much more`a that."

As Doc relaxed and worked his fingers to restore their circulation, beads of perspiration began to form on Birdie's face.

"I don't feel sa' good, Doc," she whispered.

The bed-sheets, already soaked with amniotic fluid, began to stain red.

Birdie's sister, May Belle, leaned against the door frame and their mother stood with one hand on the headboard of the bed looking worried. Though Birdie's face was indistinct in the flickering shadows of a kerosene lamp, the two women had attended enough births to know she was in "a heap a' trouble."

Doc held Birdie's hip and pushed his hand hard into her pelvis.

"Oh, Doc! Owe, Ooooo! Stop that!"

Birdie tried to pull away, but her feet slipped on the soggy bed-clothes. She turned her head toward the wall and vomited. May Belle bolted from the doorway, grabbed the edge of the bed sheet, and wiped Birdie's face.

"Stop writhing around so, Birdie," she said. "Ya' got ta' hold fast. Doc's trying to help you the best he can."

"Lordy Jesus, God have mercy!" Birdie pleaded.

Doc worked his fingers through the partially dilated cervix, slipped his forefinger over the fetal knee and slid his fingertip down the front of the shin. Wrapping his finger around the ankle and, with his thumb pressing on the tiny heel to extend the foot, he delivered one leg into the vagina. Birdie held her breath and strained.

"I'm fixin' to shit on you, Doc," she groaned.

"No, you're not, Birdie. Stop pushing now and relax." Doc fumbled in the bundle he had brought with him and pulled out a long piece of gauze. With two quick maneuvers he slipped a clove hitch over the baby's foot and pulled the buttocks down against the hemorrhaging placenta. He increased the traction until the bleeding stopped, then eased off just a little.

Birdie labored deep into the night. Rain pelted the tin-roof and the thin walls of the shack. The air grew heavy with sweat and body odor. Doc's hands and shoulders ached unmercifully.

"I'm fearsome tired, Doc. Cain't you do something?"

Dr. Sizemore smiled wearily.

"I ain't never had no baby born'd like this. I cain't stand much more, Doc."

"Hang on, Birdie, hang on."

"Ain't they something you can do 'sides just sitting there, Doc?"

"It won't be long now, Birdie. You're doing good. You're doing real good."

Birdie's heart rate stayed around one-hundred-and-forty between labor pains; her systolic blood pressure never dropped below ninety. Her retching stopped; the perspiration on her forehead evaporated. She drifted off to sleep between pains and resumed her appeals as soon as the next contraction began.

"Cain't you just knock me out, Doc?"

"No, Birdie. That would be dangerous for the baby."

"I'm hurting awful bad, Doc. They must be something you can do more'n just sitting and waiting."

Doc noted the fetal heart rate varying normally as the intensity of the contractions changed. The only sign the baby might be in distress was the black, meconium stain on the bedclothes, but that was not uncommon with a breech delivery.

The wind brushed tree limbs against the side of the house, rattled the rafters and fluttered the lamplight where it pierced cracks in the wall. Rain pelted the tin roof and dripped in a bucket in the kitchen. Doc nodded and recovered intermittently, and changed his grip to give his hands and shoulders and his neck a rest.

When the cervix finally dilated and the baby's buttocks began to ooze into Birdie's vagina, Doc eased the body out until he could slip his fingers up under the chin. He suctioned the mouth and nostrils with a rubber syringe, slipped forceps over the temples of the after-coming head and delivered a lusty boy followed by a rush of dark fluid. He lay the baby on a clean blanket on his lap, tied the cord, handed the bundle to Birdie's mother and reached back into the blood-filled vagina.

His hand slipped easily through the flabby cervix. With educated fingers he probed the wall of the uterus for fragments of the afterbirth. Dusky-colored blood ran down his arm and dripped from his elbow.

He looked up over Birdie's flaccid abdomen. Her hair was soaked with sweat; her face an ashen mask. He placed a finger on her pulse. It was too weak to count. He pumped up the sphygmomanometer cuff and listened at the elbow: nothing. His fingers trembled as he took the red rubber tube out of its tray and placed it on the sideboard.

"May Belle, lay yourself down here beside Birdie. We have to give her a transfusion right away. There's no time to waste. Do you understand?"

May Belle hurried around the bed while Doc slid Birdie to one side of the mattress. He wiped their arms with alcohol and wrapped a cord around Birdie's arm - nothing. He rubbed and slapped the skin - still nothing. He stuck a needle into her mottled skin and a faint trickle of blood oozed up into the hub. May Belle's veins stood out like blue snakes and when he slipped the needle into her arm the rubber tube attached began to throb. Pinching it gently between his thumb and forefinger to measure the flow, he watched the second hand on his pocket watch.

After removing the needle from May Belle's arm, he held the tube above his head to let the remainder drain into Birdie's circulation. Then he removed the needle from her vein and cast the hose into a shallow pan. He wiped the blood off his watch with the edge of the sheet and watched the second hand while he checked to see how she had tolerated the procedure. Her pulse was one-hundred-fifty-five, her blood pressure eighty systolic. The transfusion had helped. He just prayed that their blood was compatible. He was gratified that no reaction occurred during the procedure.

"Now you be sure to let me know right away if Birdie starts running a fever or has a lot of pain over her kidneys or anything like that," he said to Birdie's mother.

May Belle's pulse was ninety-five, her blood pressure one-hundred-and-ten over sixty.

Doc patted Birdie's arm. "He's a healthy boy, Birdie."

Birdie's mother held the baby up and folded the blanket away from his face.

"He sure is funny lookin'," Birdie said. "I cain't thank you enough, Doc. That's for sure."

Doc had his hands on his hips. Every muscle in his body ached. His joints cried out for movement.

The air hung heavy with the odor of bowel gas, vomit, decaying blood and kerosene. Birdie's grandmother, sitting in the kitchen, nudged a wad of tobacco with her tongue, spit into a coffee-can on the table and wiped her chin with the palm of her hand. The midwife, who had been standing in the shadows, smiled at Doc and moved closer to the bedside. May Belle slipped quietly off the side of the mattress and seated herself in a rocking chair.

"How do you feel, May Belle?" Doc asked.

"I feel right well thank you, Doctor Sizemore." She grasped the arms of her chair and rocked back and forth as if to prove the extent of her vigor.

Doc stretched his arms above his head and leaned back to relieve the tension in his spine. Moonlight, filtering through parchment-covered windows, cast a yellow tint on everything it touched. The rain had let up, and the wind had died down.

"Best I get out of here, I could do with a nap before the clinic opens," he said. He gathered up the big metal pan, the sheets, forceps, and various other instruments he had brought and placed them in a cotton feed sack. "I'll come back up here to see you in a few days, Birdie. I'll circumcise that boy for you then. I don't want to hear of your getting out of bed `til I say so. You hear?"

"I do feel a might peak'ed, Doctor Sizemore."

"I didn't have time to check for compatibility between your blood and May Belle's so you might run a fever sometime in the next day or two. If it's more than a hundred, or if you get sick, send someone to fetch me. You understand?"

Doc patted her leg, gathered up his medical bag, threw the sack over his shoulder, and headed out the door. He crossed the muddy yard and placed the medical equipment on the back seat of his new Plymouth. He lit his first cigarette in almost twelve hours and inhaled deeply. Energy crept back into his body and the tobacco's fragrance dispelled the sanguineous stench from his nostrils. He rotated his head to relieve the cramp in his neck muscles and massaged his scalp with the tips of his fingers.

There was a thin line of dawn hovering just on the horizon, the moon stood crisp in the lightening sky and tree frogs chirped in the surrounding forest. The little shack with lamplight flickering through the opaque windows and rusty tin roof buckling up on the ends like a ramshackle pagoda, leaned into the hillside as if afraid it would fall down in the next gust of wind.

Doc tossed his cigarette into a puddle. *I've got to stop woolgathering and get myself down off this mountain,* he thought.

Heavy downpour in the night had turned the road into a treacherous quagmire, so he drove in first gear with his hand lightly retracting the emergency brake. Oversize flange wheels and the extra leafs in the springs had been worth the wait, the undercarriage of the stock Plymouth in the showroom would have dragged impossibly.

When he pulled onto the hard road the car slid across the mid-line, but the new treads quickly bit through the muck clinging to the tires and he avoided slipping off the berm. He threaded his way along the narrow strip of highway clinging to the hilltops without seeing another car. He lit another cigarette and flicked ashes into the small tray tilted out of the dash board. As he topped the crest of a rise, a sign - almost obscured by foliage - appeared by the roadside. A stranger hurrying along the highway between Clendenin and Gauley Bridge would hardly notice the turn-off.

"No one gets to Wattsville unless they's coming here. And that's right fine by me," Beatrice Parker often remarked. "Last thing a body needs is some city-slicker wandering into some place he's not invited and poking his nose in your business."

Doc put his cigarette between his teeth and used both hands to turn the steering wheel then quickly shifted down to second to save his brakes.

As he approached the row of company houses, the sun peeked over a notch high in the hills to the east. There was a nip in the air he had not noticed when he was up on the ridge. A faint drizzle glistened on the macadam surface that stretched from the hotel to the schoolhouse. Before he got to the bus station mud from his tires started pelting the underside of the fenders. Driving past the hardware, grocery and dry goods store, barber shop, service station, Shorty's Bar & Grill and the Lyric Theater (which had been closed for five or six years) he wondered why he had returned to this dying town. After crossing the bridge to the clinic parking lot, he turned off his headlamps.

He slowly mounted the steps and unlocked the door. In his office he sagged heavily into the big chair behind his desk. His head slumped forward and he began to snore softly.

He could not guess how long he had slept when he was awakened by the rattle of something striking the window and the sound of a voice at the side of the building. He hobbled to the door rubbing his eyes. Hilda Mollohan stood on the porch with Leroy, her youngest, in her arms. Her face was red and her neck swelled from the strain. Doc covered his mouth with his hand and yawned.

"Guess I was sleeping pretty sound."

"Leroy's in right smart of distress, Doc," Hilda wheezed. "He fell out a' the loft. Climbin' when he shoulda' been gatherin' eggs."

Leroy, whimpering softly, clung tightly to his mother's neck and his foot turned off at a grotesque angle. Just then Bert Mollohan came around the building.

"Beg pardon for knocking sa' hard on the winder, Doc. We hollered out here in front for quite a spell. We knowed you was inside. We seen your new automobile out front.

"Bring Leroy on in here. We'll get him something for that pain." Doc stepped away from the entrance.

Hilda hoisted her son up onto the examination table as gently as she could.

"Now don't be afraid, Leroy. This will stop your pain."

Doc held a mask loosely over Leroy's face and dripped Ether from a screw-topped can directly onto the cotton. Leroy tried to push Doc's hand away. "Hold still now, Leroy," he said. "Take a deep breath, son and the pain'll be gone directly." Leroy only resisted briefly before he began to snore. "Here Bert, hold this over his face," Doc said. Bert leaned forward and placed his fingers around the mask.

Doc reduced the fractures and applied a long leg cast with a split to accommodate swelling. "Bert," he said. "That's a bad break, we need to get a picture of Leroy's ankle. You just take this slip over to Clendenin and Dr. Butterworth will X-ray the fracture so we can tell if it's in proper alignment."

"Looks good to me. Don't know as we can get over to Clendenin any time soon, Doc."

"Sure would be helpful if you could get your boy over there within the next few days. If he needs surgery, it would best be done right away."

"We'll try our derndest, Doc." Bert looked at the floor. "The company hit me right hard this month, and we ain't hardly getting by as it is. If it wasn't for the check-off at the mine, we couldn't'a even come in here."

"I understand, Bert. It's tight with me, too."

Mrs. Sidenstricker came up the steps. "Hi Bert. Hello Hilda," she said. "Looks like you had an accident there, Leroy. I bet you'll be better right soon."

"Thank you, Mam," Leroy answered, his voice hoarse from the ether.

"And a good morning to you, Doctor Sizemore." Mrs. Sidenstricker slipped past Doc and walked down the hall, removing her coat as she went.

Doc went into the bathroom, splashed cold water on his face and straightened his clothing.

"Been sleeping in the office again, I see," Mrs. Sidenstricker said as she handed him a cup of coffee with just the right amount of cream. "Won't do anybody any good for you to kill yourself." She stood for a moment with one hand on her hip then turned and walked heavily to the window and slid back the frosted glass. "Who's first?" she asked.

After quickly downing his coffee, Doc picked up the chart Mrs. Sidenstricker had placed on the counter. Leroy's X-ray request lay next to it. Doc dropped the slip into the waste container, scanned the top page of the chart for the chief complaint, knocked, and entered the examination room without waiting for a response.

"Hello, Mrs. Sweeney," he pronounced it "Swinny" as local custom demanded.

"Good morning, Doctor Sizemore." The patient sat on the end of the examination table, both hands gripping the handle of the imitation patent-leather purse that rested on her thighs. The tissue around her ankles bulged out over the tops of her shoes. Doc pressed his thumb into the front of her leg leaving a dent in the flesh.

She pulled her leg away from the pressure. "Owe, that smarts, Doctor Sizemore."

"Ankles swelled up again I see. I thought those digitalis pills would take care of that for a lot longer than they seem to have."

"I run out of `em, Doctor, and they was over a dollar I didn't have." Her lungs rattled when she talked. "Had to prop up on four pilla's last night to get any rest a'tall." She stopped twice before finishing her sentence. "What're you able to do about it, Doc?"

"Well, first of all, I'll have to give you a shot to get some of the water out of your lungs," he said. "But most important, you got to go back on digitalis and stay on it." He gave her a mercuhydrin shot and a prescription for digitalis pills with instructions to triple the dose for three days before going back to one pill a day.

"Don't let those run out again, Mrs. Swinny. Like I explained before, you'll have to be on digitalis the rest of your life. You need to follow the directions I wrote on this note." He held the paper before her face and poked at it with his finger for emphasis. "Do you think you can follow these directions, Mrs. Swinny?"

"I'll do my best. You can bank on that. Yes-sir-ee, Doctor Sizemore, I'll do my level best. Sometimes a body cain't do everthing what's recommended, but I'll try my dernedest."

What might appear to some to be a lack of cooperation Doc knew was a sign of independence. Less than a generation before, the people in these hills had relied on home remedies such as brews of ginseng roots, ramps, or tree bark, sugar mixed with lamp oil or camphor, stupes and poultices or vapors of eucalyptus leaves in boiling water, or sassafras tea. They were smart enough to know modern technology was better, but they were still not comfortable with all the ramifications of accepting that fact. Probably, Doc respected their hesitancy to change as much as anything about them.

Mrs. Sweeney handed him a brown paper sack with a heavy jar in it. "Thank you kindly for your attention, Doctor Sizemore. I brought you some of my elderberry jelly. I know you like that a right smart."

"That's mighty thoughtful of you Mrs. Swinny. I appreciate it."

"Be careful of the bottom of the poke, Dr. Sizemore; and say hi to your lovely wife. I still miss seeing her in the office now and agin'."

"I'll tell her you asked about her. She'll be pleased." He lay the chart on the counter and put the jelly on his desk.

Doc worked through dinner and dragged himself home late in the evening. Shirley heard the car pull into the driveway and met him at the front door.

"You look tired," she said after they kissed.

He plopped down on the couch. "I am worn to a frazzle, honey," he said. "Mrs. Swinny sends her regards and this jar of her elderberry jelly."

"How is Mrs. Swinny?"

"Tolerable." Shirley crossed her arms and waited, but Doc did not go on.

"I put the twins to bed," she called over her shoulder as she went to the kitchen. Later, when she called him to supper, there was no answer. She came into the living room and found him sound asleep. She removed his shoes and socks, lifted his feet onto the couch, removed his tie, loosened his collar and covered him with a blanket. She sat in a chair and watched him sleep. Finally, she went to bed.

Doc turned on his side and almost fell off the couch. The suddenness of the movement startled him. He sat up and ran his hand over his scalp. His hair felt thick and oily, his mouth was dry, his teeth rough on his tongue.

He heard Shirley stirring around in the kitchen. "Did I fall asleep again, honey?" he called.

Shirley came into the living room wearing an apron with ruffled shoulder straps and carrying a cup of coffee. "I'm afraid so," she answered.

"Did you say you already put the boys to bed?" She placed the cup-handle in the crook of his finger. The aroma of bacon wafted in from the back of the house.

"Dear, they are half-way to school by now. You haven't stirred since you came in last night."

"I'm sorry. Did you have supper waiting for me?"

"It's all right. You were worn out. You needed your sleep more than you needed food."

Doc lit a cigarette and slid over on the couch to reach the ash tray. He blew out the match and deposited it as he squinted to keep the smoke out of his eye. He drew the pleasant warmth into his tired chest and sipped the hot coffee.

"You need a rest, Earl," Shirley said. "We need a vacation."

They had not been able to leave Wattsville since they moved there. He was the only doctor in town except Dr. Baumgarten who was going blind, could hardly hear and probably drank too much.

"I'd like to take a few days off, but I don't have anyone to take care of the patients."

"What about Dr. Baumgarten?"

"Honey, you know I can't sign out to him."

"Even for one or two days?"

"He's dangerous, Shirley. Hardly anyone goes to see him any more; except the coloreds." Doc flicked his ashes in the ash tray and handed the cigarette to Shirley. She inhaled and handed it back.

"I saw him come out of his house the other day. He stood there for a long time with his medical bag in his hand, looking at two cars. They didn't even resemble one another. And they were different colors to boot. Finally, he just went back inside. He's so addle-pated, he probably forgot where he was going anyhow."

Doc looked at the floor through a wisp of smoke drifting up from his cigarette. Shirley put her hand on his shoulder for a minute, then pressed her face against his cheek and hugged him.

"You're working yourself to death," she whispered.

"Are you sorry we came here?" he asked.

"I knew what you wanted before we got married."

"Sometimes I think it's unfair for me to even have a family."

"You'll feel better after you've cleaned up and had your breakfast." She touched his cheek with her open hand then turned and went back to the kitchen.

When he had finished his smoke, Doc stood wearily and shuffled to the bathroom. He leaned on the sink and looked at his haggard face in the mirror.

"I don't have time for breakfast, honey," he called after looking at his watch. "I'm all ready late."

When he came into the kitchen, he kissed her on the cheek.

"You need some nourishment," she protested.

"The clinic will be crawling, and I'll never get caught up." He hurried out the door, across the porch and down the steps. ***God! You'd never know that car is only two months old,*** he thought.

He was right about the office. When he arrived, the waiting room was all ready full and Mrs. Sidenstricker was standing in the hallway.

She held her hair back with knitting needles. When she was upset she moved the long needles around and fussed with her bun. She took his coat, slung it over her arm, and held out a chart.

Doc waded into the day's work. At dinner time, he made a house call down past Nick Novak's beer joint and up the hollow called Duck.

* * *

Nick Novak's *Bucket `a Blood* sat on the creek bank down toward Duck and took its nickname from the split lips and broken noses so commonly resulting from the social gatherings on Saturday nights. It was a poolroom but the table had become ragged and was hardly ever used any more. Nick was a big man, bald with black hair running around the back of his head from one ear to the other. His neck was bigger than his head and his crown came to a shiny bullet on top. Nick was fat, but his hairy arms were muscular and he was a formidable adversary in the inevitable Saturday night brawls. There was a hand-lettered "help wanted" placard in the front window under the Open/Closed and Red Top Beer promotional neon sign provided by the brewery.

Nick had been unable to get reliable help since Winona Jackson quit to get married. He was a hard man to work for; he expected more from an employee than just waitressing. His penuriousness made it necessary for a waitress to turn a few tricks on the side, which he encouraged and may have even profited from. He also demanded to be serviced himself and Nick was a man of big appetites, and violent ways. Consequently, that hand lettered help wanted sign showed considerable wear.

A few battered vehicles parked at all hours in the muddy lot on the creek bank. Often an owner could not get his car started after an evening of drinking and the vehicle might sit in the parking lot for a month or two.

Nick's customers were local men who generally started the evening as friends. Commonly a fracas began with good natured kidding that escalated into hurt feelings, then a brawl. The next day no one would be able to remember what it had been about; consequently nothing ever got settled. Mayhem usually boiled again when a few drinks resurrected the previously forgotten animosities.

Nick was the bartender, but he would have no idea how to mix a drink. He sold Red Top, Old Oxcart, and Falstaff and an occasional bottle of Nehi Cola. If you wanted anything else you were in the wrong place. Nick could be found leaning over the bar seven days a week. He swept once in a while but never cleaned more than that. There was no door on the toilet and customers usually finished buttoning on their way back to the bar. There was no place to wash one's hands, the sink had fallen off the wall long ago. The place smelled of putrid urine, flat beer, second-hand tobacco, rotten breath and stale bodies.

Talk was punctuated with profanity, belching and other body noises, and bursts of nervous laughter usually followed by coughing. It was not a place to seek meaningful relationships or memorable experiences. There was violence regularly but only one death in all the time Nick ran the place and that was a drunk who had passed out in the parking lot. Someone drove over him in the dark.

"He was a *Bohunk* what worked the mornin' shift at the tipple and lived in a shack down there in Duck," one of his former drinking partners reminisced. "He weren't noticed `til the sun come up the followin' day."

There were so many bald-tired vehicles in and out of the place, it was impossible to tell whose truck did the damage. They only knew it was not Lyle Crabbe because he had new tires on the front of his pickup and there were no tread marks on the body. It did not really matter anyway, so no one pursued the investigation past a cursory questioning of those who could remember being at Nick's on the night it happened.

"Do you remember anything unusual on said night?" Deputy Sheriff Don Chapin queried seriously and jotted on his spiral notebook with his saliva-primed pencil nubbin. He interviewed everyone who came forward, and noted the standard answers.

"No, Don, cain't say as I can remember much that was out of the ordinary. `Course, I never had me that much to drink. I was sober as a judge when I drove outta' that parking lot. If I'da backed over a body, I sure would'a knowed it. You can rest your soul on that. No sir, it weren't me what drove over that *Bohunk*."

He probably got the same answer from some witnesses who were so drunk that night they thought they were at Nick's and were actually someplace else.

"I only treated him once," Doctor Baumgarten recollected at the general store. "And that was a couple of winters ago - thick headed - never understood a word. Had the flu. Gave him a penicillin shot as I recall. Made kind of a fuss. Bohunks are a lot like niggers; show 'em a needle and they get crazy."

They buried him up in the cemetery where the Negroes were interred at the head of Dogtown hollow. A couple of the regulars at Nick's made a coffin and dug the grave. When they came back to the beer joint Nick gave them each a beer *"on the house"*.

Nick was sitting on a chair leaning back against the side of the building as Doc drove by on his way back to the office. He waved, started coughing and tipped the chair forward so he could spit.

Back at the office Doc took care of the rest of the afternoon's patients and completed his notes. Mrs. Sidenstricker handed him another chart and nodded her head to indicate the back of the clinic.

"Pearly Mae White's been waiting in the back, Doctor Sizemore."

Doc walked to the room at the far end of the hall. There was a separate entrance to that part of the building. He scanned the chart and entered without knocking.

"Hi, Pearly Mae. How're you feeling today?"

"I's got the brownchitis again, Doctor Sizemore." Sweat glistened on her black skin and stained the edges of the bandanna covering her hair. She was not much more than a bag of bones with a goiter the size of a grapefruit. "Lord - a - mercy, I coughed sa' hard all night I broke the blood veins in my eyes." The whites of her grotesquely protruding eyes were dappled red with fresh hemorrhages. "I's feeling rite poorly, doctor."

She shivered slightly when Doc examined her chest. The room was not adequately heated and she had been waiting with the door closed. Her temperature was 104.2 degrees, and she had scattered rales and depressed breath sounds in her right upper lobe. Doc gave her a shot of long acting Bicillin and a prescription for a bottle of Elixir of Terpin Hydrate with Codeine.

"Pearly Mae," Doc said. "You got to get over to Clendenin and get that chest X- ray we talked about last month. I'm worried you may have active T.B. I can't do a skin test, you all ready had a positive several years ago so you have to get a chest X- ray."

"I's going to do that very thing as soon as I can scrape up the money, doctor Sizemore, but with my man out of work..."

"Well, Pearly Mae, you see if you can't figure some way to do it pretty soon or I got to report you. Your children're going to be sick next thing."

"Please don't report me, Doctor Sizemore. They's likely to take my chi'dren if you was to do that."

"Have you thought of going down to that clinic in the colored section in Charleston? They do X- rays and things like that for you folks for just what you can afford to pay. They may be able to fix that goiter, too."

"It's awful hard to get all the way down to Charleston, Doctor Sizemore."

"Well, don't put it off much longer, Pearly Mae or I'll have to report you to the health department as a probable active T.B. case."

Pearly Mae got up off the table and headed for the back door. "Don't do that, Doctor Sizemore, I'll try real hard." As soon as she went outside and inhaled her first breath of cool air, she started coughing uncontrollably. She stumbled down the back steps holding her ribs to lessen the pain. Doc watched her pull her ragged coat around her shoulders as she crossed the bridge and turned toward Dogtown.

Chapter Two

Wattsville was a coal town perched on the edge of obsolescence, abandoned by its young and its talented. Its constant was decline. The coal tipple, the railroad yard, the washery and the power house were the most imposing structures in Wattsville. When coal flowed down the mountainside on noisy conveyer belts from the tipple to the rail yard, or when a steam engine came up the hollow to pick up a line of gondolas, the whole town trembled. Everything not moving was covered with a thin layer of coal-dust.

Some folks in Wattsville worked for the government in one capacity or another so they had regular incomes. Or they were coal miners, whose pay was usually mortgaged to the company store. But, as Beatrice Parker liked to say. "Lots'a folks don't have jobs a'tall, leastwise not so's you could notice."

Bea as everyone called her, was the entire staff at the hotel for visiting dignitaries from Pittsburgh or New York where the mine officials had their offices. More like a large house, and never given a name other than "The Hotel," it was often empty or rented to railroad employees to defray the expense of upkeep. It was as white as anything could be in a coal town. Trimmed in green, its beauty was marred by peeling paint, coal dust and by the plumbing and wiring added to the outside of the building. Several steps led up to a large front porch with a swing, two rocking chairs and a glider. The ornate front door had a brass butterfly handle that activated an old fashioned brass bell to announce the arrival of a guest. In its heyday it had accommodated many distinguished visitors.

The Hammond-Newcastle Corporation had acquired mineral rights on twenty-eight thousand acres along Buffalo Creek for fifty cents an acre in 1893. When the Baltimore & Ohio Railroad initiated service along Elk River, a spur was extended up Buffalo Creek and the Newcastle coal seam was opened. Operations began in 1912. The mine was one of the most modern in West Virginia and Wattsville was considered to be a model mining camp. The height of its prosperity was in World War I when so-called smokeless coal was in great demand for allied ships so they would be harder to spot by German submarines.

Hard times in the years following the war and during the great depression had not been kind to the town, however. Hammond Enterprises, the parent company in New York stopped up-dating the mining equipment and they were gradually selling-off their holdings. The miner's houses were first to go on the auction block and the company service station was next. The operation returned pennies on the company's dollar and the up-surge in coal production during World War II did not change company policy. For five years coal was frantically blasted out of one of the richest seams in the country with little regard for maintenance or safety.

After the war, production limped along with an ever dwindling interest from the investors and Wattsville suffered increasingly under the cloud of a one-employer economy. The movie theater closed, the furniture store went out of business, the mine president moved to Pittsburgh, and company contributions to municipal services dried up.

About the only social activities remaining in the community were church and high school football. Doc attended the football games and recently he had been promising to accompany Shirley to church services. He was not a religious man, but sometimes he enjoyed the sociability of mingling with his patients in a pious setting.

The men touched the brims of their hats, smiled at Shirley, mumbled "Misses" as the good doctor and his wife crossed toward the steps.

"Why, good morning, Doctor Sizemore," several of the men said in unison. "Fine looking automobile."

"Thank you kindly, Homer, and good morning to you, too. How are things with you, Anse? How you been, Merle?" Doc nodded, waved his hand slightly and made eye contact with as many of the loiterers as possible. "Been a long time, Moles."

"It is ever so pleasant seeing you in church, Doctor," a patient would say. "I always admire the way the Lord guides the hand of those who heal the sick, don't you, Doctor.?"

"I do that, Misses Whipple," Doc would answer. "I truly do that!"

Doc took an honored place in a front pew on the men's side, held the hymn book in front of his face and sang louder than anyone else with the exception of Miss Thornton, the H.S. English teacher. Shirley sat with Alice Wilson and Thelma Humphries across the way.

"Thank you for coming, thank you for coming, thank you for coming," Preacher Samples intoned to each parishioner as she left the church.

"Fine sermon," Doc said. "Fine sermon."

"Thank you, Doctor Sizemore. It's gratifying to see you in the Lord's house. We don't have the honor of your presence near often enough."

"Been real busy, Preacher. Been real busy."

* * *

The church buildings served the community in many ways, not the least of which was the regular quilting get-togethers.

"A body can sleep better under a quilt what's been made by a lovin' hand," Dora Pitman said to Shirley at the regular quilting session. "And you rightly got the gift. Now me, I make a `rag' rug or a `crazy quilt' rite fine, but for fancy quiltin', you got the gift."

"Well thank you, Mrs. Pitman, that's kind of you," Shirley answered. "The ladies of the church taught me everything I know."

Shirley's quilt had won first prize at the fair in Bluefield and the one she made with Alice Wilson took second place. She decided to surprise Doc with the news and a special supper. She got out his favorite recipe:

SHIRLEY'S BEEF STEW AND VEGETABLE SOUP

Start with beef stew the night before

> 1-2 lbs beef stew meat - cut in small pieces
> salt & pepper - dust with flour
> Brown in oil (enough to absorb flour)
> Add 1 package of Lipton onion soup after browning

In pressure cooker (large pan if no pc) heat to boil:

2 water and 2 red wine (about 2" depth - maybe a bit more, you decide)

(This should almost cover the meat) When boiling:

Add meat mixture - reduce heat after coming to pressure - or when comes to boil.

Keep at pressure - (or simmer longer if you don't have pc)

4 red medium red potatoes per lb - peel and quarter

4-6 carrots per lb - depending on size - peel and cut 3" lengths - split thick end to match

Add (pots first) to meat when pressured about 20 min. - 35 min. in reg. pan (just lay vegetables on top)

Bring back up to pressure (or to boil) Cook/simmer 15 min (pc) 45 min (reg pan)

Enjoy for dinner tonight, served with cornbread!

After dinner chill this whole mixture together overnight to make soup.

SOUP RECIPE

put Into large regular pan:

Dice potatoes and carrots - I usually cut meat to smaller size

Rinse container (moderate amount of water - enough to get the contents) pour into soup - you probably will need more water later.

Depending on amount of meat/vegies - 1 can (size?) of whole tomatoes - cut up to shred.

1/2 to 3/4 cup each:
frozen corn & green peas; green beans (not canned - I like to use fresh)
diced celery (about 2 stalks)
1 small can tomato sauce - add one can water
salt & pepper to taste - about 1 tablespoon sugar
In herb mortar/pestle grind: about 1 tsp each:
    Basil; Rosemary; Thyme, Tarragon (check for correction - may
want more)
I usually don't add onion - but do if you want. Small dice.

Add water to consistency you want - stir often. Simmer until celery
is tender, about 1 hr.
    The soup is even better the next day.

She waited up for Doc until almost midnight. Finally, she folded her quilts, tucked the ribbons in the drawer out of sight, put
away the stew and went to bed.
    "How did you do at the fair, honey?" Doc asked the next morn-
ing as he came into the kitchen.
    "Oh, we did all right," Shirley answered.
    "What do you mean all right?" he teased, but Shirley seemed
to be unwilling to join in. She went about her morning chores
without answering. Doc finished his coffee and started to leave,
but Shirley raised her shoulder when he tried to kiss her on the
cheek. He stood in the kitchen looking at his wife's back for a few
minutes before he realized she was crying. He put his arms around
her shoulders and she turned and put her face on his chest.
    "I'm sorry," he whispered.

Shirley pulled away slightly and wiped her eyes with her hand.

"I am too," she said. "I was so happy last night and when you didn't come home, I guess I just felt neglected."

"I'm sorry, darling. I just couldn't hurry up that..."

"I know," she interrupted. "You don't have to explain."

"But I want to," he said.

"But I don't want you to," she answered. "I'm not mad at you. I was just hurt."

They embraced for a long time without talking and they kissed.

"I love you, Shirley," Doc said.

"And I love you, too."

They looked into each other's eyes, then Doc asked, "How did you do?"

"Oh, what would you think of it if I told you the quilt Alice and I made won second place?" She smiled and waited for his response.

"Second place!" he exclaimed. "Second place! Congratulations, honey. That's wonderful."

"And mine won first," she added in a quiet voice.

"Oh, Shirley," Doc said as he pulled her to his chest. "I really do love you! Do you know that?"

"Yes, I know that," she said. She paused before adding, "Most of the time."

* * *

"I hear your misses won the big prize at the fair," several patients announced as Doc came into the examination rooms at the clinic later that day.

"Not only the big one, but the second prize, too," Doc beamed.

Chapter Three

When the phone rang, Doc was reading a new medical journal. He was absorbed in an article about Rheumatic Heart Disease. He picked up the receiver. "This is Doctor Sizemore."

"Hi, Doc." It was Minner Wilson, superintendent of the mine. "Doc, a few of us are getting together Saturday night at my house for a little poker. Can we include you in?"

"You certainly can," Doc answered. "I'd love that! What time?"

"About seven, bring money. I'm planning on your paying for my hunting trip."

Doc chuckled. He replaced the phone in its cradle. Doc's relationships had become restricted to five or ten minute office visits, brief snippets of conversation with Mrs. Sidenstricker followed by wearily struggling to stay awake through supper with Shirley and naps on the weekend so he could get through the next week. He savored the thought of an evening of conversation about something other than illness or fatigue. He hoped the patients would let him have an uninterrupted evening.

Saturday was an easy day, Doc got caught up on his journals. He paid special attention to an article about a new diuretic, acetazolamide, being studied by Lederle. Acetazolamide was a compound to reduce edema that could be taken by mouth. That would revolutionize the treatment of heart failure. Doc went over an article about chloramphenicol twice. Disturbing reports of serious blood dyscrasias were beginning to surface with its increasingly popular use. The article cited an account of a teenager dying after taking the drug for acne. He wrote a note to Mrs. Sidenstricker to ask the pharmacist to make a list of those who had been put on chloramphenicol so he could get word to them to stop the medication if they showed any sign of problems. He included a reminder to inquire about any unexplained fevers or sores in the mouths of anyone who had ever taken the drug. He completed some left-over paper work and went home for an early supper.

"I didn't know the boys would be gone tonight, honey," he said. "I'll just call Minner. They won't miss me."

"No, it's all right. I can finish canning those tomatoes that I started on this morning. You go ahead and have fun. You deserve it."

"I am not going to be very late," he promised. "What do you say we go to church tomorrow morning?"

"I was planning to," she answered. "It would be nice if you could come along." He kissed her and left the house. On his way to Minner's, he vowed to pay more attention to her. *Shirley seldom complains,* he thought. *She deserves better than I give her.*

He parked in the driveway so he could not be blocked in. Evidently he was the first to arrive. Alice opened the door; she was drying her hands with a small towel.

"Hi, Earl," she said. "How're Shirley and the boys?" She stood aside for Doc to enter, and closed the door.

"They're fine, Alice. Shirley's finishing up some canning, and the twins are spending the night with friends. I declare those boys are going to grow up to be strangers. I hardly ever see them except for coming and going." Doc looked a little distant for a moment. "They'll be off to college soon, then probably move away for good."

"They grow up before you know it. Seems like yesterday they were just little tykes." She paused. "I'll never forget driving Shirley to the hospital in Charleston because you were off somewheres making a house call," she said. "Delivering one of the Parker kids as I recall." Doc looked sad and shook his head.

"Minner's downstairs." She turned to go back to the kitchen. "You know the way," she said over her shoulder.

"Thanks, Alice."

Minner was sitting at a felt-topped table shuffling cards when Doc came down the stairs. He called the part of his basement he had converted his rumpus room.

"Sit yourself, Doc. Can I get you a drink?"

"You got an R.C.?"

"Sure you won't have a bourbon? I've got some good stuff."

"Better not, a patient might call."

"One won't hurt."

"An R.C. would be fine."

Minner returned from the refrigerator with the bottle. Ed Humphrey and Bill Arbogast came down the stairs as Minner handed the soft drink to Doc.

"Sure you don't just want the rest of us to get high so you can win our money?" Minner said.

"As my daddy always said, `Poker is a game for a clear mind'," Doc said. He held the bottle up in front of his face and took a sip. They all laughed.

Ed was the local pharmacist, and Bill the school principal and Mayor of Wattsville. Coach Nellis rounded out the group a few minutes later; and after drinks had been poured, they sat down around the game table. Before long, the basement smelled of cigarette smoke and the popcorn Alice served in a big woven basket.

Conversations revolved around the economy, friendly ribbing, feigned accusations of cheating, high school football, the weather, hunting and politics. They agreed Wattsville was going to have a good team this year, hunting licenses were getting outrageously expensive, and business was being smothered by taxes, rules and paper work. It's going to be a cold or a warm winter seemed to be the only disagreement. Momentarily, the game was interrupted by the differing predictions.

"I was down to the company store the other day, the calf tongue in the meat case was all white-like instead of darker; you know kinda' purple," Coach Nellis said. "And that always means a cold winter."

"Well, I was talking to Alf Wills just last Tuesday," Minner said. "He says his hogs are not gaining as much fat as usual, and he says that means a warm winter."

"I heard tell if the pie-plant don't turn real red, it means a warm winter, and Thelma's pie plant's greener than I can ever remember," Ed Humphrey remarked.

Doc leaned his arms on the table and shuffled the cards. "I go by the almanac. My daddy always went by the almanac and I don't remember a time his garden wasn't planted just right. Anybody know what the almanac says?" He looked around the table and everyone shook their heads. "Well then, let's play some more cards." He placed the deck on the table, Minner cut and the game resumed. In the course of the evening a hunting trip was set up and Doc was urged to come along.

"Hell's Bells, Doc," they all agreed. "You got to have some time off."

"Anything comes up can't wait, they can always go over to Clendenin," Minner said. "Doc Butterworth or Doc Glass can take care of `em if old Baumgarten is under the weather."

"Phone call for you, Earl." It was Alice. She went back up the stairs and Doc followed. "Got to go," he said when he came back down. "Got a baby to deliver."

"Think about it, Earl," Minner said as Doc left.

"I will," Doc answered.

He lit a cigarette as he drove out of town. He told himself he would like to go but somehow it just didn't seem possible. What if something bad happened while he was away? Besides, how would a hunting trip look after the way he had neglected Shirley and the boys for so long? *I wonder if I'm just using my obligations as a doctor to avoid the other obligations in my life?* The thought troubled him.

The next morning, he arrived at the breakfast table before the twins were finished eating. "How are things in school, boys?" he asked. There was a knock at the door and the boys hurried to join their friends. As he looked back to his breakfast, Shirley turned her head and looked out the window. He picked at his food. Shirley smoked and mechanically stirred her coffee. Doc went around the table, bent over and kissed her cheek. She did not look up.

All that week the emptiness of his personal life ate at him. He was standing by his desk on Friday afternoon looking at the day's paper work when he decided to call home. Shirley answered.

"Get a nice dress on, honey, I'll be home in half an hour," he said. There was silence at the other end of the line. "Are you there, honey?" He waited. "Say something!"

"I can't. I'm speechless. What am I supposed to be dressing up for?"

"We're going to go to Clendenin. I'm taking you out to supper."

"How're we going to do that? Who's going to watch your precious patients while we're gone?"

The hint of sarcasm stung, he swallowed hard.

"Never mind about that. We're just going to let the minor stuff wait. Nothing important's going to come up in the next four or five hours."

"I'm sorry, Earl. I didn't mean to sound so..."

"That's all right, Shirley. I understand. We'll have a good time. I promise."

He took care of his last patient, a simple cold, he left a message on the wire recorder, stacked the paper work on his desk and drove home. He hosed off the Plymouth before he went into the house.

"Where are the boys?" he asked.

"They went to the Baptist Youth prayer meeting in Gauley Bridge," Shirley answered. "Mr. Arbogast took the Christian Youth Club over in the school bus.

"They were excited to go and I called to see if it were all right with you but you were out making a house call," Shirley said.

"I'm surprised Mrs. Sidenstricker didn't say something to me about it," he said. "That house call was before dinner and I have been in the office all afternoon."

"Oh, it was not today," she said. "I called early last week and it was almost time for Mrs. Sidenstricker to leave the office. She must have assumed I told you that evening when you came home, but you were so late I forgot." She paused as if that were all she were going to say. Then she added, "And you have been coming in so late and going out so early since, I..."

Doc squeezed her hand, then went into the bathroom. He washed his face, changed shirts, slipped on a sport coat and came back into the kitchen. He took Shirley's arm and placed it over his.

"Come on, honey!" he said as he guided her through the front door and down the steps. "We're going out to supper come hell or high water!" He opened the door of the car and held her hand as she climbed onto the front seat. She smiled as she seated herself.

"Well, thank you kindly, sir. You must be new in these parts and right successful, too. This is a fine looking automobile you have here, if I do say so myself."

"Pretty spiffy, eh? The best money can buy. Picked it out to order and it's bought and paid for. Cash on the barrel head."

Doc had got a lot of comments from patients about his new car.

"Looks like Doc's doin pretty good, new car an' all. Gettin' our check-offs ever month whether we git any medicine or not...," a person might say in the waiting room. Often, uttered loud enough to carry into the examination rooms for Doc to hear. The people in Wattsville did not know it, but Doc's new car was a gift.

He closed the door, leaned in the window and kissed Shirley. It had been a while since he had thought about how attractive she was when she was dressed up and happy. He lingered with his hands on the window-frame. Her skin was flushed, a smile lit her face. **My God, she still looks like a young girl,** he thought. "You are a lovely lady," he said. "I should tell you that more often." A tear drifted along her lower lid. She blotted it with her handkerchief and patted his hand.

The car hummed smoothly up the hill to the main road. He turned toward Clendenin.

"I am going to cut down somehow," he said. "We can't go on like this. We deserve an evening to ourselves now and again." He glanced across at his wife and placed his hand over hers on the seat. She moved closer. She put her hand on his thigh and leaned her head on his shoulder. Doc felt a warmth for her he had almost forgot. It made him sad. He put his arm around her shoulders.

They drove into Clendenin, crossed the iron truss bridge over the Elk River and pulled into the parking lot at Rose's Diner. Doc went around the car, opened the passenger door and offered his hand. They crossed the parking lot holding hands and walked up the path to the entrance of the former trolley car. Their shoes crunched in the fine gravel. The hand-operated metal door at the front still had the black rubber strip where it previously opened down the middle and the mechanism for the driver to operate it from his position behind the throttle. The big, red neon rose bud on top of the restaurant flickered in the waning light and emitted that electric sound characteristic of such contrivances.

Inside, the diner had a long counter with stools on one side and booths by the windows. The homey warmth, the smell of gravy and frying chicken greeted them as they entered and climbed the steps.

Jed Rose, famous for his chicken fried steak, meat loaf, mashed potatoes and gravy, and green beans, often had customers from as far away as Charleston. He stood in front of the grill with a spatula in his hand and a stained apron reaching to his knees.

"Sorry Doc, they was a phone call for you not ten minutes ago," he said.

"What was it about?" Doc asked.

"Was about a boy name of Parker," he answered. "He's real sick. His pa said you better get right back because the boy's having a lot of trouble breathing."

"Can I use your phone, Jed?" Doc hoped he could avoid going back to Wattsville right away. "Could be a couple hours won't make a lot of difference," he said.

"Won't do no good to call," Rose answered. "He weren't phoning from home. Said he was getting right back to be with his woman. Said you should come right away."

Doc still had hold of Shirley's hand. He looked at her. Her face was turned away. He gripped her fingers. She turned to look at him and shrugged her shoulders. They left the restaurant, climbed into the car and drove back to Wattsville.

When he stopped in front of the house, Shirley got out before he could turn off the engine. He started to say something, but she ran up the steps and across the porch without looking back. He barely got the window rolled down in time to hear the door bang shut behind her. When he recovered from the shock, he turned the car around and headed down toward Duck.

"Hi there, Billy. What seems to be the trouble?" Doc asked. Billy's face was strained as if he had a headache.

"He's awful weak, Doc," his father said. "He's been puking and he cain't go to the privy - number one or number two."

Doc looked at the thermometer that he had stuck under Billy's tongue. "103," he said. "Let me see you sit up, son." Billy struggled to a sitting position and rested back on his hands. "Lie back down, Billy and let me lift you up this time." When he lifted the boy by his shoulders, his head fell back. Doc motioned for the parents to follow him into the living room.

"I think I should do a lumbar puncture," he said. The parents looked at each other. "You know, a spinal tap," Doc explained.

"What do you think's wrong, Doc?" Parker said.

"I'm not sure, Bill, but I would like to make certain it's not meningitis."

"You don't mean spinal meningitis do you, Doc?"

"Let's see what his spinal fluid looks like before we start worrying about a diagnosis. It may be nothing. I'll need your help to hold him while I do this," he said. The tap was easy and when he held the vial up to the light it looked clear.

"This looks pretty good," he said. "I don't see any pus cells, but I gotta' take this to the office for further examination. While I'm gone give Billy some sips of water and see if he can urinate - you know, pee."

In the office he stained a portion of the fluid and under the microscope it showed a few leukocytes, but not many. ***Damn***, he thought, ***probably polio!***

"Has he voided yet?" he asked when he returned to the Parker house. The parents looked blank. "You know, number one, pee."

"No, he ain't been able to a'tall, Doc."

Doc inserted a catheter and drained it into a bag he hung on the bed. He pinched it off and drained the urine slowly. When the bag filled, he emptied it and re-attached it to the catheter.

"I want his feet propped up, his knees bent, and I want him to rest. And I want both of you into my office tomorrow to have gamma globulin. And everyone else he has been in contact with for the past few days. I'll call the health department in Charleston and get enough to give everyone who needs it."

Later, when he climbed into bed, Shirley turned on her side and faced the wall. He lay awake for a long time.

Three more cases popped up in the following five days. He ran out of gamma globulin twice and had to call the health department for more. The next week seven more children, two teen-agers and an adult developed symptoms. He sent five to the hospital, one died and three developed severe respiratory symptoms and could not come home. Billy Parker got better and Doc took the catheter out in two days, then Billy got worse and had to be sent to Charleston. Doc worked day and night giving gamma globulin, teaching parents physical therapy, inserting catheters, giving enemas, showing the best body positions to avoid deformity, encouraging early passive then active exercise to prevent muscle wasting. For three weeks new cases continued to occur. He grabbed a sandwich or a fried egg at a patient's house, a nap in a chair by a bedside, a cup of coffee and a quick cigarette here and there. At one stretch he was not home for five days. He brushed his teeth in the office, changed clothes and washed haphazardly on the run and went to sleep twice while driving.

"You are a sight," Shirley said when he finally got time to come home and sit on the couch.

He dozed off without answering. Shirley covered him with a blanket.

Chapter Four

One evening as Doc was about to leave the clinic, the phone rang. He walked back down the hall, picked up the receiver and answered casually. "Hello."

"Is this the doctor?" the voice inquired.

"Yes, it is."

"This is Preacher Pattison, Albert Morgan is sick. I'm worried about him. Could you come see him?"

"Do you think you could bring him into the clinic? I'm sure I could do more for him here." Doc was puzzled. He tried to remember who Preacher Pattison was but he could not conjure up a face.

"He's really too sick, doctor. When you see him, I'm sure you'll agree."

"I'll come as soon as I can," he promised, and copied the directions. He locked the clinic and drove down the narrow lane to Duck.

The road was sprinkled with puddles, it had been raining but it had slacked up. Bare trees lined the road and covered the hills. The coke ovens, with their fires banked, sizzled in the cold mist creating thick white clouds of steam. The steep slopes ascended into low lying cloud banks. The subdued light on the hillside muted the colors. Damp cold penetrated his clothing until the heater warmed the car.

The weather-beaten house sat back from the road in a line of similar shanties in need of repairs. Weeds in the yard were so tall they created mounds where they had grown in clumps and fallen over. Doc parked his car and stepped up onto the porch. He was surprised when a Negro man opened the door.

The man was small, about Doc's age, and appeared to be trim and muscular. He extended his hand; his smile revealed perfect white teeth. "Hello doctor. Thank you for coming so promptly. Albert is in the bedroom." Doc followed to the back of the house.

The man in bed was Caucasian. He looked very sick. He sat propped up gasping for air; his eyes were sunken deep into their sockets; his shoulder bones protruded against his skin. His face was so emaciated Doc could see the imprint of teeth through the skin around his mouth. His lips were blue, his skin almost transparent yellow-white.

"You look short of breath. Is it all right if I ask your preacher some questions instead of making you more uncomfortable?" Doc leaned forward as he made the inquiry so the man in bed could understand. Morgan protested by shaking his head, but his wind failed him. He could not get his answer out.

"What are you trying to say?" Doc asked.

"He is saying, I'm not his preacher. I preach at the Mount Carmel Baptist Church." The reverend's explanation was dispassionate.

Doc looked at the preacher for a moment, then turned back toward the man in bed.

"How long have you been sick?" he asked.

"Albert has been sick for some time," Preacher Pattison answered. "He has a problem with his liver. I think it's all right with Albert for me to answer your questions." He looked at Albert for confirmation. The sick man nodded feebly.

Doc examined Albert, who seemed to be in the final stage of cirrhosis. His abdomen was bloated so much he could not move his diaphragm to breathe properly. His feet and legs were swollen, the jaundiced skin was shiny and taut. Doc explained that a mercuhydren shot and a paracentesis would give only temporary relief, but it was all he could do.

"I'm sure Albert would appreciate anything to help his breathing, even for a little while." The preacher looked at his friend who moved his head slightly.

Doc gave the diuretic into the swollen buttock and anesthetized the skin in a spot below Albert's shrunken liver edge. He made an incision and inserted a large bore needle. Soon the dish-pan he held under the needle was half full of straw colored fluid.

"If I drained too much it could aggravate his all ready precarious nutritional status," Doc explained. He had drained just enough to give a measure of respiratory comfort. After he finished the procedure, Albert's breathing became regular, less labored. He drifted quietly into deep sleep, soon he was snoring softly.

Doc placed a bulky dressing over the incision. "This is likely to continue to drain a bit. Just change the dressing when it gets soaked. Any cloth will be OK as long as it's clean." The preacher nodded and after he arranged the pillows to support the patient's head, he followed Doc to the front room.

"There will only be temporary relief, but you must know he hasn't much longer anyway?" Doc posed his statement as a question.

"Yes, I know," Pattison answered.

Doc turned to leave without further conversation, then as he reached for the door-knob, he could not resist asking. "He used to be a fighter, didn't he?"

"Yes," the preacher answered. "He fought as Black Jack Albert Morgan. Do you remember him?"

"Yes, I saw him fight many times. I knew he lived somewhere around here, but I haven't seen him in years. I remember he always wore rabbit fur on his trunks," Doc said.

"That was Albert all right." The preacher laughed. "He was one of a kind."

"I always thought he could have been good, if he had trained," Doc said. Black Jack was well known for his excesses.

"Yes Albert has always had a mind of his own. He could have lived a lot longer, too, if he had just taken the advice of his friends. He has not even stopped drinking yet. I don't know how, but he still gets something from time to time. I guess it doesn't matter anymore though, does it?"

"No, I'm afraid it's too late for the Black Jack," Doc answered wistfully. "What about you? You look like you have taken good care of yourself."

"Yes, I'm still in pretty good shape."

"I remember you, too, you know?" Doc said.

"Oh?" The preacher smiled.

"You're Red Pattison, aren't you?"

"Well, I was a long time ago." The preacher rubbed his palm over his hair.

When Doc confirmed who the patient was, he had naturally recognized the preacher. He and Black Jack had fought as teammates on a boxing club called The Wattsville Brawlers. Pattison had hardly changed since Doc had seen him in the ring twenty years earlier; except his hair no longer had the red tinge that gave him his nickname.

"I'm surprised we haven't run into each other before now. I saw you at the Armory in Charleston when you and Noel Kelly fought the Lopez brothers."

"I been away for a few years," Pattison answered. "I do remember that fight. Kelly had some trouble later as you probably recall."

"I always thought you would become champion some day. Why did you quit?"

"I got smart. I got tired of the exploitation. I didn't want to end up like Albert or Kelly. I didn't fit in with the fight crowd." It sounded as if he had not thought of the subject in a long while. Each statement was separated by a pause, as if he thought of another reason each time he finished the last.

"I'm glad I stopped." He was pensive. He looked at his hands. His white fingernails were manicured.

"Well you were too good for everyone I ever saw you in the ring with. You could have gone all the way. You had the talent."

Pattison smiled. "Thanks for the thought, doctor, and thanks for coming to take care of Albert. I wish we could have reminisced under different circumstances."

They shook hands. "By the way. Have you heard anything about Noel Kelly lately?" Pattison asked.

"Someone told me he was out in California painting houses or something."

"He could have been champion of the world," Pattison said.

"He was never the same after that bullet in his abdomen," Doc said.

"Nasty business," Pattison agreed.

As Doc drove back to town, the rain picked up again and the coke ovens gave the darkening sky an eerie glow. When he got home, Shirley was asleep.

* * *

A few weeks later, Doc was just finishing supper when the phone rang.

"Dr. I'm sorry to bother you this time of the evening, but do you think you could come to my house right away?" It was the Reverend Pattison.

"What's wrong?" Doc asked.

"It's Albert, Albert Morgan. He's worse again."

"Sure, I remember the way. I can get there in twenty minutes." Doc was surprised Albert had hung on so long.

"No, he's not at the same place, doctor. We moved him." Doc wrote the directions down on a note pad Shirley handed him.

"That's Dogtown," she said. "I wonder what a white man is doing there?"

"The last time I saw him, he was in Duck. I didn't ask Preacher Pattison why he's been moved."

The dirt road below the coke ovens clung precariously to the hillside until turning up the narrow hollow. Doc drove slowly, looking for "the fifth house on the right after you pass the church."

The structures in Dogtown were all the same, unpainted shacks on both sides of a dirt road; front porches separated by little more than the road itself. No electric or telephone lines came up the hollow, each shanty had a privy close by. The official name was "National Hollow," but Doc had never heard it called anything other than Dogtown.

Preacher Pattison was walking by the side of the road returning home from making his call. He directed Doc to turn into the yard. His shack, built against a steep hillside, had a cellar dug in beside the house and a corrugated metal roofed privy in between.

"Thank you for coming, Doctor," he said. His manner was somber. He extended his hand to show the way, the porch groaned with their weight. "Albert's having a lot of trouble getting his breath."

As they entered the house, a woman came out of the back room. Doc could see that someone had been sleeping in the living room. A daybed seemed to have been shoved back into position to serve as a couch. The edges of a blanket protruded beneath the skirt of the slip covers. A kerosene lamp provided the only light. The odor of burning petroleum permeated the air.

"This is my wife, Mary belle, Dr. Sizemore. Honey, this is the doctor I told you about."

Mary belle, was a small neat woman, with light skin. Her features were delicate, her eyes almost oriental. She smiled, lowered her eyes and stood aside for him to pass.

Albert was propped up in bed, his jaw hung loose. Thick saliva drooled out the corner of his mouth and down his neck. His eyelids were open, his stare frozen at some point in the hereafter.

Doc listened for heart sounds. With his stethoscope still in his ears, he looked into the concerned eyes of Reverend Pattison.

"Black Jack has fought his last fight, Preacher," he whispered. A tear ran down the preacher's cheek. His wife wiped it away. He hugged her close to his side. Doc put his stethoscope back in his bag. They walked out into the front room.

"We can never thank you enough for your kindness," the preacher almost whispered. Mary belle nodded, looked at her husband with a wan smile, and Doc started to leave. At the door he turned.

"Why did you move him here, into your house, into your bed-room?" Doc asked.

"He had no one to take care of him. He couldn't pay his rent any longer so he had to move." It was a simple explanation. There was no sorrow or suffering in it. That was just the answer to the question.

Doc must have looked puzzled.

"You're thinking about the other evening aren't you?" The preacher smiled. He glanced at his wife. She looked distant. "I know he didn't want you to think he went to a Negro church. I didn't think anything about that. Albert was a proud white man, but I always considered him a friend." He paused and took his wife's hand in his and looked at her for a minute. Then he offered his hand to Doc and when they shook he leaned forward, smiled and said, "My wife and I have a good life here. You needn't be concerned."

Doc waved as he turned the car back down the road. Soot from the coke ovens had settled on the hood. The wind striated it as he drove.

Chapter Five

Logging was no longer profitable in W.Va. and farming was out of the question on the available terrain. The brightest and the most creative had moved away. Many of the servicemen had been killed or had gone to work in industrial cities, or used their G.I.Bill to go to college instead of returning to Wattsville. Much of southern West Virginia was in the doldrums until the Korean War and an expanding economy injected an element of enthusiasm into the coal industry. The Wattsville mine returned to three shifts a day, seven-days-a-week. The miners were rotated from shift to shift on a five week cycle and again coal poured down the big conveyers night and day.Over Minner's objections, tailings from the mine were used to create an impound dam across the head of National Hollow to provide water for the coal washing plant. It was put in operation to reduce the cost of transporting coal to market.

Things were looking up in Wattsville and everyone said so. However, because the seam had begun to take a downward pitch, chain-breast machines were replaced with post punches which were not as efficient at undercutting the coal so miners started to use more powder in their blasting charges. Instead of a smaller charge bringing down a face of coal that had been properly under-cut, a larger charge was placed to make up for the inferior removal at the bottom of the seam and to displace more coal in smaller, easier-to-load lumps. This change resulted in more violent explo-sions which occasionally penetrated through the seam to the face. These "blow offs" created more coal dust suspended in the air and, under conditions of low humidity, explosions into the room at the face were inevitable. Sometimes men were killed in the blast, usu-ally the shot-firer. The more intense explosions occasionally weak-ened the roof causing it to fall on a loader as he cleared the coal away from the blast area. In one five-year period Doc pronounced thirty-two dead and twice as many injured.

February twenty-seventh, a little after midnight, Vittie Pitmen checked the sprags at the face, set the charge, tamped the damp clay in the hole with his wooden tamping rod, attached the cable to the ends of the detonator lead wires and backed out of range of flying debris. He checked his safety lamp, made a final inspection of the position of the roof supports, connected the wires to the bat-tery terminals, inserted the key necessary to complete the circuit and pressed down on the two firing buttons. The earth rumbled. Coal dislodged from the face with only slightly more dust than usual. An eerie quiet, broken only by the sound of water dripping from the ceiling, engulfed the tunnel.

Vittie crouched, waiting for the dust to settle and listened for the sound of movement in the roof of the room at the face. The drip, drip, drip continued but no other sound. When he was satis-fied the mountain had not been disturbed and there was no dan-ger, he stood and walked around the corner, just in time to see a wall of water pouring through the face of the shaft. He turned to run but he never had a chance. The palisade of water swept through the mine killing him and three other men who were entering the area to begin clearing the coal.

Doc was startled from a sound sleep by the siren. He climbed out of bed and dressed quickly. Shirley warmed-over some coffee and handed him a thermos as he left the house. He kissed her on the cheek at the front door.

"Thanks, honey," he said.

"Be careful," she called after him as he ran down the steps.

"I will," he answered.

He sped out of the driveway and headed for the main entrance to the mine. As he drove down the road toward the bridge he was struck by how high the water was and that the creek seemed to be filled with debris. As he crossed the bridge and drove along the railroad tracks to the mine office, he saw water running out the air shafts into Buffalo and Mill Creeks just below the town.

Minner and Carle Frink met him at the gate. Carle was Minner's assistant superintendent. Their dress indicated they had hurriedly got out of bed and rushed to the mine.

"The entire south main section of the mine is flooded at level three and four," Minner said, as they walked toward his office. A small crowd had all ready assembled outside the fence and as they passed Dora Pitmen grabbed Carle Frink's arm. Doc and Minner continued on through the gate. Doc could hear Carle explaining that it was too early to be able to tell her anything.

"Are there any survivors?" Doc asked.

"So far we've got five missing. No one's been recovered," Minner said.

"Who?" Doc asked.

"Vittie Pitmen's gang," Minner whispered. The phone was ringing when they entered the office and Minner picked it up. "Superintendent's office," he answered. "Oh, My God! No!" he exclaimed. "Oh, God! No!" He replaced the receiver and leaned heavily on the phone for a minute before he said anything. "Oh, God," he whispered. He shook his head in disbelief. "We better get on down to Dogtown, Doc. There's been a flood."

He pulled on a red sweater, canvas jacket, heavy boots and a cap, and grabbed a big flashlight and the keys to his truck. "You better ride with me in the truck. Road's washed out just below the bridge."

Doc went to his car to get his bag and medical kit, and Minner gave Carle instructions to direct operations at the mine. As they drove out of town, Minner explained. "Our impound dam above Dogtown failed and washed everything out of the hollow. No one had time to get out."

Minner turned off at Duck and drove to the head of the hollow. "Debris has trapped water behind the bridge at National Hollow and created a lake, so I'm going to go above it if I can find a way. If we can help anyone, they'll be above that water."

"You suppose the water..."

Minner looked at him with an expression that answered the unfinished question.

They crawled up the almost undetectable remains of an old logging trace and crossed over the ridge into the hills above Dogtown. As they descended into a clearing at the head of the hollow, Doc could not believe his eyes. The impound dam was gone and what had been the bed of Mill Creek was a lake. Minner stopped the vehicle and they got out. The ground was still wet from a light drizzle the day before. A dog howled in the distance, the water glistened in the faint sliver of moon-light. Someone called from the far side of the hollow. It was not a cry for help, it was more like a wailing sound.

Minner grabbed a shovel, some blankets and a rope, Doc brought his medical bag and they climbed down the steep hillside toward the edge of the water. Minner's boots were appropriate for the occasion. Doc wore no tie, but he had on a suit and dress shoes. He fell several times. By the time he got to the road, the seat and the knees of his pants were a mess. Four houses on one side were hardly touched, but across the road three others were severely damaged. They stopped at the water's edge and Minner scratched his head. "My God, there must be fifteen or sixteen houses completely covered."

"Or washed away," Doc added.

About that time, four adults and a child came out of the woods with a wailing woman in tow. Their identities were indistinct in the darkness, and the woman stumbled along with her hands over her face. She was crying and half-walking, half-swooning at the same time. The leader of the group emerged from the shadows. It was Walker Robinson, the janitor at the high school. He was a big, soft-spoken man who was well-liked by the entire community.

"Been a real calamity, Doctor Sizemore and Mister Wilson," he said. Walker always bowed when he spoke to a white man and he continued the habit even under the circumstances. "Was no warning a`tall. No sir'ee, none a`tall."

Doc didn't recognize the agitated woman; with her face buried in her hands.

"We trying to settle her, but she's powerful hopeless," Walker said. "She cain't find her man and her three chid'ren."

"Lordy oh Jesus! Lordy oh Jesus! Lordy oh Jesus!" she cried, bending forward at the waist repeatedly and straightening at the end of each outburst

"Help her up the path to my truck and we'll take her to town," Minner said. He placed a blanket over her shoulders and Radsey Johnson, Walker's common-law wife, straightened it into position. "I don't think there's anything we can do here tonight, Doc," he whispered. "Look," he said to Walker. "Bring the rest of your bunch, too, and come with us. We'll take you into town and find a place for you to stay. I'll send people up here at first light to see what we can do to help whoever's left."

"We bin all around," Walker Robinson explained. "If they's anybody left they's on their way to town all ready. I suppose we might's well go, too. They's nothin' more we can do here. I's sad to admit that, but it's true for certain."

Doc climbed back to the truck with great difficulty because of his leather-soled shoes and Minner and Robinson helped the others up the slope and aboard the pickup. By the time he got to where the truck was parked Doc had grass stains and mud on the front of his shirt.

Minner negotiated the damp hillside skillfully while his passengers clung to the sides of the truck-bed. The "Oh, Lord Jesus'es" settled down to a whimper; otherwise no one spoke. They stopped several times to pick up confused Negroes stumbling along in the dark, most of them partially dressed and bare-foot. When they got back to town a faint light was filtering over the hill-tops and more survivors straggled toward the Buffalo Creek Interdenominational Temple where ladies from the church and others from town had pushed the pews against the wall and set up cots or spread quilts on the floor.

Doc climbed out of the vehicle. Shirley smiled as she spotted him through a window in the back of the church. There was no joy in the smile. It was just habit. She was holding a baby in her arms, feeding it a bottle. The infant looked content. Doc helped several women out of the back of the truck and he and Minner drove to the mine.

Two bodies had been found, Hobart Price and Ernst Birkinbine. Vittie Pitmen and Bert Mollohan were still missing and Adam Clowdus had survived.

"We sent Clowdus over to Clendenin. He was banged up pretty bad," Carle Frink reported to Minner. "He blew out through number two air shaft into Buffalo Creek. Might have a broken leg. Was carried almost a quarter-mile before he crawled up onto the road." Carle shook his head in disbelief just relating the story. "Judd Parrish heard the siren and was on his way to the mine. Said he damn near run over Clowdus in the dark. Layin' right smack dab in the middle a' the road like that."

While Frink related the events to Minner, Hilda and Leroy Mollohan, Dora Pitmen, Minnie Price and Vera Birkinbine stood with a small clot of women near the wire fence. There appeared to be no conversation between them. They looked stunned. Several men milled around a short distance away, smoking and casting worried glances, first in the direction of any change in activity, then at the women. It was as if they were concerned about the disaster, but more concerned about the women's possible reaction to it.

The sound of a big diesel generator, the bright lights, and the people wandering in and out of the shadows gave an air of unreality to the scene. The panel truck that served as a back-up ambulance sat on the far side of the road near the railroad tracks. The doors to the cab were open and two men wearing fire hats, sat half-in and half-out of the vehicle. One was chewing tobacco and every once in a while he punctuated some observation with a stream of brown juice. Several men in dirty work clothes with solemn black faces and arms crossed tightly across their chests slouched around the truck or leaned against an empty gondola nearby.

A clot of worried-looking females stood at the gate, sometimes on tip toes straining to see what was going on.

"Why are the wives of the dead men still out there?" Minner asked.

"We thought we'd better wait until you came back to tell them about their husbands," Frink answered.

Minner straightened his tired back, ran his fingers through his hair and turned toward the door. "Damn, I hate this job sometimes," he said.

"I'll go with you," Doc whispered.

"Thanks, Doc."

Light was breaking over the hill-tops as the two men approached the women and in a soft voice, Minner told them what he knew. There was almost no reaction. Every day of their lives these women had lived with the foreboding that their husbands, fathers, brothers or sons would not return home at the end of a shift. They all had relatives and friends who had been killed in the mines.

Vera Birkinbine's lip quivered when Minner said Ernst's body had been found. "It was quick, Vera. He never knew what happened," Minner whispered as consolation. For a minute or two she seemed on the verge of breaking down, but she didn't. She returned his look of despair with a half-smile and she wiped her eyes with her hand.

"Ever'day he was down under that mountain, I knew this could happen." She looked at Doc. "I tried to be a good wife and keep the worry off a' him while he was at work. Looks like my life has been just one sorrow after another."

Minner touched her arm. Vera's expression stayed fixed straight ahead as if she were talking to no one in particular. Her eyes remained dry.

A younger woman, the wife of one of the Birkinbine boys, put her arm around Vera's shoulders and guided her across the dirt road toward home.

"I cain't feel no sorrow no more. My sorrow is crushed under a heap a worry," Minnie Price told Minner when he said he was sorry about Hobart. "I done lost a father and a son down there under that mountain diggin' the rich man's coal. I got no sorrow left."

Minnie's daughter-in-law, the widow of Hobart and Minnie's boy, George, took Minnie by the arm and led her across the tracks to the hard road. The workers lounging nearby looked away, and Doc stood watching them disappear into the darkness. At times like this, he wondered what good it was to be a doctor.

Minner put his hand on Doc's shoulder, they stood there for a few minutes. Then Minner said, "Why don't you go home and get a few hours sleep, Doc. I'll call you if we find anybody you can do anything for." Doc looked into the drained face of his friend and suddenly he realized how tired he was.

"Are *you* going to get any rest?" he asked.

"I'll get a few winks in the office after I find out what's going on down there at Dogtown," Minner answered. "I got a feeling you're going to be up to your ears at the clinic starting pretty soon. There's nothing you can do right now anyway." He shoved Doc's shoulder gently as if to propel him toward his car. "Now go on."

Doc seated himself behind the wheel, suddenly he was overcome with the feeling of impotence. He could not press the starter with his foot without trembling from the effort. When he got home he sat in the car and cried. Finally, he wiped his eyes, blew his nose, replaced his handkerchief in his back pocket and climbed out of the car. Shirley was not home when he went in, so he set the alarm to go off in two hours and draped himself across the bed.

Doc took a bath, shaved and brushed his teeth, then on his way to the clinic, he drank some of the coffee from the forgotten thermos. The waiting room was empty; Mrs. Sidenstricker informed him that a large crowd had gathered at the Dogtown bridge to look at the lake.

Several workers with minor injuries reported to Doc that the debris was being removed near one bridge abutment to create a spillway. The plan was to drain the lake slowly so the bridge and the railroad trestle would not wash away.

For the next three days, the people of Wattsville were almost in a state of suspended animation. They wandered around in silence. A total of twenty one people were dead or unaccounted for. The third and fourth levels of the mine were sealed with Vittie Pitmen and Burt Mollohan inside.

Shirley spent most of her time at the church, cooking, cleaning, distributing clothing, comforting those in distress.

On the second day of the tragedy, a committee of town's people, including Dora Pitmen and Minnie Price, approached Reverend Romel Goad with the admonition that it would be inappropriate for "The Coloreds" to be using the "Lord's House" when it was needed for the service of three of the dead miners. Ernst Birkinbine's ceremony would be conducted at The Tabernacle of Zion across the road.

Mayor Arbogast opened the high school gymnasium and had the survivors moved onto the basketball court. Walker Robinson was told the move was chosen because of superior bathroom and cooking facilities. He accepted the information graciously and passed it on to the congregation he seemed to have inherited in the absence of Reverend Pattison. Shirley told Doc she was certain Robinson knew better but held his tongue to spare everyone else's feelings.

The newspapers in Charleston and Beckley reported Buffalo Creek had been "*inundated by a flash flood with loss of life to some local inhabitants. The town of Wattsville was spared, but four men were presumed dead as a result of the water that flooded the lower levels of the Hammond Newcastle Mine. Company investigators reported that the water entered the mine through an air shaft.*"

Follow-up reports in southern West Virginia newspapers lauded the way the community had pulled together and assisted those who were displaced by *the tragic blow Mother Nature had dealt to their fellow citizens.*

As the water receded, twelve bodies were found but nothing remained of eleven houses and the High Holy Mount Carmel Church. Walker Robinson asked if he could conduct his ceremony at the high school but the school board was reluctant to set such a precedent. When Shirley learned of the school board's ruling, she and Alice Wilson opened the theater but it was too late. The funeral was held under a large Elm tree on the hillside above the former site of the impound damn.

A group of Negroes from Charleston and Bluefield carried the coffins up the hillside to the burial site where they had prepared graves for each family. Hand carved markers were placed at the head of each site whether the body were present or not. The wood working class at the Stephen Douglas Vocational School in Charleston made the markers as a class project.

At the last minute, it was decided that all four miners would have their service at the Buffalo Creek Interdenominational Temple. Two men from Adam Clowdus' shift carried his wheel chair up the steps and pushed it to a place down front where he could see his friend's caskets. A reporter stood in the back of the church and took notes.

The cemetery was a mile out of town on the road to Clendenin. Doc dropped Shirley off at the house after the burial. "I'll try to be home before dark," he promised. Shirley closed the car door, and stood in the driveway until he was out of sight.

Doc parked on the hill above Duck, picked the wreath off the back seat and walked along the ridge. He could see the water had drained out of Dogtown Hollow leaving the seven houses and several feet of mud resembling a lava flow in the receding light. He knelt before the marker at the empty grave site marked Pattison, The Reverend Martin and Mary belle. There were no dates of birth and no maiden name of Mary belle, only the date they were presumed to have died.

Doc placed the wreath against the marker and whispered the message he had written on the card: "*A garland for the brow of a gallant warrior and a man who knew how to be a friend.*" Then he stood and looked at the reddening sky in the west and wiped a tear from his cheek. He took his handkerchief from his pocket and blew his nose. He realized he was sobbing.

He started to walk back up the hill to his car. **Pattison and Walker Robinson may be the only colored men I have considered as individuals,** he thought and that realization deepened his sadness. He paused on the ridge, leaned against his car door, lit a cigarette and watched the last rays of light subside behind the hills. A bobwhite called from a nearby tree. A slight breeze blew up from the hollow. Doc shivered and pulled his jacket close, though it was not really cold. It was past dark when he got home.

Shirley hugged him when he came into the kitchen. He picked at his food and then lay awake looking at the ceiling. Shirley cleaned the kitchen and came to bed. She put her arms around him and drew him close.

A few days later, a meeting was held at the Lyric. The coloreds had to be dealt with and soon. Mayor Arbogast protested against moving them out of the gymnasium.

"There's no place suitable to move them to that I know of," he said.

Henry Knopp shouted from the back of the theater. "Well, they cain't just stay where they are forever." It was soon obvious there were two factions at the meeting, neither willing to hear the other's viewpoint.

"I can't believe we're even having this discussion," Bea Parker complained. "I think you ought to be ashamed of yourselves." She pointed her finger directly at Earl Braxton who appeared to be one of the most vocal spokesmen for the group intent on ousting the *coloreds*. Earl's face turned red and for a minute it looked as if he were going to sit down, but momentarily he squared his shoulders and regained his courage.

"Now, look here, Bea," he sputtered. "You been running that hotel too long. You're beginning to sound like one a' them out-siders what comes in here from New York or Pittsburgh." He looked at the faces in the crowd to see how he was doing. He must have sensed approval because he pressed on. "You ain't got no children what's getting ready to go back to school, so you'd best stay out of what don't concern you to begin with."

Quite a few "yeah's" emanated from the assembly and a lot of heads shook in agreement with his position. Bea looked around and made eye contact with several hostile faces. She sat down.

Nothing was decided at the meeting, but Mayor Arbogast told Minner afterward he knew he had to do something about the Negroes soon.

Minner was summoned to Charleston where Governor Morris Archer personally presided over the formal hearings to "get to the bottom of this terrible tragedy." The official verdict was that the disaster was caused by an "Act of God."

The Charleston newspapers reported that "*as terrible as the event had been, the people of West Virginia could close this sad chapter of their state's history with the certain knowledge no laws had been violated and no safety rules ignored.*"

Charles W. Moran, president of the Hammond-Newcastle Collieries, called the newspapers to personally express his sympathy for the families of the miners, "...who were struck down by the unprovoked act of nature." He patted Minner's shoulder, shook his hand vigorously, assured him he knew none of this was his fault, and boarded the train for Pittsburgh confident the matter was concluded.

"I feel kind of dirty," Minner said to Doc the evening he returned from Charleston.

"I'm sure there was nothing you could do," Doc said.

"You may be right, but that doesn't make me feel any better. One thing did come out of the hearings," he said. "And it's really kind of funny. Nothing was said about the Coloreds. Nothing! Their situation seemed to just lay there like a dead cow in the middle of the table. It was like it didn't exist if it was not brought up. But after the meeting the Governor told me he was sending tents for the survivors."

"Do you think he meant it?" Doc asked.

"I think so. I believe the Negroes' situation was on everybody's minds. They were just afraid to talk about it. It was like, if they didn't say anything, no one would find out what really happened."

"That's politics," Doc said. "Politics as usual."

That night at the supper table, Doc was pensive. Shirley asked about the hearings. "Is the Governor going to do anything to help the Negroes?" she asked.

"He's going to send tents," Doc answered.

"Oh," Shirley said. "And what about the next snow storm?"

"Maybe they'll be winter tents," Doc answered.

A few days later, as Doc crossed the parking lot at the office, a stranger stopped him. "Did you treat any of the victims of the mine disaster?" he asked.

"Who are you?" Doc asked.

"I'm a reporter."

"The only injury of importance was the one miner and he was sent to Clendenin," Doc answered. "I have taken care of him since he came home, but most of those I treated had minor injuries."

"Then his injuries were serious?"

"Not really. He was pretty shaken up, but luckily he'll have no permanent disability."

"How is he emotionally?"

"Well, he had a bit of a fright," Doc hedged.

"What about the wives of the dead men?"

"What is your name?" Doc asked.

"Stein. Morris Stein."

"What paper are you from?"

"Oh, I'm not from a paper around here," Stein answered.

"Where are you from?"

"Detroit."

"You're a long way from home, aren't you?"

"I just want to ask a few more questions," he said.

"Well, they'll have to wait. My wife is expecting me. My supper's getting cold while we stand here."

"I'll walk along with you."

"I'd rather you didn't," Doc said, and walked away.

There had been rumors floating around of some "city-fied" newspaper man poking around town, but this was the first time

Doc had encountered him. Minner said he was trying to stir up trouble.

"We need to put this behind us," Mayor Arbogast said. "Granted, the Negroes have not been as well treated as some would have liked, but the tents seem quite acceptable to them - at least for the present. There has been enough dissension in the community all ready."

When Doc discussed it with her at supper, Shirley said, "Well, I think ignoring a problem does not make it go away. Those poor people have been treated as if they don't exist. What are they going to do about their church and what are they going to do about school?"

"I don't know," Doc said. "Preacher Pattison was the school teacher. He was the only one with any education and he only finished high school."

"Mayor Arbogast proposed that the colored kids attend class with the white students but the school board over-ruled him. Now, he's trying to get the county government to pay Lessie Williams to carry on classes at the theater. She's almost fifteen. She was Preacher Pattison's best pupil, and, of the nine other students remaining, the oldest was in the fourth grade."

"I guess a fourteen-year old is better than no one," Doc said.

"Lessie is quite mature," Shirley said. "She had two brothers and a sister and she was the oldest. She's got no one now."

"Where is she living?" Doc asked.

"With her grandmother in one of those tents," Shirley answered.

The next morning, Mayor Arbogast flagged Doc down as he drove past the General store and showed him a newspaper. "Minner gave this to me this morning," he said. "Charles W. Moran sent it to him by special courier late last night."

Doc took the folded newspaper through the car window and opened it. The masthead said, The Detroit Free Press and under it, the headline, "*The Dogtown Massacre!*" The story ran over the byline of Morris Stein. He started by calling the impound dam a "*hastily constructed Gob Pile, thrown up in defiance of proper engineering standards and with total disregard for law or human life.*" He went on to say "*there had been many warnings of impending disaster. Warnings, officials of Hammond-Newcastle and the state and federal inspectors, charged with policing such structures, had ignored.*"

The following pages pilloried the governor, mine officials, state and federal mine inspectors, and the people of Wattsville. "*If the company had attempted to construct a mine refuse dam with such flagrant disregard for the lives of white people there would have been an out-cry heard all the way to Washington. This disaster was entirely man-made and predictable!*" He concluded his report with an account of the disgraceful treatment of the Negroes at the hands of public officials and citizens alike. He called the "*White elite; people who live in two story houses,*" and he faulted them for identifying more with the absentee mine owners than the citizens of their own community. He went on to say they could have influenced the other white residents to make humane accommodations for the unfortunate victims of the flood, but did not do so because the victims were Negroes. Doc handed the paper back to the mayor.

"I think Shirley would agree with him," he said.

"How about you?" Arbogast asked.

"I'm kind'a sorry I didn't speak up. You know, Mayor, I have sort of stayed out of most of the political affairs of this town." He paused and looked at the steering wheel then back to the mayor. "I always thought it was because I was above politics. But I should have said something."

"I'm just as guilty. I'm supposed to be a mayor, and the principal of the school, for God's sakes. I should have resigned. When the school board voted to keep those Negro children out of the school, I should have resigned as principal and mayor both. Right on the spot!" He took the paper as Doc handed it back through the window. "Minner was really low after he read this, Doc. If you get a chance you might try to cheer him up some."

Doc started the engine and sat there looking straight ahead. Then he looked at Mayor Arbogast, smiled a sad smile, put the car in gear and drove away without rolling up the window.

The next day the governor announced that, *"Due to the irresponsible and inflammatory reporting by out-side agitators and foreign communists from as far away as Detroit, the Wattsville area will be off-limits to all reporters until further notice."*

Chapter Six

"Hosey White wants to talk to you, Doctor Sizemore," Mrs. Sidenstricker said the following day at the office. "Says he can't rouse Pearly Mae out of bed."

Doc handed the chart he was finishing to her and went to the back of the clinic. "What's the matter with Pearly Mae, Hosey?"

"I don't rightly know, Doctor Sizemore," Hosey answered. "I cain't get her to wake up and she don't seem to be breathing right."

"Is she gasping or breathing real hard or what?"

"She don't seem to be breathing hardly a'tall. I shook her and shook her and she just keeps on laying there looking at the ceiling. She's kinda' foaming at the mouth."

"You meet me outside. I'll get my bag and we'll go see what's the matter." Doc picked up his bag, told Mrs. Sidenstricker where he was going and walked to his car.

"Well, I never," Vernetta Shawkey said when she saw Doc climb into his automobile with a Negro and Mrs. Sidenstricker told her she would have to wait until the doctor got back from a house call. "Things is coming to a pretty pass when an upstandin' white person has to wait while the high-an-mighty doctor traipses off to take care of one of them niggers."

Hosey looked out the car window and mumbled as they drove to the tent village at the mouth of Dogtown hollow. Doc had trouble keeping up with the worried husband as he scurried between the tents to a place on the edge of the clearing. Hosey threw back the tent flap and held it up for Doc to duck under. Pearly Mae was lying on a cot with her eyes wide open. Her mouth was open and foam covered her teeth. Doc took out his stethoscope but he knew it was no use. He listened for breath sounds, there were none. He looked at Hosey and shook his head.

"I'm sorry, Hosey."

Hosey sat down on the cot. He touched Pearly May's face. Tears ran along his eyelids and drifted down his cheeks.

"I wanted her to thumb down to Charleston and see if she could get that X a'ray picture you wanted, Doctor Sizemore, but she was afraid what it would show." He patted her face gently and wiped his eyes with the palm of his hand. "What's I going to do without my Pearly Mae?" He fiddled with the covers and brushed her hair back from her forehead.

Doc stood in the middle of the little tent. Hosey leaned forward with his head in his hands and rocked back and forth.

"What's I going to do? What's I going to do?" he mumbled.

Doc motioned to a woman standing outside. She let go of a little girl's hand, ordered her to stay where she was and entered the tent.

"Where's Pearly Mae's children?" he asked.

"They's staying with me. Hosey brought them over before he come for you," she said.

"Can you get someone to stay with Hosey while I go to town for the ambulance?" Doc asked.

"My man'll stay with him."

"Thank you. I'll send the ambulance right away. Might be best if Hosey goes over to your tent when they come." Doc placed his hand on Hosey's shoulder, patted him gently, then drove back to town.

"Pearly Mae White died today," Doc said to Shirley when he got home that night.

"Pearly Mae couldn't have been more than thirty," Shirley said. "What did she die of? Not that goiter?"

"Pneumonia, probably, but I'm afraid she had active tuberculosis. That's all we need in that tent village."

* * *

Rumors circulated that Walker Robinson had been seen talking to that "New York Jew reporter from De'troit," and was most likely the source of those lies about the events.

"Probably wants to get government welfare for the lot of `em," Woody Woodrum announced at Nick Novak's place after a few bottles of Red Top Hardy Pilsner.

A voice from the darkness at the far end of the pool table mumbled, "Might be `at nigger needs to learn to keep his mouth shut." He leaned forward to line up his shot. It was Mule Ears Goad.

Novak snickered from behind the bar.

"That nigger'd slap them big ears a' yours up `side your head so hard they wouldn't stick out for a week."

Mule Ears made the nine ball, walked around the table, screwed up his face to keep the smoke from his cigarette out of his eye, and lined up on the ten.

"Sounds like you're scared a' that nigger yourself, Nick," he said. He scratched on the ten. "Shit! You caused me to scratch. Shit!" He banged the heel of the cue on the floor in disgust.

"I ain't scared a' nobody," Nick answered. "But I'm warnin' you. You go after that nigger, you better have help or he'll treat you like three coons on a pup. And quit banging the pool cue. I just put new tips on `em."

Later that night, Walker Robinson was awakened by a commotion outside his tent.

"Who's `at out there?" he whispered.

"Never you mind who it is," the voice answered out of the darkness. "You don't want us to burn down ever tent in this holler, you keep your voice down and come on out here right now."

Walker Robinson slipped on his shoes, put his finger to his lips and shushed his wife, Radsey.

"Don't make no fuss now, honey. I gots to go talk to some white folks. I'll be back as soon as I can. Now, don't you worry." He leaned down and kissed her. She clung to him.

"Don't go out there, Daddy. They goin' to hurt you for sure." Robinson pulled her hand loose from the front of his overalls and separated the tent flaps. He paused in the opening, staring into the gloom. A sullen voice instructed him to walk onto the trail where the road had been.

"Now, you just go up toward the head of the holler and don't make no commotion, and nobody's going to get hurt," the voice said.

"What you want?" Robinson asked.

"Never mind about that, nigger. You just do what you're told. We just want to talk to you. Now get yourself on up the holler." The voice seemed to be getting angrier and more confident with each remark.

The big Negro walked slowly into a clearing near the head of the hollow and stopped as he was commanded. He stood trembling in the faint light of the moon, staring into the darkness. He could not see his antagonists, but he was sure there were several of them. Bushes rustled all around him. A cricket chirped nearby.

"O.K. now, nigger boy, strip."

Robinson bent forward at the waist and turned slowly in a half-circle. He studied the blackness for movement and backed slowly toward a big tree. He straightened to his full six-feet-four-inch height, arms hanging loosely at his sides and in a pleading voice, he said.

"I don't want no trouble from you and it'd be better if you all'd let me go on back to my tent." There was less fear in his voice than before. The order to strip meant they intended to whip him and Walker Robinson knew if they got close enough to do that he would most likely give a good account of himself. When he was in the Army, Walker Robinson had been in the ring with Joe Lewis. There were no four or five white men in Wattsville who wouldn't have to pay dearly for any whipping they tried to administer to a riled up Walker Robinson.

"You better do what your told and be quick about it, boy."

"I ain't strippin' for no man and I ain't your boy neither," he growled. "Now, you white boys go on home and leave me alone. I's going back to the tent." With that he turned quickly and swung his massive fist in the darkness, but at that instant someone jumped him from behind. He whirled around and threw the body into a tree trunk. He swung again and hit someone in what must have been his face. He felt a bone cave in and a body sag to the ground. He swung again, but something hit him on the head. Lights danced in front of his eyes, electricity shot through his brain. That was the last he could remember until Radsey's face came into focus.

About three in the morning, Doc got a call from Merle Prowse that there had been an accident. Mule Ears squirmed on the examination table when Doc touched the swollen cheek-bone.

"That's a nasty bruise you got there, Goad," he said.

"Owe, owe, be careful, Doc. You're hurting me," Goad protested.

"How'd you get hurt, anyway?" Doc asked.

"I fell down," Mule Ears answered.

"Pretty nasty fall, you ask me," Doc said.

"Well, never mind about that. Is anything broke?"

"Looks like you broke your cheek bone at least. Could have a fractured skull. You need some X-rays. I think you'll have to go to Charleston to get that cheek bone fixed and your nose don't look so hot either. I'll call an Ear Eye Nose and Throat specialist and you can drive him down there tonight in your car," Doc said to Merle.

After a phone call to be sure the specialist was available, Merle and Doc helped Goad down the steps and across the parking lot. Doc looked at the two men waiting in the back seat of the car.

"You look kind'a skinned up, Coyner," he said to one of the men. He could not tell who the other one was, but whoever it was, he grunted with pain when he scooted into the shadows.

"Fell trying to help Mule Ears up the hillside," Coyner explained without being asked.

"You ought to come in here and let me take a look," Doc said.

"I'll be O.K.," he answered.

"Have it your way," Doc said. "Any signs of infection, get yourself in and let me have a look right away. You hear?"

"I'll do that very thing," Coyner answered. Merle climbed into the driver's side, turned the key and put the Ford in gear.

He pulled out of the parking lot across the bridge and turned toward the road out of town.

Three days later, Doc sat at the table, smoking. They had just finished supper and Shirley was clearing away the dishes. There was a knock at the front door. It was timid at first, then as Doc crossed the living room, a second knock was louder.

Radsey Johnson stood on the front porch with a stricken look on her face wringing her hands. "You gots to come and see my Daddy, Doctor Sizemore. He's down in bed and he ain't been up on his feet for more'n two days now. I's sorry to be knocking on your door this time of the evenin', but Daddy ain't never been so sick before and I'm powerful worried on his account."

"Wait `til I get my coat and I'll be right with you, Radsey." He kissed Shirley and headed for the door. "Be back as soon as I can, honey," he said. Radsey waited on the porch outside the screen door, a worried expression on her face.

"Sorry to bust in like this, Misses," she said when she saw Shirley following Doc to the door. Shirley nodded.

Radsey sat quietly in the passenger seat as Doc drove down Buffalo Creek to the tent village in National Hollow. "Radsey, tell me what happened to Walker,"

"Some white men called him out the other night and he ain't been hisself since," she answered. "But he weren't down in bed `til yesterday. He just ain't able to get on his feet a'tall."

Doc thought about Mule Ears and Prowse but he figured it best to say nothing. He parked outside the first row of tents and Radsey led the way. The mud was so deep they had to walk on planks strung between the tents. Radsey pulled back the flap and Doc stuck his head into the little room. The formerly-white canvas was muddy near the ground and grimy-black above, the only light was a kerosene lantern and a coal stove salvaged from the flood was vented through the back of the tent. The floor was the packing crates the tent was shipped in. Two children about eight or ten occupied one cot in the back of the room, Walker and Radsey had a small bed on one side and an elderly lady sat on a cot against the opposite wall. Doc recognized the Robinson children; he had given them shots for ear infections.

"I's sorry...," Walker whispered as Doc bent over to enter the tent.

"Don't apologize, Walker," Doc said. "Probably should have called me sooner." He pulled a Nehi drink crate up by the bedside and sat down. "Tell me what's the matter." Walker looked at him with a blank expression and opened his mouth. He seemed to be forming a word but it never materialized. He put his hand up as if he wanted to reach out. His elbow stayed bent, the hand frozen in position, half open.

Doc held the lantern in front and then away from Walker's eyes, there was very little reaction. His face was a mask, the left pupil larger than the right. Doc checked for toe movement, reflexes, pain response and heart sounds. His blood pressure was 170/110, his heart rhythm was regular. Doc had trouble doing a thorough neurological examination because of the circumstances, but after he looked into Walker's eyes at his blurry optic disc, he motioned for Radsey to follow him outside.

"Radsey, I think Walker's got a subdural hematoma. His fundi, that's the back of his right eyeball is shoved forward and that means something is pushing on it." He waited for his explanation to register before he went on. "He needs to go to Charleston and see a Neurosurgeon right away."

"Is my sweet Daddy gonna' die, doctor Sizemore?" Radsey leaned forward, grasped Doc's hand in both of hers and hung on. She looked Doc straight in the eye waiting for his answer.

"No, Radsey, he's not going to die. Not if we get him to the hospital right away." Doc knew Robinson was bad-off, but he was strong and healthy and though he might have some permanent damage, he should live if that blood could be sucked out of his skull. "I'll send the ambulance as soon as I get back to town," he said. "And I'll call the doctor in Charleston so he'll be ready for Walker when he gets there. Now don't you worry, Radsey. He'll be all right."

Doc drove to the clinic and called the mine office. Carle Frink answered the phone. "Sure, Doc, we'll get the ambulance right down there and get Robinson to the hospital right away. Which one do you want us to take him to, Doc?"

"Mercy," Doc answered. After he hung up the phone, he called and talked to the resident. He explained that Walker had a sub-dural and recommended the resident call a Neurosurgeon right away to alert him.

"Yeah, yeah," the resident responded. "I'll take care of it." He started to hang up the phone but he heard Doc still talking and put it back to his ear.

"I have examined Mr. Robinson and I assure you he is going to need surgery very soon. The sooner the better," Doc said. "I would appreciate it if you would consider that very seriously."

"Yeah, yeah, I'll take care of it. Now if there's nothing else, I'd like to get an hour's shut eye while the so-called sub dural is getting here."

Doc lowered his voice and softened it as much as he could.

"Wait a minute," he said. "This is not an it, nor is this a so called sub dural. This is a human being. His name is Walker Robinson. He is a fine man, his wife and children love him..." Before he could finish the sentence, the phone went dead. Doc called back and the operator at the hospital switchboard informed him Doctor Ellison was busy and would return his call when he could get to it. Doc sat with both hands on the telephone for a long time.

The next morning, Doc called the hospital and talked to an intern who was assigned to the case. "Yes, doctor Sizemore, Mr. Robinson was admitted here last night, but he is being transferred as soon as the ambulance gets down here from Beckley."

"An ambulance from Beckley? What in Hell's going on? Has he been operated on yet?" Doc could not believe his ears. That hematoma should have been evacuated hours ago.

"He's a vet," the young voice explained. "Got to transfer him to the Veteran's Hospital by their ambulance. He's been ready to go for quite a while. Some delay with the paper work, but Dr. Huddleston's trying to clear that up right now. That's all I know except they think it's a sub dural."

The next day was Friday and Doc called the Veteran's Hospital. The Nurse informed him the doctor was busy and the patient, Walker Robinson, was being evaluated. "We are very busy, why don't you call us next week," she said.

"Because next week he will be dead," Doc answered. "Why can't I talk to the doctor?"

"Because, as I told you before, he is busy. Now I have work to do so I must terminate this call." With that, she hung up the phone. Doc tried to call all weekend without success. Once he got the janitor, who sounded no more confused than everyone else he had talked with. Monday morning he finally talked to an Intern who seemed accommodating.

"Dr. Menendez, who admitted him Friday, went on vacation so no tests were ordered. Can't get anything done around here on weekends, but I'm starting to request some studies today. The doctor in Charleston sent a note, he suspected a sub dural so the patient," he paused. "Let's see, Robinson isn't it? Yes, it's Robinson. Well, anyway, he's probably going to need surgery."

"What kind of shape is he in?" Doc asked.

"Well, I just came on. I'm reviewing the chart now but as soon as I finish, I'm going to see him right away." He reassured Doc he would call him back as soon as he had something to tell him.

"His wife is worried sick," Doc said. "She went to Charleston and spent two days waiting before she was told Walker was discharged from the hospital. She thought he was sent home. If she comes over there, can she visit her husband?"

"I'm not sure about that. Tell her to call and ask the switchboard operator. She knows about that stuff."

Radsey was told visiting hours were four to eight except on weekends and holidays when visiting hours were ten A.M. to seven P.M. Shirley drove Radsey over to Beckley in Alice Wilson's car. Walker was in X-ray until seven-thirty so Radsey was allowed to go into the room for only a few minutes.

"Alice said she could bring you back tomorrow, Radsey," Shirley said. "Maybe they will let you see him earlier." Radsey did not answer, she cried quietly all the way home. When Shirley opened the car door, Radsey seemed to be in a trance. "We're home, Radsey," Shirley said.

"He gonna' die," Radsey said. It sounded like a pronouncement. There was resignation in the statement and no room for contradiction. Shirley just stood there looking at the forlorn little figure. Suddenly, Radsey looked about fifteen years old. Shirley wanted to hug her but she could not bring herself to move. She stood there until Radsey turned and shuffled out of sight between the tents.

"How is Walker?" Doc asked as soon as Shirley came in the door.

"I didn't see him," she answered. "But Radsey said he's going to die." Doc did not answer. He knew she was right.

The next day just before noon, Mrs. Sidenstricker was waiting in the hallway when Doc came out of an examination room. "Doctor Sizemore," she said. "You just got a call from the telephone operator at the hospital in Beckley. She said to tell you that Walker Robinson died at one o'clock in the morning. Only she called him Walter Rogers. She asked us to inform the *deceased's* widow."

"I'm afraid they'll have to do that themselves. She's on her way over there now," Doc said.

* * *

The funeral was held in that well-used spot under the elm tree. The Negro community was accompanied up the hill by Mayor Arbogast, Doc and Shirley, the Wilsons, Coach Nellis and several school teachers. Deputy Sheriff Chapin was parked at the foot of the hill when they came back to their cars. Doc asked Shirley to wait in the car while he talked to him.

"How's things, Doc?" the Sheriff asked.

"Not good, Don. I hate to tell you this, but I know who killed Walker Robinson."

"That right? Could I trouble you for a smoke, Doc, my pack seems to be empty." He took the package out of his pocket, twisted it elaborately as if to demonstrate how empty it was and threw it on the ground. Doc tapped several cigarettes up out of the top of the full package and reached it out to the Sheriff.

Don Chapin was a tall man with big hairy arms, a paunch and wisps of long hair combed across his shiny scalp. He had the look of a man in need of a shave even though he had done that a few hours before. He was almost ordinary looking except he had a sinister air about him.

"Are you sure you know as much as you think you do, Doc?" He bent close to Doc's match and sucked in to ignite the tobacco. At the same time he looked up sharply at Doc.

"I saw four men, been in a fight and lied about it," Doc answered.

"Is that all, Doc?"

"What more do you need, Sheriff?"

"Proof," he answered. "Proof, Doc. I need proof." He turned and climbed into the police car and drove away.

"He's not going to do anything," Doc told Shirley on the way home. "They are going to get away with it. Just as sure as we are sitting here, they are going to get away with it."

Shirley placed her hand on his thigh and after a few minutes she patted his leg and looked out the window.

Chapter Seven

"I'm afraid we're in for a long one this time," Minner announced from behind his cards in his rumpus room. "If we knuckle under to this, there'll be no end to it. The union has demands we just can't oblige."

"What do they want?" Doc asked.

"What *don't* they want? They want the company, I guess." He looked at his cards indifferently.

"When is the vote?" coach Nellis asked.

"Next week," Minner answered. "We're getting ready for the operators to take over. I guess we'll be living at the mine `til it's resolved."

"Why's that?" Nellis asked. "You're not expecting trouble are you?"

"We have a feeling this is going to be the biggest showdown since the vote to unionize," Minner answered. "And you know the violence *that* caused. Wouldn't be surprised if the governor calls out the national guard before it's done."

"You don't expect bloodshed do you, Minner?" Doc asked.

"Never can tell. Wouldn't shock me any if almost anything happened. Don't say I told you, but the operators would like nothing better than to break the union." Minner's declaration caused the card game to be forgotten. The players placed their hands face-up on the table. Doc had two aces and the coach had three tens. Minner stood up. "Let me get another round." His high card was Nellis' other ten.

"I think I'll have a beer this time, Minner," Doc announced. The others pretended surprise.

"Whose going to drive Doc home tonight?" Coach laughed. "Boozin' like that, the man's gotta be taken care of by someone's only had four or five bourbons. Cain't have you wrecking that new car now can we?" They all laughed at the joke.

* * *

Doc was used to the comments about his **"NEW CAR"** *mostly implying how rich he must be getting, but actually the car was a gift from Ramsay Southard. It had been almost two years since Doc first met the Southards. Bernard Southard had been diagnosed with Friedreich's ataxia, and his parents told his paralysis would progress and he would die in his teens.*

Ramsay Southard had taken his son to every highly regarded specialist in Charleston, several Midwestern clinics, even a famous neurologist in New York. Each confirmed the diagnosis and agreed with the prognosis. Ramsay had grown wealthy from the sales of a special type of drill bit he invented. He had leased the manufacturing rights to Hugheston Drilling

Tools Inc. of Houston, Texas, and every mining and drilling operation in the world was busily switching their equipment over to his innovation. Money was no object to Mr. Southard, and he would have given everything he owned to see Bernard healthy.

While traveling in the Midwest, Southard had seen an article in the Cleveland Plain Dealer. The headline read: "Rural Practitioner Saves Man's Life." The article was accompanied by a picture of a man, with a knapsack on his back, standing on the top of Lover's Leap looking out over the New River Gorge. Under the photo the caption read, ***"Avid hiker continues recovery!"*** *The article went on to report,* ***"Mr. Quenton Parker, a technician in a piano factory in Cincinnati was told by a leading cardiologist that his heart valve had been irreparably damaged by Rheumatic Fever and nothing more could be done for him. Mr. Parker, believing he had only a few months to live, returned to his parents' home in the rural community of Wattsville, West Virginia. Dr. Earl Sizemore, the village physician, conducting an examination in the patient's home, using only the rudimentary tools of a rural general practitioner, corrected the mistaken diagnosis."***

The article went on to explain that Doc had sent Parker to the Cleveland Clinic where his diagnosis of constrictive pericarditis was confirmed and the pericardium surgically removed.

"With the removal of the confining sac from around the heart, the patient was cured," *the article concluded.*

Ramsay Southard had called from Cleveland and asked if Doc would see his son. He cut short his business trip, rushed home to Fall's View, and brought Bernard to Wattsville. Bernard Southard had been carried into Doc's office because of paralysis in his legs and severe downward flexion of his feet. When questioned carefully, however, the boy described a progressive weakness rather than ataxia. There were no eye signs and his upper extremities were totally uninvolved. Doc suspected a benign tumor pressing on the spinal column instead of Fredreich's Ataxia. Bernard's deformed feet had probably helped to fool those previously consulted. Doc called the neurosurgeon in Charleston and asked him to re-think his diagnosis. He explained his reasons for questioning the opinion. The specialist, though reluctant to withdraw his previous judgment, was sympathetic to Doc's argument. He agreed to perform a myelogram.

Doc had charged for an office visit, refused the higher fee offered and sent the pair on their way. The X-ray showed a benign tumor pressing on the spinal cord and it was removed within a month. Bernard began physical therapy as soon as he recovered from the surgery. He was getting around a month after that and walking normally at the end of a year-and-a-half.

The notes from Bernard as his condition improved, and the boy's testimonial that someday he was going to be a doctor "just like you" meant more to Doc than any material gift,

"You gave us our son back and this token is nothing compared to that!" Ramsay said. Doc was proud of that car but not for the reasons his patients suspected.

* * *

On his way home Doc slowed as he drove by Shorty's Bar. A group of miners sat in a booth near the front, several others stood solemnly nearby. It looked like a meeting to Doc and he remarked about it to Shirley when he got home.

"There's talk," she said. "At the quilting club today Sarah Fowler said Orville warned her there's going to be violence."

Orville Fowler, Sarah's husband, was secretary of the union local and should know the mood of the workers if anyone did.

Over the next few days it became obvious trouble was brewing. Clots of miners congregated everywhere at the most unlikely hours. People started putting in supplies. Essential commodities and ammunition were gone from the shelves at the company store almost overnight.

Minner and his salaried employees had not left the mine area for almost a week when the miners walked out and established a picket line at the gate. Minner contacted the head office and asked for help. Workers from Cannelton were sent over by bus, but they refused to cross the union picket line and were turned away. The miners on the line set up a roar of approval when the bus backed around to leave.

Fresh supplies were blocked at the mine entrance the following day. The next day it was learned that workers and supplies were sneaked in on the locomotive that had come to tow away the already filled gondolas sitting on the tracks below the tipple.

Bud Sweeney hastily called a meeting in the back room at Shorty's.

"If we don't stop that railroad from bringing in scabs and supplies, we might's well give up now," he said.

"How we going to do that?" someone questioned. "They ain't going to stop no train for no miners with signs."

"We got guns ain't we?" someone else shouted. The roar of approval changed the mood of everyone in the room and tension in Wattsville seemed to escalate after that meeting.

Probably because of his friendship with Minner, Doc's sympathies were mostly with the operators but he kept his opinions to himself. A few days into the strike he crossed the line to treat a foreman for an injury; the seriousness of which turned out to have been exaggerated. After he dispensed some aspirin to the ailing miner, he went into Minner's office.

"I've been thinking of quitting this job and moving away," Minner said. "I dread what it's going to be like for me and Alice when this is over." Doc shook his head. He could not think of anything to say.

It was learned through a leak from within that Doc had smuggled in some bourbon. He was searched from then on before being allowed to cross the picket line. A note was sent in to Minner warning that an exaggeration of the seriousness of another illness would end the privilege of having Doc cross at all.

Before the strike was three weeks old, a truck driver was shot on the road into town. The narrow lane winding through dense woodland made vehicles and their drivers easy targets for sharpshooters who could sit on a hillside unobserved and take potshots at any unwanted traffic. A week later a railroad engineer was killed by gunfire. The truck driver died in Charleston General Hospital three days after that.

Minner's superiors appealed to the governor and the telephone lines to the mine were cut before the governor could contact Minner to find out about circumstances inside the mine. For the time being the governor postponed any response.

The economy of Wattsville had not been good for a long time. With the miners on strike the check off paid to Doc from their wages dried up and his income dwindled. Folks began leaving town to stay with relatives and businesses started closing their doors so everyone began to suffer. The two bars managed to stay open but school was shut down.

"Collections are next to nothing," he remarked to Shirley one day."Maybe I should go back to work in the office," she said.

"We're still getting by," Doc said. "Let's hold out a while before doing that."

They dipped into their meager savings, economized where they could, and put off purchases. Weeks dragged into months. Still the operators held out.

Conditions in Dogtown became even worse than they had been and some of the coloreds moved away. Doc diagnosed four cases of tuberculosis in the tent village. Hosey White and three others were sent to the sanitarium and his children went to stay with their grandparents in Gamoca.

After five months of violence and signs the stand-off was nowhere near to a solution, the governor sent in the national guard. Word of their assembly in Charleston leaked to the miners from someone in the Governor's office the day it was decided to mobilize. The trestle across Mill Creek was destroyed the next night. The troop's train had to stop two miles before it got to Wattsville.

The civilian soldiers with their campaign hats perched jauntily on their heads disembarked from the train and hiked toward town. Their uniforms smelled of mothballs, and wrinkles far outnumbered creases. The shades of their olive-drab clothing varied according to the number of times it had been washed and along with a random attention to fit, created the impression of a disorganized affair rather than a military detail. Their march deteriorated quickly into a stroll and cigarettes appeared along with gripes about the footing on the rail-bed.

They sounded like a hive of bees swarming along the creek bank until they came through the narrow pass toward the mine entrance. As they scrambled into the ravine beside the remnants of the trestle, shots rang out from a hill on the opposite side of the creek. No one was hit, but the detachment was pinned down all afternoon and into the night. Morale, not very high to begin with, took a severe downturn during the uncomfortable night. The next morning patrols scoured the woods but found no sign of the snipers. The soldiers bivouacked and set up machine guns between the pickets and the mine entrance. They set their tents behind the protection of a row of gondolas and dug their latrine along the bank of Mill Creek.

As their little settlement became more comfortable, laughter could be heard drifting along the creek-banks and eventually music echoed through the hollows. An accordion, a banjo and several guitars appeared by campfires and their melodies issued from inside tents. Early in the evening it might be, *When the weather's kind of chilly and we start to kiss and hug/everyone thinks she's silly 'cause she wants to cut a bug...* or *When it's peach pickin' time in Georgia/apple pickin' time in Mississippi/everybody picks on me...* and as the sun went down and it was about time for taps, *In the Blue Ridge Mountains of Virginia/on the trail of the lonesome pine/in the pale moonshine our hearts entwine...*

Mornings started with Cpl. Guthrie's cornet sounding reveille followed by the rumble of coal down the mountainside. Evenings ended with the melancholy notes of taps. Some of the troops came into town when they were off-duty; but mostly they went over to Clendenin. There were a couple of fights at Nick's and one in front of Shorty's, but they never escalated into anything major. Doc treated some minor wounds among the guards, a few insignificant illnesses and once he went to the camp and checked their facilities because of an outbreak of dysentery. He submitted vouchers for payment.

It was quiet for almost a month and nearly half the contingent was sent home. Two days later an Army truck was set ablaze and when its fuel exploded, a Lieutenant was severely burned on his chest, both arms and his face. Much of his hair was singed away and his bronchi must have been seared because he developed pulmonary edema.

Doc covered his burns with cold wet dressings and ice. He administered morphine, started intravenous fluids, gave him a shot of penicillin and an injection of mercuhydrin. Shirley volunteered to go in the ambulance with the wounded soldier to the hospital in Charleston. She was to inject more morphine if the patient became uncomfortable on the trip.

"Keep that I.V. just barely open, Shirley," Doc instructed. "He needs fluids mighty bad because of the burns, but the water in his lungs worries me that we may overload him if we're not careful."

"I'll be careful," Shirley said.

"If his pulse gets over a-hundred-and-fifty or if the wet rales in his lungs get worse, slow the I.V. down and give him some more morphine. You got that?"

"I understand," she answered as the ambulance doors were closed. Doc watched the ambulance out of sight before he drove home. He felt good having Shirley accompany the patient. She had not practiced in a long while, but she was a good nurse with good instincts. He waited up for her return, and when she got home later that night she assured him the patient had arrived at Mercy in good shape.

"His lungs were clearer than when he started and he was comfortable with the morphine. Dr. Wescott in the E.R. said he was pleased with the care you provided. He said he had a lot of experience with this type of injury in the war and he was certain the Lieutenant would recover with minimal scarring."

Oh God the war, Doc thought. *I can't believe that soldier got his war wounds in Wattsville.*

After they were in bed, Doc put his arms around Shirley.

"Thanks for helping out, darlin'," he whispered. "You are a wonderful nurse."

"And we work well together," she said. "I must admit I felt a little rusty, but it was exciting to be able to help." It was late and they were both tired, but they made love for the first time in weeks.

Doc lay awake after Shirley was asleep and smoked a cigarette. He dreamed of the war and awakened in the morning as tired as when he went to bed.

The following week, federal marshals were sent into Wattsville to search for firearms. No weapons were found except a Civil War musket in the back of the second hand store and a shotgun belonging to ten-year-old Dana Carper.

There were twenty of the marshals some of whom doubled up in the rooms at the hotel. The rest stayed over in Clendenin. It was hard to tell them apart, they were about the same age, had similar haircuts and they all dressed in dark suits. They took over the theater, set up desks, chairs and file cabinets and brought miners in for questioning in what appeared to be an aimless exercise. At first they were polite but as they experienced the escalating resistance, their mood degenerated through coldness to outright hostility. They seemed intent on intimidating the strikers but, in fact, they intensified the violence.

A marshal's car was hit by rifle fire the fourth week after their arrival. The windshield and two tires were shot out. One marshal got off three shots and was certain he had hit something. The following morning blood was discovered on a tree and along the path leading away from the site where several shell casings were found lying on the ground. Evidently, someone had beaten a hasty retreat through the woods. It was the first time evidence of a sniper's location was left behind.

Doc was sure Alf Martin was moving gingerly when he watched him get off the barstool at Shorty's a few days later.

"Got a problem I can help you with, Alf?" Doc asked.

"No, Doc. Ain't nothin' botherin' me. Nothin' at all," he said as he skittered out of the bar and up the street.

The next day, Doc treated Hobart Skidmore for a gunshot wound of the thigh that looked as if it were several days old. Hobart said he shot himself that day while hunting.

Looks like a strange wound to be self inflicted, Doc thought, not to mention that Hobart was supposed to have turned in his weapons. He heard rumors later Hobart and Alf had been hit while they were running from the attack on the marshal's car.

Doc worried about what he should do. He knew he was supposed to report the gunshot wound but he also knew that would mean serious trouble for him and his family. Since no one was seriously hurt in the incident, he decided to say nothing. He did not talk to Shirley about it.

The next night, one of the federal marshals was on guard duty near the power station that served the coal tipple. He was walking along the railroad tracks alone. There was no moon; every sound and every movement caused him to flinch and the darkness escalated his anxiety. When he thought he heard a metallic sound as though someone were cocking a rifle, he dropped quickly to the rail bed and pulled his pistol. His forearm rested on the cool metal of the rail as he stretched out on the ground. He held his breath; his hand trembled; sweat formed on his lip; his eyelid twitched. Suddenly, he detected a rustling of the bushes on the other side of the tracks. He quickly yanked the gun-barrel in the general direction of the noise and jerked the trigger. The weapon recoiled and air escaped from his lungs simultaneously with the sound of breaking glass.

The lights came on in Carper's shack on the creek bank next to the railroad tracks. Ralph Carper rubbed his eyes to accustom them to the light. Thelma was all ready out of bed.

"What was that?" Ralph asked.

"Sounded like a winda' in the back of the house," Thelma answered. Ralph reached under the bed for the rifle he had hidden from the marshals and hurried to the front of the house in his underdrawers.

"Oh! My God!" Thelma screamed from the back of the house. "Oh! My God!"

Ralph ran through the house to Dana's bedroom. Thelma stood in the middle of the floor, screaming. Dana's bed was covered with blood.

Woody Woodrum had been walking along the creek on his way home from Shorty's when he heard the shot. He came around the house just in time to see a man in a suit and tie running along the tracks toward town. He stuck his head in the broken window and saw Thelma standing in the bedroom screaming and Ralph bending over the bloody bed.

"I'll get the doctor," he yelled and took off toward Doc's house.

"What is it?" Doc called as he headed across the living room toward the front door.

"Somebody's been shot over at Carper's house, Doc," Woody yelled through the door. "You got to hurry." Doc ran back to the bedroom to get his pants. He slipped his shoes on without sox and buttoned his shirt as he ran across the porch. Woody had all ready sprinted into the darkness back toward Carper's place.

When Doc arrived, Ralph had Dana uncovered and the boy was gasping for air. Doc listened with his stethoscope, there were diminished sounds in Dana's right lung and his left was quiet. He had his hands around his neck and at first it looked as if he were choking himself. His face was swollen, bluish and mottled, his lips purple. Doc took a sixteen-gauge needle and stuck it into the left upper chest wall and air rushed out. Dana's breathing began to improve immediately and Doc started an I.V. into the left arm with a large bore needle. Dana whimpered softly.

Doc took a rubber glove and fixed it to a fifty-cc syringe with a rubber band. He cut one finger-tip off the glove, attached the contraption to the needle protruding from the chest wall and put Ralph's hand under the barrel of the syringe. The rubber expanded allowing air out of the chest space when Dana exhaled and flopped down preventing the flow back in when he inhaled. Dana's breathing improved with each inhalation.

The ambulance roared up the railbed backwards, two wheels bumping noisily on the ties and the other two crunching in the gravel. Woody was the first out of the vehicle and through the back door of the little house. Doc took Dana's blood pressure, it was eighty-five over zero, his pulse a steady one-twenty. The entrance wound was just below the left lower rib margin and the exit was out the back. The scapula was shattered along its inferior edge but the wound appeared to be sealed.

"I'm worried about his spleen so get him to Charleston as quickly as you can," Doc instructed Bud Albright. "I'll call Dr. Wescott and tell him to get surgery ready. Now get outta' here. Speed that I.V. up if he gets shocky."

"O.K., Doc," Bud answered. "I finished my ambulance training. I'll let Anse drive. I'll take good care of him, Doc. You can count on me."

Ralph and Thelma slipped on their clothes and climbed in the back with Dana. Doc checked Dana's pulse, listened to his heart and took his blood pressure. He looked at the bluish tint of the skin just below Dana's ribs. The discoloration was still localized in the left upper quadrant of his abdomen, but the capsule of Dana's spleen was certainly stretched to its limit.

"Speed's important, Anse, but if you hit a bump too hard his spleen could really let loose." Doc climbed out of the ambulance and closed the door. He was pleased that Anse eased the vehicle down the tracks, drove slowly across the bridge and did not speed up until he reached the smooth road on the opposite side of the creek. Doc climbed into the Plymouth and drove home.

Dr. Wescott returned his call almost immediately.

"Dana Carper is ten, Dr. Wescott. He has a punctured spleen and a tension pneumothorax. Gunshot wound. Went in the left upper quadrant of his abdomen and shattered his left scapula on the way out. I put a sixteen gauge needle in his chest with a one way valve and started an I.V. with an eighteen needle in his arm. He was stable when he left here."

"Sounds like you did all the right things. I hope they take it easy with that spleen."

"I told them speed was not as important as being gentle."

"Great! I'll let you know when I have something solid," Wescott said. Doc hung up the phone, his hands trembled. He was too nervous to sleep. He heated some left-over coffee, sat at the kitchen table and smoked a cigarette. When he crawled into bed, Shirley put her arms around him and he felt better.

The phone rang, but Shirley picked it up before Doc could get out of bed. She had been working in the kitchen.

"It's Dr. Wescott."

"Hi, Dr. Wescott," Doc said. "How's Dana?"

"He's going to make it, Doctor Sizemore. We took out his spleen, you had already re-expanded his lung so I just converted your makeshift valve to a tube with a water trap. The capsule of his spleen was still holding when he got here, he did not even need a blood transfusion. You did a good job, Dr. Sizemore."

Doc was sitting on the side of the bed with the phone on his thigh and his hand on the receiver. Shirley bent over and kissed him on the forehead. His shoulders trembled, all of a sudden he felt weak.

Two days after the incident, Hobart Skidmore was arrested and charged with every crime that had been committed, including wounding Dana Carper, probably in an effort to get him to name others. He was warned the killings would get him executed at the Moundsville State Prison.

"Hanged by the neck until dead," was the way the threat was reportedly delivered, with facial and respiratory gestures and sound effects included. Rumor was he was scared to death and had begun to point his finger at everyone he could think of in an attempt to bargain for a deal. Everyone in the union, who had anything to do with the shootings, was getting nervous.

Woody Woodrum's insistence that he saw a federal marshal running away from the scene of Dana Carper's shooting did not convince anyone, even the staunchest supporters of the Union's cause. Marshals investigated the shooting but the bullet was never found. When Ralph Carper returned from Charleston, he swore he had seen the bullet in the door facing and sure enough a piece of wood had been gouged out. The federal marshals postulated that one of the miners must have cut out the evidence so it could not be used against the "no good slime who would commit such a dastardly deed."

"I don't think anyone could have cut that bullet out except the marshals," Doc said to Minner when he crossed the picket line to treat Carle Frink for a back injury. "They had that house covered tight as a drum. Wouldn't even let Don Chapin in."

Minner shook his head in disgust.

"That's all we need. A bunch of federal cowboys riling everybody up even more than they all ready are. If I get out of here alive, I don't know if I'll ever come back."

"Minner sure is low," Doc said to Shirley that evening. "He's talking about quitting the mine and moving away."

"Alice never said anything to me about that," Shirley said.

"Probably doesn't know," Doc said. Shirley put her cigarette out in the ash tray and placed her hand on top of his.

"Do you suppose he really means it?" she asked.

"I don't know, but don't say anything to Alice."

A week after Hobart Skidmore's arrest, Doc got a call to go to the William's house. Oscar Williams was having trouble getting his breath. Doc was not surprised. The heightened level of anxiety in the valley was taking its toll on the already precarious pulmonary status of its inhabitants.

"Probably stress causing his asthma to act up," Doc said to Shirley when he kissed her at the door. As he drove down the narrow lane toward Duck, Bill Stricker stepped out into the road and flagged him down.

"OK I ride down the road a piece with you, Doc?" Bill asked.

"Sure, Bill." Doc said, as Bill walked around the car to the passenger side. He glanced into the woods before he opened the door to get in. Suddenly, three men stepped out from behind bushes growing next to the roadside and pushed their way into the automobile. They wore masks and carried rifles.

"Now git out of here," one of the men ordered Stricker. "And if you say anything, you'll be sorry'er than you ever believed you could be." Stricker turned and ran up the road toward town without looking back.

"What is this?" Doc exclaimed. "Get out of my car." The leader, who had sent Stricker scrambling, pointed his rifle at Doc's temple.

"You're not in no position to be ordering nobody around so just you shut up and drive on down past Dogtown and up the next holler." His instructions were issued in a guttural tone of voice. Doc did as he was told. He turned off into the woods where the leader indicated with his gun and stopped as he was directed. With the rifle in his back, Doc was ordered out of the car and shoved into a clearing where he was pushed into a sitting position on a log. The masked man pressed the barrel of his shotgun into Doc's shoulder.

The cleared area was the recently vacated site of a still. Signs of extensive cooking and the dregs of spent corn and grain and empty sugar sacks littered the forest floor. The sour odor of mash clung to the foliage and mingled with the sweet smell of the discarded sacks. The moonshine industry had taken the brunt of guardsmen and marshal's forays into the countryside. For the time being, the locals were out of business.

Doc recognized his captors, but he was certain he would be better off pretending to be fooled.

"Well, Doctor, we are mightily disappointed in you." The throaty delivery, accentuated pronunciation, and scarf-muffled projection was almost funny. Doc caught himself starting to smile but he succeeded in suppressing it. Ansel McCoy's play acting may have sounded humorous, but Doc was sure his intentions were not. "We knowed you was thick with the super-in-ten-dent," he over pronounced. "But we was su-prised to no end to learn you cain't be trusted."

"What are you talking about?" Doc almost said Anse, but he caught himself in time.

"You know good'n well what we're talkin' about," Anse answered, sliding back into his more normal pronunciation. "A person name of Hobart Skidmore - now we don't know the man personally, since we're not from around here - but we been told he was arrested on account of you turned him in for a gunshot wound what he got whilst he was hunting."

"No! I did not!" Doc answered emphatically.

"I tol' you. I tol' you. I knowed we'uz wasting our time," Marlus Coyner piped up.

"Shut up," McCoy ordered. "You want him recognizing your voice? Let me do the talking."

"I don't know who turned Skidmore in, but it was not me. I guarantee you of that. I live here. I'm not that stupid." Doc was more confident after Marlus' outburst.

McCoy was silent. At the meeting the previous night, Anse had been the only one in favor of blaming Doc. His accomplices were reluctant participants who followed Anse's lead out of habit. He was so sure Doc was the villain, he had expected him to be intimidated. He had not counted on Doc's denial being so convincing. Anse stammered something incoherent, then motioned for the others to follow him to the edge of the clearing. They conferred for a few minutes, seemingly without much argument, returned and ordered the doctor to get into his car. Anse directed him to drive back to the spot where they had invaded his automobile and ordered him to stop.

"Now, you git yourself on back to town and forgit this ever happened. We'll be a heading on back to our homes in Montgomery, see?" He stuck his head into the passenger compartment. "You understand?" He closed the door without waiting for an answer.

Doc let up on the clutch as the three men disappeared into the bushes. He drove slowly up the road toward town and at the first turn-off he pulled over. He backed in out of sight and lit a cigarette. Not more than five minutes passed before McCoy and Coyner went by in Coyner's pickup. As soon as they were out of sight, Doc pulled onto the road and drove out past the spot of the high-jacking and turned off at Duck. He drove up the hollow to the Williams shack and stopped. He knew the third member of the group had been Oscar Williams. He walked up to the house, but before he climbed the steps to the porch he felt the radiator of Oscar's old rattletrap. It was so hot he almost burned his hand.

Oscar must have been in a hurry to get home, he thought.

Bella answered the door with her usual taciturn, "Vat ya vant?" Bella Williams was from Rumania. She came to West Virginia as a mail order bride and she had lived up that hollow going on to twelve or thirteen years, but she was still known as "Oscar's Bohunk Wife."

"I got a call to come out here to see Oscar," Doc explained. "Sorry I'm late, but I was detained." He placed special emphasis on the last part of the sentence as Oscar stuck his head around his wife's shoulder. Oscar, obviously wide awake, pretended to be recently aroused. He yawned and scratched his head.

"We been here all evening Doc, and I was in bed asleep when you drove up. I don't know who could'a called you." There was a hint of panic in Oscar's voice. He looked at his wife for confirmation but she remained as stoic as ever. She refused to enter into the interchange in any way. Oscar had never been able to get her to lie for him so he just pretended her silence was verification.

"Voice on the phone said you were having trouble breathing," Doc said. "Sounded legitimate to me."

Oscar Williams had been left holding the bag. The conspirators, not expecting Doc to continue on his mission, had devised no cover for that eventuality.

"Well, I ain't sick," Oscar protested. His wife walked away leaving him standing fully clothed in the very same attire he wore at Doc's interrogation. The sound of the radio or a phonograph swelled from the living room soon after Bella disappeared inside.

It sounded like a mazurka, played loud enough to drown out the conversation at the front door. Oscar attempted to fade into the shadow of the partially open door but his embarrassment was too pronounced to camouflage.

"Cain't figure who'da said I was," he stuttered.

Doc stood impassively watching the discomfort increase, then without another word he turned and walked down the porch steps to the car parked in the yard. He placed his hand on the hood and turned back toward the house. Oscar was peeking through the partially opened doorway and when Doc looked straight at him he jerked his head back out of sight.

"Got an overheating problem there, Williams," he called. "Need to get that car in to Mr. Legg's place. Going to cause you trouble, you don't get it fixed."

He walked slowly back to his car, seated himself, lit a cigarette, took a couple long drags and let the smoke drift out of his nostrils. He started the motor, slowly backed out of the yard and drove onto the road with the lively music fading into the background. He rolled up the car window after he shifted the Plymouth into third gear. He drove up past the dark, cold coke ovens and the hotel and turned off toward home.

The next day Doc passed Ansel McCoy walking along the road. He stopped, rolled down his window, stuck his head out and called. "Hey Anse, like a ride up as far as the clinic?" Ansel, who had been trying to pretend he did not see the Doc's car, stood still for a moment looking confused.

"No, thank you just the same, Doc. I was going the other way." And with that, he turned and walked in the opposite direction.

"You're entirely welcome," Doc called after the rapidly retreating figure.

Two nights later, Minner's house burned to the ground. Alice barely got out with the clothes on her back. The families of other salaried employees had all ready moved when threats of reprisals against them were first rumored. Alice spent two nights with Shirley and Doc, then left for Charleston to stay with her sister. Doc tried to cross the picket line to let Minner know that Alice was all right, but Orville Fowler held his hand in front of Doc's chest.

"You don't go in there for nothing but if somebody's sick," he said.

The next night after Minner's house burned, the assistant superintendent's residence caught fire and an explosion destroyed a company building outside the gates. Luckily, Frink's family had all ready moved and the company building was unoccupied.

The violence became sporadic with time and eventually petered out. The strike dragged on for over a year and ended with both sides making concessions they had vowed to resist. There were no raises, but the union negotiated royalties on each ton of coal produced. The union officials got what they wanted, more power and more control over the money generated by coal mining. The operators got concessions from the union leaders that there would be no strikes for the foreseeable future, and the coal miners got squashed further under the yoke of both factions. They also got debts from being off the job.

Doc never did get paid for the work he did for the national guard but he got a lot of paper work to fill out and each time the forms came back stamped, "denied for insufficient information." Finally, he just started throwing the forms in the trash.

Minner moved to Clendenin and every day afterwards he passed the burned out remains of his house on his way to his office at the foot of the tipple. The charred rubble and partially melted masonry of the finest house in town stood untouched. The back wall of the rumpus room still supported the hillside and the partially charcoaled deer antlers that had once attested to Minner's hunting skill. Carle Frink rebuilt and his family returned to Wattsville.

* * *

"What happened to Hobart Skidmore?" Doc asked Minner on one of those rare evenings when he stopped by the office for a chat. Since the end of the strike they seldom saw one another unless Minner was working late and staying overnight at the hotel.

"How'd you like a snort, Earl?" Minner reached the bottle across the desk and when Doc refused he shrugged, took a stiff drink and leaned back in his chair with the lid in one hand, the bottle in the other.

"Don't know," he said. "No one has seen hide nor hair of him since the federals let him loose. He's probably scared shitless of Anse and his boys. They've been making noises about getting even with anyone that cooperated with the marshals."

"Do you think he really did cooperate with them?"

"It's my understanding he sang like a bird. But, since they figured they could not get a conviction anywhere in southern West Virginia, they let him plead guilty to the charge of destroying property. He got off with the time he had all ready served and probation for a year. If he'd kept his mouth shut, he wouldn't even got that. They had no evidence tying him directly to any of the crimes, and if they'd gone to court with what they had, the judge would have thrown them out for sure."

"Doesn't seem very just to me; people killed and injured and property destroyed," Doc said wistfully.

"To me neither," Minner agreed. "But, that's not even the worst of it. The governor pressured the coal company to accept the union's demands and in the long run everyone's going to suffer. The union's having control of more of the coal money is not going to help the miners, you can bet your bottom-dollar on that."

"Why did the company go along with the settlement then, if it's not good for anybody?" Doc asked.

"Because they had no choice. Hell, the union officials were willing to break the company and the governor wouldn't do a dad-blamed thing about the violence. He was afraid it would cost him his union support." Minner extended his arms, palms up in a gesture of futility, then took a long drink. "Mining's on its last legs in West Virginia anyway," he predicted. "Before long, all the coal is going to come from non-union, surface mines in Montana and places like that, and half of West Virginia's going to end up on the dole. Hell, they're striking over in Widen now and I hear tell Prince is next. They shot a truck miner down near Shinnston last night and burned a foreman's car. Don't seem to learn much." He took another drink, screwed the lid back on the bottle and set it on the desk.

"Minner, I don't remember your being much of a drinker. Do you think drinking that much is a good idea?"

"How do the twins like it out there in Arizona, Doc?" Minner asked.

"Seems like they like it fine," Doc answered.

"I'm worried about Minner," Doc said to Shirley, later that evening. "I think he's drinking too much."

"Alice is worried about him, too," Shirley agreed. "She said he won't listen to her at all."

"When I tried to talk to him about it he just changed the subject," Doc said. Shirley patted his hand and reached out her cigarette. Doc inhaled deeply and handed it back. He ran his fingers through his hair, closed his eyes and exhaled. "I'm tired I think I'll go to bed."

Chapter Eight

The miners went back to work, school re-opened and the mine payroll began to flow back into town. Businesses in Wattsville that were marginally successful in the past became even more dependent on the whim of the coal industry. Slowly, life returned to normal except several stores never re-opened and most of the kids were a year behind in school. The monthly card games were not resumed.

Shirley had been helping distribute surplus commodities from the government and clothing donated by the Salvation Army. She worked evenings at the church turning out quilts for the families living in tents, mornings helping get the children, orphaned by the flood, fed and clothed and weekends petitioning businesses and government for supplies to help the residents of Dogtown rebuild.

"Honey," Doc said one evening. "Do you have to be gone so much? I really miss you." Shirley put her arms around his waist and rested her head on his chest. Then she gently pulled away and looked into his eyes.

"Everyone depends so much on you, I guess we forget you have needs, too, darling. I'll stop helping so much in the evenings from now on." She moved her hands to his face and kissed him. They went to bed and made love.

After Doc fell asleep, Shirley got up and stood at the window and smoked a cigarette, then she went back to bed and sat up watching him sleep. Finally, she lay down beside him and whispered, "I love you." He smiled and put his arm around her.

The next morning Shirley was bent over the sink scrubbing potatoes when Doc came up behind her and put his arms around her waist. "I love you, Shirley," he whispered. "And I have really missed you."

"I'm glad," she answered.

"I don't know what I'd do without you," he said.

"Don't worry. You'll not get rid of me very easily." She kissed him and snuggled close with her head resting on his chest.

He laughed and pulled away. "But we better stop this or you'll give me ideas and I gotta' get to the clinic."

"All right, but don't you work too late. I'll be waiting tonight."

Doc turned on the radio in the car, Montana Slim was singing. *No letter today/ I've waited since dawn/ I've waited each day since you have been gone...* Doc hummed along.

Later, at the office he was listening to a patient's heart and did not hear the knock on the examination room door. The patient got his attention by tapping on the bell of the stethoscope as Doc moved it to a new location on the chest. Mrs. Sidenstricker had her head interjected into the room, an urgent expression on her face.

"There's someone here to see you, doctor." She motioned with her head to indicate the person was in the hall.

"I'm busy," Doc protested. "Can't it wait? I'll be out in a little while." From the hallway, a masculine voice mumbled something Doc could not understand.

"He says it can't wait," she answered.

Doc removed the other earpiece from his ear canal, snapped the stethoscope from around his neck and hung it on a hook.

"You can button up your shirt, Angus. I'll be back in a minute." He looked at Mrs. Sidenstricker, who was still holding the door half open, and went into the hallway. Her insistence had annoyed him but he supposed she would not bother him if it weren't important.

A stocky man in a blue suit and grey felt hat stood in the corridor as if he were on guard. Doc recognized John J. Loomis, the head of the Southern West Virginia Chapter of The Miners Affiliates of America. Loomis' hands hung down but his arms were spread accentuating his manliness, his face jutting forward like a bulldog's. He had a red tie knotted tightly under his chin a little off the midline as if it were a noose, and the ends of his collar stood up against his flabby jowls. The front of his hat brim was snapped down over a forehead dominated by huge eyebrows. He wheezed when he talked; his voice sounding as though his larynx had been injured.

"I'm a busy man and I need to talk to you," he said. "It's important."

"What about? I have patients to take care of." Doc glanced at Mrs. Sidenstricker to let her know he was upset with her for disturbing him for such a purpose.

"That can wait. Is there someplace we can talk in private?" Loomis was evidently not used to taking no for an answer. Doc motioned toward his office, Loomis indicated he would follow. When they had seated themselves, he removed his hat and started to talk. "I am here to tell you about the new union rules. We have organized..."

"Wait a minute, wait a minute. I am busy here with a clinic full of patients to see and..."

"I can see that. You listen to this now and stop buttin' in and we'll get it over with in no time." He leaned back in the chair he was too wide for, and placed his hat on Doc's desk.

"Medical Hygiene Inc. has been contracted with by the Miner's Affiliates of America to provide medical care for all the miners and their families in the southern part of the state. We just negotiated a contract with the operators to pay us a royalty on ever ton of coal we deliver. That royalty'll be administered by the Union Family Welfare Fund to pay docs who work for us." He paused, took out a cigarette and lit it after a few seconds hesitation, as if he expected someone else to do it for him.

Doc had momentarily forgotten the patients. He sat at his desk, at a loss for anything to say. Then he picked up an unsharpened pencil, held the ends between the forefinger and thumb of either hand and leaned back in his chair.

"By the way, what is your name?" Doc was angry about Loomis' attitude. The question was calculated to put him in his place. "And, what about communities where Medical Hygiene has no clinic?" he asked, satisfied he had placed the union representative on the defensive.

Loomis looked surprised. He wheezed to get air into his lungs.

"My name is John J. Loomis, if you don't all ready know, and there ain't going to be no communities without no Hygiene Clinic." He took one last puff on the remainder of the cigarette and stretched in front of Doc, across the desk for an ash tray. He put his hand inside the front of his coat and removed a document.

He spread it out on the desk and reached a pen across the top with his other hand. Up close, Loomis face was grotesque and he was shorter than Doc expected.

"We're paying you a fair price and from now on you're working for us." Doc looked at the front of Loomis' shirt. It bulged out between the buttons and hair showed through the openings.

"I can't just sign this without knowing what's in it," Doc protested. Doc had heard of Loomis' union tactics and his business practices.

"Why *can't* you sign it? Ain't nothing in it. It's just a standard contract."

"I need to read it first. That's why I can't sign it."

"Well, read it." Loomis sat back down, lit another cigarette and extinguished the match in the ash tray he had moved to the arm of the chair without asking permission. He tried two or three times to cross his legs but because of his bulk, he couldn't, so he gave up the effort.

"I have patients waiting," Doc protested.

"Let them wait!"

Doc leaned forward and held the paper flat on the desk. He read the first few paragraphs, then looked up.

"You expect me to go on a salary to the union?"

"To Medical Hygiene Inc. And when was the last time you made thirty two thousand dollars in one year?" He hesitated, looked at the end of the cigarette to see if the ashes needed flicked into the ash tray, and smiled. No answer was necessary. Doc had never made fifteen thousand dollars in a year.

"When was the last time you had a specialist come here to see a patient? We intend to make this a group practice with you at the head and visiting specialists to come here regularly to see patients you need advice about." He paused to let that sink in and then he said… "And when was the last time you had a vacation?" Again, no answer was forthcoming.

"What kind of a vacation?" Doc inquired after the pause.

"Two weeks a year," Loomis answered. "And one weekend a month."

"How does that work?" Doc asked.

"*Locum tenens*," Loomis explained. "We pay an intern or resident from a hospital in Charleston to come up here and take your place while you're away. And," he paused as if to gauge the softening of Doc's resistance. "One week a year to go to a medical meeting of your selection." He had delivered the *coup de grace,* and his posture indicated he knew it.

"What about this building and the equipment?"

"We pay you rent."

"What about my employee?"

"We pay all employees." Loomis was enjoying himself. He evidently liked the magnanimity of this part as much as he did the process of intimidation.

"What if I say no?" There was no way he was going to, but he could not help asking.

"You may be dumb, but you're not that dumb," Loomis answered. He stood up, leaned over the seated physician with his face so close Doc could feel his breath, offered the pen and reproduced his intimidating expression for just a moment. "Now, sign the paper." His voice was almost a whisper, but the words still constituted a command. The odor of after shave drifted across the desk.

His breath smelled of cigarettes.

Doc took the pen, hesitated, looked up at Loomis hovering over him and smiled. Loomis smiled benignly in return. His bushy eyebrows raised slightly as the muscles in his face relaxed.

Shirley is really going to be pleased. This is the answer to all our problems, Doc thought. He signed the paper. Loomis folded it, replaced it in his jacket pocket and patted Doc's shoulder.

"Good doin' business with you, doctor." He picked up his hat and placed the ash tray back on the desk. "Be seein' you," he said and left.

After Loomis had gone, Doc sat there for a few minutes. He was suddenly drained.

Maybe I should have taken the time to discuss that with Shirley, he thought. Mrs. Sidenstricker stuck her head into the room.

"You have an office full of patients, doctor. What was that all about?" she asked as he walked around the desk and passed her in the doorway. He gave her a perplexed expression but no answer. The rest of the afternoon was a blur, but Doc got through it without any complaints from her, so he must have been all right.

Doc was late getting home. Shirley was sitting in the kitchen, reading. They had not tried going out of town together since their ill-fated sojourn to Clendenin. Nor had they talked about it. She looked up as he entered the room, took her cigarette out of her mouth and offered her cheek. Doc kissed her and when she stood to get his supper from the oven, he put his arms around her waist.

"Amorous after such a hard day?" She laughed and pushed him away.

"It has not been a hard day at all," he said. "It was a wonderful day." He attempted to swing her around the kitchen but she resisted and started laughing.

"Watch out for my cigarette," she scolded. She held her hand away from her body to avoid burning herself. "Have you been drinking, doctor?"

"No! I have not been drinking!" he answered. He hugged her tightly to his chest and swayed back and forth. "Come outside with me. I want to talk to you."

"What's wrong with right here?"

"It's more romantic outside. Spring will soon be in the air. It's a clear night and you can see the aurora borealis."

"I saw the aurora borealis before you got home." She hesitated, then repeated. "Before you got home, doctor."

"Come on." He pulled her by the hand. "How often can the northern lights be seen this far south?" She extinguished the remainder of her cigarette and allowed herself to be pulled along, still protesting mildly. When they reached the back fence where they could see the milky sky to the north, Doc put his arm around her shoulders. "Honey, do you remember that piece of property at the end of town? The flat piece you like so much?"

"How could I forget? It's the best land in town."

"Well, I want you to buy it."

"What for?"

"So we can build a house on it."

"What are you talking about? You know we can't afford to do that."

"Yes, we can. And you better be thinking where you want to go on a two week vacation, too." He spread his hands out to his sides with his fingers locked through hers. He leaned back to better observe her reaction.

"What in tarnation are you talking about? You know that's not possible."

"You, my dear lady, have not heard of *locum tenens* I dare say, or you would not be so negative."

"And you are feeling mighty superior, darling. Or have you gone out of your senses? What is this *locum tenens?*"

"Today, my skeptical bride, I became an employee of Medical Hygiene Inc. Today I signed a contract that will allow us to lease out the clinic and draw a salary of thirty-two thousand dollars a year. And *locum tenens* is what will allow us to take two weeks' vacation, and one week study time a year, and a weekend off a month. That is what *locum tenens* is. How do you like that?"

Suddenly, she became serious. "I don't understand and I don't believe it," she answered. "The coal companies have never done anyone any favors. Are you sure you can trust them?"

"This is not the coal company. This is the union and I have a contract."

"Where is it?"

"Well, they have it, but I signed it."

"Did you read it?"

"Most of it."

"Most of it?"

"Some of it."

"How much rent will they pay?"

"Fair market value."

"What is that?"

"Well..."

"What about Mrs. Sidenstricker?"

"They will pay her."

"How much?"

"Well..."

"Who pays your replacement for this big vacation?"

"They do."

"You got it in writing?"

"I got his word."

"Whose word?"

"John J. Loomis."

"Don't you know how he got to be head of the local? Don't you remember how he got that last contract negotiated? Have you forgot the violence?"

Doc did not feel so good all of a sudden, but the feeling passed quickly. There was no way he could be taken advantage of. "I am the only doctor in town," he said.

"What about Baumgarten?" Shirley asked.

"Nobody'd go to him."

"Not even if they were told to?"

"We're still in the driver's seat." He was becoming sure of himself again. "I don't have to worry," he said. "They need me more than I need them. Who could they get to take my place?"

"Have you never heard of *locum tenens?*" Shirley asked as they returned to the house.

Doc did not sleep very well that night and in the morning he had trouble getting out of bed. Shirley came into the bedroom with a steaming cup of coffee in her hand. Doc rolled over on his back and sat up. "Thanks, honey," he said. She waited until he had taken a sip.

"You better get yourself out of there pretty soon or you'll be starting behind. Mrs. Sidenstricker will be fit to be tied." She shook her finger playfully. Doc managed a tired smile.

The first thing he did after he arrived at the clinic was to call Minner. "Could you stop in before you go home this evening, Minner?" he asked.

"Sure, Earl. Is anything wrong?"

"Not really," Doc answered. "I just need your advice about something."

"See you later," Minner said. Doc sat in his chair for a few minutes after he had hung up the phone. Finally, Mrs. Sidenstricker stuck her head in the door with a disgusted look on her face.

"Are you planning to begin work sometime today?" she asked. Doc got up and took the chart she thrust into his hand. It was a long day before he finished.

Minner seated himself, crossed his legs and worked the bottle of Green River out of his hip pocket. He unscrewed the lid and extended the half-empty bottle over the edge of the desk tentatively. Doc held his hand in a position of rejection. Minner shrugged and took a long swig. His eyes were bloodshot; his hand shook when he replaced the lid. Doc started to say something but he hesitated.

"What's bothering you, Earl?" Minner asked. His speech was slightly slurred.

"You driving home tonight?" Doc asked.

"That what you got me over here for, doctor?" Minner leaned back in the chair.

"No," Doc answered. They studied each other as if they were meeting for the first time. Finally, Doc relaxed. He realized the question had put Minner on the defensive. He decided to postpone his concern. "No," he repeated. "I asked you to stop by to get your advice."

"What about?" Minner pulled himself erect in the chair. He concentrated to correct his speech and to appear alert.

"I just signed a contract with the union to let them take over the clinic."

"And, you want to hear what I think of it?"

"I was hoping to. I've had second thoughts after thinking about it."

"How long are you locked in?"

"What do you mean, locked in?"

"I mean, if you don't like it, how long will it take you to get out of it?"

"I don't know."

"You mean you haven't read the contract?"

"Not exactly."

"Well, let me take a look."

"I don't have it."

"You mean you haven't signed it?"

"No, I mean I haven't got a copy."

"And you signed it?"

"Yes."

Minner took the lid off the bottle and reached it across the desk again.

"Here, Earl. I think you'd better take a drink."

Doc took a sip. He handed it back and Minner took another healthy swig.

"You think I shouldn't have signed it so quickly?"

"Who'd you talk to?"

"Loomis."

Minner shook his head.

"I don't know what to say, Earl. Maybe he'll be fair with you. After all they can't very well run this clinic without you."

Doc didn't mention *locum tenens.*

"You look worried, hon," Shirley said when Doc came in the kitchen later. "I'm probably wrong about the contract. They'll probably be fair." She kissed him and smiled.

"I'm worried more about Minner's drinking than I am about that," he said. Shirley frowned and put her arms around him.

After they finished supper, Doc and Shirley walked out onto the porch and looked at the stars. He put his arm around her shoulders and kissed her cheek. They didn't talk much and when they went to bed he lay awake for a long time.

* * *

Mrs. Sidenstricker stuck her head in the doorway one evening a few days later. "There's a man on the phone wants to talk to you, doctor Sizemore. He says he's from Medical Hygiene." She looked puzzled. "He said something about a new employee."

"I am sending a new employee by to be oriented," the voice explained. He did not introduce himself other than to say he was calling from Medical Hygiene Incorporated's Charleston office.

"I have not heard anything about any new employee," Doc protested.

"I assure you we need another employee in the front office," he said.

"Don't you think I should have been consulted about this?" Doc protested.

"I was caught up in some administrative work and did not have time to call you, but in the future all hiring will be handled through you. This lady has worked in a doctor's office before. She'll move over from Gauley Bridge as soon as she can find a place to stay."

A week later, Mrs. Sidenstricker was informed by the new Clinic Administrator that he had hired two women to assist in the back office. When he arrived to introduce himself, Doc complained about the oversight. "I thought I would hire any employees or at least have something to say about them. The man at the main office assured me of that."

"Those people in the main office are a bunch of paper pushers," the administrator answered. "They don't know how to run a clinic. Don't you worry your head about it. I'll take care of the business. You just practice your medicine and we'll get along fine."

The administrator was a prissy little man with wispy yellow hair and silver-rimmed glasses. He wore a bow tie that bobbed up and down on his Adam's apple when he talked, swallowed, or cleared his throat, which he did often. His name was Tyree B. Cox. He sat in Doc's chair with a ledger opened on Doc's desk. He had moved Doc's papers to the extra chair so there was no place for Doc to sit.

Cox had graduated from the Chicago Correspondence School of Business with the third highest grade they ever awarded. He was certain he was destined for better things than overseeing the finances of a bunch of jerk-water clinics in hick-towns in West Virginia. He felt disdain for the kind of white trash who lived in such places and those with some education who did nothing better with their lives than return there to work out their miserable existences.

"I can understand the niggers, they don't know any different," he told his mother. "But white people should try to do better." His mother listened to every word her brilliant son uttered without so much as missing a stitch in her crocheting. He was right, of course. She was certain of that and would acknowledge her agreement with the slightest nod of her head and just the hint of a smile. She was not one for wild emotional displays.

"I don't know what I'll do with two people in the back office," Doc said. "Besides, those women have no training. One nurse would have been better. At least she could have taken some of the work off me."

"They'll be needed for the increased work load," the administrator explained. "You can train them the way you want and you won't be able to complain about any lack of competence on their part. After all that's partly what we pay you for. With the visiting specialists, dispensing medicines and taking your own X-rays, you will need more help. Not to mention the increased patient load we expect to service. I've learned that some of the miners' families have been going to Clendenin and Gauley Bridge for their care. From now on they will be funneled into Wattsville. We have decided to make Wattsville a regional group practice. You will no longer continue your usual check off pay from the operator. We will supply your income from the royalty on coal production. We will have specialists visit on a regular basis and we will recruit a partner for you when it is appropriate to help with the new workload."

"But a lot of the patients live closer to those other places. It would be difficult for them to come here," Doc protested.

"We will put a stop to patients just going wherever they decide to get their medical care. You can bet your bottom dollar on that." The administrator picked up his pencil and went back to his ledger. Doc stood there for another minute or two before he realized he had been dismissed.

At first, things were not very different for Doc except that Miss Porter, the new employee in the business office, spent all her time on the increased number of reports to fill out and Wampler and Sturgill did not have much to do. It was not long before that changed, though. An X- ray machine was moved in, a laboratory set up and the store room converted to a pharmacy.

At the first business meeting, the administrator announced that, "We will have different specialists visit the clinic on a rotating basis so your complicated cases can be taken care of right here."

"What if an illness cannot wait?" Doc inquired.

"I don't see that as a problem," Cox answered "but let's not worry about details just now. We will handle those questions at the regional meeting where all the clinics will be represented."

"What regional meeting?" Doc asked. No one had mentioned such a thing to him.

"Once a month I'll get all the doctors together to work out any problems that come up and answer questions about new directives. We will meet at the clinic in Cedar Grove." Cedar Grove was the nearest clinic to Charleston.

"How is that?" Doc asked. He didn't like the, *I'll get all the doctors together,* as if it were some kind of an order from the boss. "Cedar Grove is almost forty miles from here. That's too far for me to come and leave the patients with no doctor."

"We will provide a *locum tenens* for the evening," the administrator answered. "Now that your questions have been taken care of, I hope we can work together to make this a profitable venture for everyone concerned." With that, he closed his folder and concluded the meeting. He stood up, folded his briefcase and snapped it closed.

Doc knew all his questions had not been answered. For the moment, however, he could not think of anything to say except, "When will you be moving to Wattsville?"

"What made you think I was going to move to Wattsville?" The executive chuckled. "I'll continue to live in Charleston. I will be supervising seven sites in Kanawha, Fayette, Logan, Greenbrier, Webster and Barbour counties. I can't do that satisfactorily from here."

"We all thought you would be managing the clinic."

"And that I will. You don't need to fret about that. I'll take care of the business. Somebody thinks they're going to get away with something has a surprise coming. Bet your life on that." He smiled condescendingly at the naive country doctor and brushed past him on his way to the door. In the hallway, where he was visible to all the clinic employees, the administrator stopped, opened his case and took out an envelope. "By the way, here is your paycheck." He held the envelope out with his arm half extended so Doc had to approach him to reach it. Doc's face reddened as he took it, stuffed it into his pocket and looked around the room. Everyone was staring.

Later that evening, Doc opened the envelope and looked at the check, twelve-hundred and eighty-six and sixty-four one hundredths dollars. He quickly multiplied by twelve and it did not come close to the thirty two-thousand he had expected. He handed it to Shirley when he got home.

"What's the matter, dear?" she asked.

"Look for yourself. That's not what Loomis promised."

She finished her inspection and handed it back.

"Maybe there's a mistake," she said.

"Probably, and I hate to think whose it is."

He called the administrator the next day after tracking him down in Hinton. He asked why the check was not larger. The administrator advised him there were deductions and he must have misunderstood Loomis.

"No one pays a doctor thirty-two thousand dollars a year. Heaven's sakes. I don't make that much, myself. It's twenty-two thousand and that's more than the going rate. He must have thought you would continue getting the *check off* of the miner's pay."

"I am certain I did not misunderstand," Doc protested. "Loomis distinctly said thirty-two thousand."

"Well, you can take that up with him if you want, but I have your signed contract for twenty two and I expect you to honor your contract." The administrator was not at all agitated. He had apparently had this conversation before or at least anticipated it.

"I don't feel obliged to live up to the terms of a contract I've been hoodwinked into signing." Doc was angry. He did not like being steam roller'd in the first place and now that he learned he had been bamboozled; he was not about to put up with it.

"Suit yourself, we can hire a Mexican or a Filipino for eleven." The administrator sounded as if he had been saving that card, and that he enjoyed playing it. There was a triumphant tone in his voice. He might as well have added, *Gotcha'* but he did not need to. Instead he said, "And if you think you can work at the clinic without our permission, you have another think coming. This payment also includes the lease on the clinic, which is binding for five years with three guaranteed extensions." He paused. Doc slumped in the chair and almost let the phone slip out of his hand.

The next words out of the administrator's mouth were delivered as if his conversation with Doc had been about the weather.

"Now that the matter is cleared up and we are in agreement, I need to conclude this discussion. I have other things to do." With that, he hung up the phone.

Doc sat in the chair holding the dead receiver for at least two or three minutes before admitting to himself the conversation had been terminated.

Mrs. Sidenstricker stuck her head in the doorway to urge Doc to get back to work. When she saw his face she closed the door softly and went back to her desk.

Chapter Nine

When Doc finished with his last patient, he went to his office to meet the *locum tenens*. Mrs. Sidenstricker turned to make the introduction. "Dr. Sizemore, this is Dr. Jordan."

"Well, young man. It certainly is a pleasure to meet you. I am sure the clinic will be in good hands while I'm away." ***He looks so young,*** Doc thought.

"Thank you, Dr. Sizemore. I'm looking forward to taking care of some real patients by myself. Seems like every time an intern looks over his shoulder, there's a resident or an attending spying on him." He smiled a little uncomfortably as if he had said too much.

"Well, young man, this is just the place to get your feet wet, so to speak." The tone of Doc's voice lessened the tension. "I'll leave the phone number of the clinic in Cedar Grove. If anything comes up that can't wait, or you can't handle, just call. I'll try to help." He paused. "Any questions before I leave?"

"I don't think so. Have a good time, Dr. Sizemore."

Doc hummed along with the radio. *The call of the highway seems faded and distant/settlin' down don't come easy to a ramblin' man...*

He drove out of town and up the winding road to the highway. He felt a little uncomfortable. ***"Kid said he wasn't used to taking care of patients by himself,"*** he thought.

The meeting was short. The administrator's mother was in the hospital and he had to drive down to Charleston to be with her.

Doc passed Fall's View on his way home before the sun had dropped behind the hills to the west. The river was running higher than usual and Kanawha Falls glistened in the slanting rays of the sun.

She flies across the desert and cruises the Alaskan sky/ starts every morning with a screaming eagle cry/Maybe I'll get lucky and be an eagle when I die... He leaned over to turn the radio up so he could hear the rough western voice of Dakota Sid and the beautiful metallic sound of the dobro. The song continued: *Time to an eagle is just what it seems...*

* * *

"Well, Dr. Jordan, how did it go?"

"Not too bad, I'd say." Jeff yawned and stretched to loosen the kinks from dozing in the chair. "Only one thing you need to know about. There's a woman in labor who might be calling you later tonight." He handed Doc a slip of paper with a name written on it. "Name is spelled Sweeney, I think, but her husband kept pronouncing it Swinny."

Doc smiled. "Lots of them around here," he said.

Jeff gave Doc a puzzled glance and continued. "Anyway. I checked her out. Effaced but not dilated yet, so I sent her home.

Told her husband to call if her pains got closer than four or five minutes apart. It's her first, so I think it'll be a while."

"Sounds good, son. Thanks for taking care of things while I was gone. Now drive carefully on your way home." Doc shook his hand. "Has the administrator talked to you about your pay?"

"His secretary said for me to call tomorrow and she would send a check."

"Good. Now you call me if there's any problem getting paid, you hear?" Jordan smiled as he closed the door.

When he arrived home, Shirley was waiting in the bedroom. She had bathed, her hair glistened from brushing and she was wearing a beautiful, filmy nightgown he had not seen before. She kissed him and climbed into bed. Doc took a quick bath, slapped on a dash of after-shave and crawled in beside her. They made love for the first time in almost a month. They were relaxing with a shared cigarette when the phone rang. It was Henry Sweeney.

Chapter Ten

The administrator sent word that Doc was to report to his office right away. He used Doc's office when he was at the clinic and referred to it as, "*My office.*"

"Have the doctor report to my office right away," he instructed Mrs. Sidenstricker, whom he used as his messenger when he was in residence. "Tell him to hurry up. I have to pick up my mother at The Diamond Department Store in two hours, so I barely have time to drive to Charleston."

"He's with a patient," Mrs. Sidenstricker protested.

"Tell him the patients can wait." The administrator considered Doc, and to only a slightly lesser extent, Mrs. Sidenstricker to be painful afflictions in his otherwise smooth existence. He was a busy man. He was tired of hearing, "he's with a patient, he's with a patient," every time he wanted to see the doctor. He was sure it was a ruse to irritate him. No one cared that much about a bunch of illiterate hillbillies.

"Sorry to drag you away from your precious patients," he apologized sweetly, "but, I have a prior engagement and we need to clear up this vacation thing."

"My wife was hoping to go to Virginia Beach for a few days. If we don't go soon it will be too hot," Doc said.

"Your vacation is two weeks a year as agreed upon."

"Yes, that's what I understood. Is anything wrong?"

"Well, you haven't been an employee of Medical Hygiene Inc. for a year yet."

"Do you mean I can't take a vacation next month?"

"No, I don't mean that at all. You have one weekend a month and we will honor that agreement, contingent on the schedule of the interns and residents we contract with of course. But your two-weeks' vacation comes after you have been here for a full year. You have not completed the full year."

Doc had not been asked to sit. He stood in front of his own desk and looked at the floor.

"Shirley was counting on it," he mumbled.

"Well, be that as it may, she'll just have to wait." The administrator chuckled half under his breath as he gathered up his belongings and headed for the door. "See you in about a week or so. Don't worry, doctor," he added in a loud voice. "You'll get your vacation when the time comes."

He breezed out of the building, hopped into his car and drove briskly out of the parking lot while Doc stood fixed, looking at the empty chair with Tyree's imprint still in the leather.

"I'm sorry about the vacation, honey," he whispered in bed later that night. Shirley did not answer, but she hugged him closer and kissed his neck. He felt the warm tears on his chest.

Later that month the administrator mandated a new policy of dispensing drugs from the office and soon after that, added a directive defining a strict formulary. "You have been using medicines without adequate regard to their cost," he announced at a regional business meeting. "From now on, I will purchase all supplies for each of the clinics in order to better control runaway costs." He handed a stack of papers to the physician nearest the chair he had selected for himself. "Pass these around and each of you take one," he said in a pleasant voice.

The administrator seemed happiest when issuing orders to his employees, *instructions*, he called them. After each participant had perused his copy, the administrator announced that the paper was a list of acceptable pharmaceuticals to be dispensed from the office. "In the future, you will be allowed to dispense only from this list, and to reduce drug costs, prescriptions for long term medicines will be mailed to our central pharmacy."

Several hands went up as he stood to close his brief case.

"I'm sorry. I would like to answer your questions, but I have a previous engagement. Save it. We can discuss it further at another time." And with that, he left the room.

His mother had been ill. He needed to get home to be sure she got her nightly medicines.

The doctors shuffled the hand-outs uncomfortably before straggling out to their cars one at a time. Doc drove home slowly. The next day he gave the administrator's list to Mrs. Sidenstricker.

"What is this for, Doctor Sizemore?"

"This is a catalog of the medicines we can use from now on and the number of pills or volume of liquid we will be allowed to dispense," Doc answered.

"Do you mean..."

"Yes, I do mean." He turned his back to her and removed the chart from the rack on the wall. "We do not have time to stand around jowling about nothing in particular. When I came in I noticed the waiting room was all ready full."

Mrs. Sidenstricker looked perplexed. She was not accustomed to such brusque treatment. As the day wore on, Doc tried to soften his demeanor by smiling when he caught her eye, at the end of the day he patted her shoulder.

With the union take-over of medical care and the miner's welfare fund footing the bill, Doc's work load had increased perceptibly. The low cinder block clinic building with its metal casement windows, tin roof and drab architecture became the center of activity in the community. The wooden bridge spanning the creek carried more traffic than it ever had before and not all of it was friendly. There were those who resented being forced to leave their previous doctors and drive out of their way through the hills to a clinic all ready over-loaded.

"Looks to me like you got enough business 'thout tryin' to corner the market. My doctor is just down the road from the house in Clendenin. I don't see why I have to drive all the way over here."

Doc soon got tired of trying to explain. Besides he didn't have time. He picked up another chart and looked at the name: Hobart Humphrey.

"What's he doing here today, Sidenstricker? I wanted him to see the Eye, Ear, Nose & Throat specialist when he comes up from Charleston."

"Says he won't wait. He's fit to be tied."

Doc opened the door to the examination room, and entered without knocking.

"How are you feeling, Hobart?"

"I reckon you know how I feel," Hobart snarled. "Ain't no different from I was last here."

"Did you get set up to see the specialist I recommended?"

"No and I ain't goin' to neither

"Getting upset isn't going to help, Hobart. Why don't you tell me what's eating on you?"

"I ain't upset," Hobart protested. "But I ain't gonna' wait no six weeks to see no quack neither. One of them new sec'etarys you got told my woman we got to wait six weeks."

Doc shrugged his shoulders.

"Well, Hobart, if you want the union to pay the bill you have to see the specialist who comes here to the clinic."

"All any of y'all wants is a feller's money." Doc resisted the temptation to say no one was likely to get much of Hobart's money because he never had any to speak of in the first place. He was all ready working himself up into a tizzy. No sense in making matters worse.

"Man could die for all any of you care."

"Well, Hobart, what do you expect me to do?" Doc's faltering patience showed in his voice. "Maybe you should take this up with your union. It's their rule."

Hobart got up off the end of the examination table.

"Well, Doc if you're goin' to take that attitude." He hesitated as if he were going to say something more, then stormed past Doc through the waiting room, and out of the clinic. The door banged into the wall, rebounded against the jam and came to rest half-open to a cold breeze. Hobart's old flivver threw gravel against the side of the building as he pulled out of the parking lot.

Hobart was not an easy man to satisfy. He would *try the patience of Job*, as the saying went, but Doc was not used to fielding patient's complaints and he had certainly never had his motives questioned prior to the union take-over. Intellectually, he knew it was silly to give it so much concern. An older doctor once told him, *"If you can't please anyone, you don't have any personality, but if you please everyone, you don't have any character."* He knew that was right, but he had to admit he did not like the feeling that things were changing between him and those he was sworn to serve.

That evening on the way home he stopped at Shorty's. Minner was sitting in a booth talking to Shorty. When he saw Doc he waved. After Shorty returned to his place behind the bar, Doc asked Minner if he were driving over to Clendenin.

"Reckon I am. Why do you ask?"

"Well, it's a pretty winding road."

"Interesting you should inform me, Doctor. As you well know I've driven it a few times myself and I have noticed that very thing."

"I just thought..."

"I know what you just thought and its none of your business."

"Minner is getting awfully touchy these days," Doc said to Shirley later that evening.

The telephone awakened him, he looked at the clock. It was midnight.

"I'm sorry to bother you, Earl, but have you seen Minner?" It was Alice. She sounded worried.

"I think he left about seven. Is he not home?"

"No, not yet. Was he O.K.?"

"I think so," Doc said. He decided to avoid mentioning the drinking. "Would you like for me to call Don Chapin?"

"I all ready did. He said he'd drive up along the ridge and take a look."

"Do you suppose he stopped to take a nap?" Doc asked. "He seemed kind'a tired when I saw him."

"I'm worried he was drinking. He hasn't been himself lately."

"I'll call you if I hear anything," Doc said. Alice hung up the phone.

"What's wrong?" Shirley asked.

"Minner's not home yet. He was not in any condition to be driving. I should have stopped him."

"Do you think he could have had an accident?"

"That's what I'm worried about." Doc started to get dressed.

"Where are you going?" Shirley asked.

"I thought I'd drive up along the ridge and see if I can find the deputy."

"Don't you think you should wait here? In case Don tries to call you. What if Minner's hurt and you're out wandering around the countryside?"

"I guess you're right," he said. "I should have stopped him, though."

The next morning, Don Chapin stopped at the clinic.

"I never seen hide nor hair of him, Doc. Drove all the way over to Clendenin. Never saw a thing. Nothing."

Shirley called Doc.

"I'm going over to Clendenin," she said. "Don Chapin called. He's going to drive over there and talk to Alice. I asked to go along."

"Call me if there's anything I can do," Doc said. He had trouble concentrating on patient's complaints, but somehow he got through the day. Shirley called before he left the clinic.

"I'm going to stay with Alice until something's found out," she said. "She's worried sick."

"I understand," Doc said. "Tell her I'm sorry."

Three days went by and nothing turned up. Volunteers scoured the countryside.

"Didn't pick up a trace," Don Chapin reported to Doc. Then it began to rain. "Going to make it twice as hard," Don said. "Won't do nobody no good to be out there traipsing about in this. Got to call it off `til the weather breaks."

Shirley came home the next day.

"I'm going back over in a few days. Thelma Humphrey's staying with Alice until then."

Two days after the rain quit, a man from Clendenin found Minner.

"Just drove straight off the road, Doc. Never hit the brake or swerved or nothing," Don Chapin reported. "Found him just sitting there deader'n a door nail. Not even a drop of blood. His leg was broke, but that was all."

"Suppose he hit his head?" Doc asked.

"Don't know. Sending him to Charleston for an autopsy. Just a accident, but since there's no obvious cause of death, got to do it. You understand?"

"Yes," Doc answered.

"You look kind'a peak-ed, Doc. I know he was a good friend. Sorry to have to bring you the news." Doc drove home to an empty house. Shirley had gone back to Clendenin the minute she heard. Thelma drove her over.

The autopsy showed the cause of death, a broken neck. Minner was buried in the cemetery over near Clay where he was born. After the service Carle Frink put his arm around Doc's shoulders.

"I know you'll miss him, Doc. I will, too."

As they drove away from the cemetery, Doc realized he didn't feel anything. All he could think of was that last night. Shirley was leaning against the car door looking out the window. "I was so worried about myself," he said. "I never even thought of Minner." She scooted over on the car seat, put her hand on his thigh and squeezed it gently.

At home, Doc lay awake looking at the shadows on the ceiling. Finally, he got up and went downstairs. When Shirley came down he was sitting on the couch, smoking. She sat next to him and put her head on his shoulder.

"I hope you're not blaming yourself," she said. He held his cigarette out and she took a puff without taking it out of his hand. "Come back to bed, darling. You need your rest," she said.

He followed her up the stairs.

Chapter Eleven

Because of the formulary and expanded work load, Doc had begun to hurriedly prescribe routine potions to the moderately ill and to hand out useless, safe nostrums to terminate social visits. The limited formulary so restricted his prescribing options that alternate drugs became a thing of the past. When a certain medicine failed to work, Doc had no choice except to say, "Maybe you haven't taken it long enough."

A major blow to Doc's pride and the final revelation that he had completely lost control of his place in his chosen profession may have come with the creation of the *Grievance Committee*. At least it was the first time he actually articulated it to himself.

"Starting this Thursday evening, you will report to the schoolhouse auditorium at seven-thirty sharp," the administrator announced during one of his regular visits. "Thereafter, the local union representative will conduct a community liaison meeting on the second Thursday of each month which you will be expected to attend. The meetings will be governed by a committee of clients; henceforth to be referred to as The Grievance Committee.”

“What do you mean community liaison? What do you mean grievance committee?” Doc asked.

“Well, there have been complaints...”

“Complaints about what?”

“About the way some of the medical care has been delivered,” the administrator answered. He stood to leave. “Resolving the complaints directly is certainly in your best interest. That way no action will have to be taken higher up.” With that, he left the room.

Doc had supposed he had seen everything.

What will they think of next? he wondered. He was certain it was something the administrator had devised to embarrass him.

On Thursday, Doc arrived at the meeting at seven-thirty. He looked around and his eye caught Earl Braxton sitting alone staring in his direction.

Earl had harbored ill will against Doc ever since he had been denied disability by the surgeon who came up from Charleston every six weeks.

The union representative sat at the front of the room. When Doc came in he stood up. “It has come to the attention of the Grievance Committee of the Affiliated Miners of America Local Number 13 that you have not cooperated with a certain patient to help him get an appointment with a specialist in Charleston. Now, why is it that you have refused to cooperate with the ag’grieving party?” he asked, seemingly carried away with linguistic self importance.

“Are you talking about Earl Braxton?” Doc asked. “Because if you are, he has all ready been seen by the specialist.”

“Is that true, Earl?” the representative asked.

“I wanted to see a specialist in Charleston. He made me wait `til one of them company quacks come to the clinic.”

"The specialist is the same one he would have seen in Charleston, and he happens to work for your union, not for the coal company," Doc said.

Earl had wanted to be disabled permanently because of hemorrhoids the surgeon said could be fixed. The doctor examined Earl and said he could return to work in a total of four weeks after the procedure. Earl pronounced him a quack and demanded to see a "real doctor."

"Is it true you have been seen by the specialist?" the representative asked again. Earl crossed his arms and clenched his teeth. He fumed and grunted and his face turned crimson. He sputtered something unintelligible, jumped up and bolted from the room.

When Earl had refused to have the surgery because "I ain't going under no knife," his disability payments were stopped. Still harboring his animus, Earl assumed a conspiracy. He had no target for his anger save Doc, and when he heard of the formation of the grievance committee, he assumed they would surely take his side. He left the meeting still convinced the company was responsible for his troubles and that the conspiracy had expanded to include the grievance committee, too.

The representative was not used to thinking on his feet and after Earl ran from the room, he stood mute for at least two or three minutes before he regained his composure then went to the next case.

"We have a complaint about pills making a certain patient sick. What do you say to that report, Doctor Sizemore?"

"What case are you talking about?" Doc asked.

"Does that make a difference?" The representative responded, as if he were baffled by such a rejoinder. He had expected to command a little more respect in his new position and he had expected not to feel so uncomfortable with the power. He had not only promised to reconcile the participant's complaints, he had boasted. Now, here he stood feeling like a fool.

"I can't very well answer if I don't know what the pills were or who the patient was, now can I?"

"The person did not want me to use her name."

"Was there anything else?"

"Yes there was. But they wanted to remain anamonimus, too."

"Well, I can't answer complaints I don't know anything about." Doc stood up. "If that's all, I've got work to do."

The representative looked at his list. Doc waited momentarily, turned and left the room.

At the next meeting most of the complaints were about having to travel to the clinic when there was an available doctor closer to the complaining miner's home. Doc advised the representative to talk to the administrator.

"It is your rule," he said. "I don't like it any better than you do."

The next round of complaints was about having to wait to see the specialists from Charleston. Hobart Humphrey sat in the front row with his arms crossed and a frown plastered on his face. When Doc said, "Take it up with the union," Hobart stood up and started yelling.

"You ain't cooperatin'! You ain't tryin' to answer our complaints. This committee ain't doin' nobody no good but you!"

Doc sat in his chair until the tirade was completed and then he stood up.

"Hobart, I am as frustrated as anyone here. I would like to help clear up your grievances but I've got no power to do so. If you don't like what is going on, you should talk to your union representative. Maybe he can help you. I certainly can't."

There were no complaints at the next few meetings so Doc did not attend. But a few months after Medical Hygiene, Inc. had started the new formulary policy, small white objects began to appear along the banks of the creek in front of the clinic. One evening, as Doc was driving out of the parking lot, he glanced at the stream. The full moon reflecting off the white rectangles caught his eye. He stopped the car, rolled down the window and leaned out to get a better view.

Damn if those don't look like pill boxes, he thought. He opened the door, walked to the end of the bridge and climbed down to the water's edge. He picked up one of the white boxes and opened it. The tablets rolled out in his hand. He squatted, gathered several more boxes and shook them. They each contained freshly dispensed medicines. He looked up and down the stream, white paper boxes lined both banks like snowflakes in the moonlight.

Doc looked at the powder in the palm of his hand. He threw the container into the water, brushed the powder from his hands and climbed back to his car. He drove slowly, trying to sort out his feelings. All he could grasp was a deep overwhelming sadness. He thought about the message but he could not decide what to do about it. He knew that his working for someone other than the patient made him beholden to an organization whose interests *conflicted* with those of the patient. Patients had a right to presume he would consider their interest and, when possible, put that above all other considerations. He had always known that. For the first time in his career though, he was unsure what those interests were. He knew every one of those boxes represented an un-met expectation. He suspected that if he were to resist the takeover, his patients would go where their union bosses ordered them and he would be without any patients. He sat in the car in front of the house and smoked a cigarette. His chest felt tight. A heaviness penetrated his neck and shoulder muscles. Getting out of the car, struggling up the steps and opening the door was a chore. He hung his coat in the hall closet and joined Shirley in the kitchen.

"Do you ever feel like a salmon swimming upstream to die?" he asked.

She put her arms around him and they stood in the middle of the room welded together until she started coughing.

"You've been coughing an awful lot lately, honey," Doc said. His sadness was immediately replaced by concern for his wife. "You should come into the clinic and get a chest X-ray."

"It's only a cigarette cough, doctor." She laughed. "I've decided I'm going to cut down starting next week on the twin's birthday."

That night in bed Doc whispered, "Just to make me feel better, come into the clinic and get a chest X-ray. Will you? The specialist can look at the film when he comes up from Charleston day after tomorrow."

"O.K.! O.K.! If it will make you happy. I'll do it, but I'm busy to-morrow. I'll do it first thing next week." She laughed and snuggled close to him. "Now stop practicing medicine and put your arms around me."

"That's not soon enough, honey. I want the specialist to look at it right away." She did not answer. He moved closer. She felt good next to him and he was aroused for the first time in weeks, but he was so tired, he fell asleep. The next morning when he awakened, she was all ready in the kitchen. He tip-toed down the hall, put his arms around her from behind and kissed her on the neck. She melted against him for a moment, then playfully pulled away.

"No you don't," she teased. "You had your chance last night and you went to sleep." He pulled her close and kissed her. She pushed her hands against his chest and giggled. She reminded him of a school girl. "Now stop that, darling." She picked up an empty mug and shoved it into his hand. "Get yourself a cup of coffee and get dressed or you're going to be late to the clinic."

Doc took the cup and filled it from the pot on the stove. He turned to leave the room and stopped.

"You look beautiful this morning," he said. She smiled and returned to her chores. "Now, you be sure to come in for that chest X-ray today. You hear? The radiologist's coming up from Charleston tomorrow. I want him to take a look at it."

"Oh, all right. I'll do it this morning," she promised. "Now get yourself off to your job. We've got a new house to build." He carried his half eaten breakfast to the counter by the sink, kissed her on the back of the neck and left for work.

That afternoon he asked Mrs. Sidenstricker to look through the pile of films on the desk and get Shirley's chest X-ray. "I want to look at it myself before the radiologist comes," he said. "I'm really worried about her cough."

Doc had read an article by a Dr. Graham in St. Louis linking smoking to lung cancer and he had become concerned about Shirley's smoking.

Mrs. Sidenstricker returned in a few minutes, placed the large manila envelope on his desk and slipped the film onto the view-box.

"Sidenstricker, do you know where my black crayon went?"

"No, Doctor," she lied. She knew the radiologist had thrown the crayon away the last time he came to read X-rays.

"I don't need some hick G.P. scribbling all over the films," the radiologist had muttered. He had pretended he was unaware of Mrs. Sidenstricker's presence, but she knew he wanted her to hear.

Doc thought the clinician had an advantage because he had examined the patient, so he often made crayon marks to give the specialist an idea where the problem was.

That very day, a group of radiologists were gathered in the doctor's lounge at Mercy Hospital. They considered their rotation through Medical Hygiene Clinics to be scut work, but they liked the extra money.

"The quality of the films is poor," one griped.

"Yes, but what really pisses me off," one of the more pompous specialists complained, "is that hayseed up in Wattsville's always putting arrows on the film and writing symptoms down on slips of paper and clipping them to the X-rays. I'd never get anything done if I paid attention to his hen-scratching."

"What do you do about it?" his less experienced colleague inquired.

"I threw his crayon away," he answered. "But if he gets another, a damp sponge'll take the arrows off, and wastebaskets are made for *L.M.D's.* notes." The important men gathered around in the doctor's lounge, laughed at the obvious solution.

The chief radiologist stuck his head in the door of the lounge and smiled sweetly. "Say, fellows, is there a chance I could talk one of you into taking my turn in Wattsville tomorrow?" He grinned and looked from face to face. No one in the room would make eye contact with him. He scratched his head and looked disgusted. "Hell, I guess I'll have to con one of the residents into doing it then.""What do you think of Greyhound stock," someone asked, shifting to a more important subject.

The next day Doc delayed his house call departure as long as he could, hoping the radiologist might be early, but he finally had to leave. He called Mrs. Sidenstricker into his office and pointed out the area he was concerned about on Shirley's chest X-ray.

He had not developed confidence in the employee's the administrator hired, so he continued to depend on Mrs. Sidenstricker when he wanted to be sure something would get done.

"Now this area right here is what worries me," Doc explained. "Be sure he checks it thoroughly. Don't let me down."

"I won't forget," she reassured him as he left the building. Soon after Doc departed, she greeted the unfamiliar doctor at the head of the hallway and ushered him into Doc's office. The chief radiologist had successfully dumped his obligation onto a first year resident who had never been to Wattsville.

This was supposed to be the young doctor's day off. He had promised his girl friend to spend it with her.

"If I turn down the chief radiologist's request to take his turn in Wattsville, I might as well find another residency," he had explained. "The chief assured me the drive will only take an hour each way and a half hour at the most to read all the films. We can spend the rest of the day together. We'll go to a movie," he promised. "I know they get extra pay for the work they do in those clinics. Maybe he'll share a few bucks of it with me." He had kissed her and smiled. She had returned his assurances with a frown.

"Doctor Sizemore asked me to be sure you pay particular attention to this film," Mrs. Sidenstricker said as the young doctor seated himself behind Doc's desk. She held the film in front of the view box and pointed to the white spot Doc had indicated to her before he departed for his house call. "It is his wife's chest X-ray. She has been coughing a lot and the doctor thinks there is a suspicious spot in the right middle lobe. He pointed it out to me right here. See? It's closer to the pleura than to the hilum. He said he would have marked it but he has misplaced his crayon."

"O.K! O.K!" he answered. He took the film down and stuck it on the bottom of the pile. The drive had taken an hour and fifty five minutes, and there was no way he was going to get through that stack in a half hour. Mrs. Sidenstricker stood by the desk until he sensed she was not going to leave. He looked up from the mound of envelopes.

"Doctor Sizemore is very worried about his wife's health," she said. "I promised I would see that you checked the X-ray thoroughly."

"O.K. O.K.! Don't worry. I'll get to it." He waved his hand in a gesture of dismissal. She hesitated, started to say something more, but the doctor looked at her, frowned and turned his back. She left the room.

Most of the films were routine broken bones, sprains, strains and arthritis studies. He whizzed through those by seconding the *"Local Medical Doctor's"* opinions from the notes he had originally intended to throw in the wastebasket, **but Hell's Bells anyone can read an X-ray of a broken bone, even a L.M.D.,** he thought. The chest X-rays took a little longer, but he hurried through them. Everyone in coal mining communities had increased markings, emphysema, old Ghon tubercles and the like, so he had little trouble getting them finished. He looked at his watch. It had taken him over an hour and a half.

Oh shit! It's going to be three o'clock before I get back to Charleston. Sue's going to be fit to be tied.

As he hurried for the door, Mrs. Sidenstricker attempted to question him about Shirley's chest X-ray.

"Yes! Yes! I paid attention to all the films. There was nothing unusual to report." He practically ran through the waiting room, across the porch and down the steps. Mrs. Sidenstricker watched him spin the wheels of his car leaving the parking lot.

"I hurried back as fast as I could," Doc said as he rushed in a little later. "I was hoping to catch the radiologist before he got away.

He didn't waste any time getting through the films. Did you point out the place where I wanted him to pay particular attention?"

"I handed the X-ray to him personally when he first arrived and explained whose it was and where you thought you saw a suspicious lesion," she answered. "I even put it up on the view box and pointed to the area you showed me." She did not tell Doc the radiologist looked like a youngster or that he had dismissed her so contemptuously.

Doc took the hastily scribbled note out of the jacket and read it three times. *Increased Bronchial Markings.* He looked at the film again. The small white irregular patch was easily visible.

He couldn't have missed that, Doc thought. "I don't recognize this name. What does that say?" He held the report up for Mrs. Sidenstricker to see the scribbled signature.

"He was not one of the doctors who has been here before," she said.

"Didn't he introduce himself?"

"No, he didn't. Not as I recall, anyway."

Doc looked at the spot for a long time before he returned the film to its envelope.

"Well, the specialist says your chest X-ray is all right," he reported to Shirley that evening.

"I told you so." She laughed. "This cough will go away as soon as I quit smoking on the twin's birthday."

"I seem to remember you were going to stop on the twin's birthday last year, too," he said.

"Stop nagging me. You know how hard I've tried. Maybe if you didn't smoke, too, it would not be so difficult."

"What do you say we quit together when we go on vacation," he said. "It should be easier if we're not under so much pressure."

"Sounds like a good plan to me." She laughed, relieved that the matter could be put off for a while.

Doc would have felt better if he had been there to show the radiologist what he saw on her X-ray, but as time went by, he supposed the specialist must know what he spent all his time doing.

Still, he thought. *I think I'll pull that film out and show it to the next radiologist in four weeks.*

Four weeks went by. The radiologist did not make it to the clinic. One member of the radiology group was on vacation and another was out sick with the flu.

"You'll just have to get by for a week or two on your own," the administrator explained over the phone. No one could make it for the following rotation as they were behind in their hospital work. When a radiologist did come, he waved Doc off.

"Look, I have more than I can get to with the new films. If you have a film that's all ready been read you want looked at again, it will just have to wait." He mumbled something under his breath about Doc's having replaced his crayon with a grease pencil and whipped an X-ray across the front of the view box and back into its envelope *before you could say Jack Robinson.*

One thing after another postponed the re-evaluation until one day Doc sat at his desk looking at the X-ray for about the fortieth time.

Maybe I should send this down to Dr. Wescott, he thought.

Mrs. Sidenstricker stuck her head in the door and said, "Dr. Sizemore, Mrs. Sizemore called and told me to remind you about this weekend"

I guess if that spot were important, he would have known, he decided.

"Dr. Sizemore, did you hear me?"

"Oh, I'm sorry, Sidenstricker. What did you say?"

"I said your wife called."

"Oh, yes. Tell her I'll check with the administrator. I've got a couple weekends coming." He put the films aside, then after a while he decided to slip them into the stack in the radiologist' locker in a fresh envelope with a fictitious name.

The administrator called back after he was located in Barboursville and admonished Doc for expecting him to schedule a weekend locum tenens on such short notice.

"The interns and residents are busy people. They can't just shift their schedules around on short notice to accommodate the whims of every clinic doctor." He paused for a moment, then just before hanging up, he said sweetly. "Call again when you can give me proper notification, doctor."

"Sorry, honey," Doc said to Shirley when he got home that evening. "I know you are disappointed. I wish we could have gone to Charleston, too. The administrator said we have to give more notice."

Doc had trouble getting to sleep that night. Not only was Shirley's disappointment upsetting, but also the administrator's harsh response grated on him.

The promises don't seem to be working out the way I'd hoped, he thought. *Sometimes, I think disappointing Shirley's expectations is more painful than her not having any.* He turned and looked at her sleeping beside him. The full moon filtered its light through the trees and the curtains, softly illuminating her face. He brushed her hair away from her cheek and kissed her. She smiled and moved closer. He put his arm around her and closed his eyes.

Chapter Twelve

Ed Humphrey called one evening as Doc was preparing to leave the clinic.

"Hi Doc. Thelma and I'd like to have you and Shirley over for supper Saturday night. Do you think you can make it?"

"I don't see why not," Doc answered. "What time?"

"Let's make it early if that's all right with you. How's about seven?"

"I am sure we can make it at seven, barring an emergency."

"All right, we'll see you at seven."

"It's about time," Shirley said when Doc told her of the invitation. "We haven't been anywhere in so long I can't remember when it was. I'll call Thelma and see if we can bring anything."

In the car on the way to the pharmacist's house on Saturday evening, Doc was pensive.

"What's the matter, darling?" Shirley asked. Doc did not answer right away. Just before they got to their destination, though, he slowed the car and pulled off the road. After he had stopped he turned to Shirley.

"I've been thinking, honey. Ed and Thelma have been scarce as hen's teeth for several months now. Everyone knows his business doesn't pay its light bills anymore. Do you suppose this is a farewell supper?"

"Oh, God, no!" she said. "I hope not." Doc reached over and took both her hands in his. Finally, he patted her hand reassuringly, turned in the seat and started the motor.

He had guessed right, it was a farewell. The Humphreys were leaving in five days. "We just can't stay here any longer. The union is taking all the business out of town. I only filled three prescriptions last week. We're going to stay with Thelma's folks in Dunbar until I find something," Ed said. "I guess we'll lose our house and the pharmacy building. We can't even pay the interest on our loans. The bank extended us twice all ready."

It was a pretty dismal evening. On the way home, Doc drove silently, Shirley smoked a cigarette and looked out the window.

"I understand several hospitals have closed up and the mayor over in Gauley Bridge told me it's getting hard to find a small town drug store in southern West Virginia anymore," Bill Arbogast said the next day. "I knew it was only a matter of time for Ed."

Shirley moped around for several days. She spent more time on the phone with Alice Wilson over in Clendenin after that, and when she and Doc were alone, he sensed her growing sadness.

"Seems like a person can't get close anymore but something happens to separate us," she whispered one night when they were in bed. Doc held her near and felt her warm tears on his cheek. He kissed her and wiped her eyelids gently with his finger. He knew he had to say something.

"What say you go over to Kaymoor to visit your mother for a few days?" he said. "You can take the bus."

"We'll see," she whispered. "I love you."

"I love you, too, Shirley."

The next day at the clinic Doc pulled out the X-rays he had slipped in with the fresh batch, once more the reading on Shirley's films came back, "Increased Bronchial Markings." He supposed he was being compulsive and he should let the matter rest but he remained uneasy. He decided he would take the films to the next district meeting in Cedar Grove and ask Dr. Hamer's opinion. He was also a G.P. but he had looked at X-rays for a good many years and knew a thing or two.

Doc put the film back in its jacket and walked down the hall to speak to Mrs. Sidenstricker. As he passed the lab area he noticed Sturgill preparing an adrenalin injection for an asthmatic with severe shortness of breath. The light from the window radiated through the pink liquid in the multiple dose vial.

"Wait a minute," Doc called. He took the vial and held it up to the light. "This medicine should have been discarded long ago." He handed it back. "Get a fresh bottle and bring it to me." Sturgill returned from the pharmacy with an unopened bottle. She handed it to Doc.

"Look at the color," he complained. "It's as pink as the other." He shook the vial. Tiny particles distributed themselves throughout the fluid. "This medicine will not do," he said. "Adrenalin is outdated long before it turns pink. You'll have to get another bottle."

"There's a case in the pharmacy, Doctor," Sturgill said. "And it's all the same color."

"Is that all there is? Don't we have any fresh adrenalin?" he asked.

"That's all there is, doctor," she answered. Doc walked into the pharmacy to check for himself and after he confirmed Sturgill's statement he picked up a large container of penicillin pills and poured some of them out on the counter. Some were crumbling, some stuck together, their color was faded to several shades of yellow, and in the bottom of the container there were a few that were mottled looking as if something were growing on them. Those white boxes on the creek bank flashed through Doc's mind. He took the pink adrenalin to Mrs. Sidenstricker along with a box of penicillin pills about to be dispensed.

"Have you noticed the color of this adrenalin or the condition of these tablets?" he asked.

"I discussed it with the administrator, Doctor Sizemore. He said they were perfectly all right." She looked sheepish. "I didn't say anything to you..." She looked at the floor for a moment, then she turned and walked away. Doc understood she was trying to spare his feelings.

The patients had started using disrespectful nicknames for the medicines Doc had begun to prescribe. Names like Black Devils for some of the pills, G.I. Gin for the Tincture of White Pine, or Elixir of Turpin Hydrate he had to prescribe for coughs, or snake oil for the Iron, Quinine and Strychnine tonic so many got for the "blahs." The Dover's Powders, dispensed for flu symptoms, were called Pirate's potion because they had originally been concocted long ago by the famous buccaneer named Dover. The patients knew the dispensing changes were to cut expenses, but they blamed Doc instead of the union.

Doc called the administrator in Charleston and protested against the policy of using out-dated medicine. "Whether you believe it or not some of these people are really sick. Now we don't even have a drug store for them. And while we're at it," he complained.

"I've been trying to tell you most of the formulary we stock at the clinic is either archaic or ineffective."

"I am a busy man. You should know better than to bother me at a time like this with such trivial matters. We can discuss this at the business meeting. That is what we have business meetings for."

"This is not something to discuss at a business meeting," Doc said. He did his best to control his anger. "This is a medical matter and it is not trivial. I am sick of using tinctures and mixtures that were old fashioned before the turn of the century. Besides, the business meetings consist of your pronouncements and little else. I don't seem to have any say in what goes on around here anymore."

"Doctor!" Cox pronounced the word scornfully. "I am responsible for running these clinics with as little waste as possible. When I find a bargain on medications, I am certainly going to take advantage of that good fortune. I am getting fed up with your constant bickering about one petty matter after another. This is not the time for this discussion. We provide an opportunity for your rebuttal regarding medical matters at the monthly meetings. I expect you to either work within the guidelines of the formulary we have gone to great effort to put together for you, or..." He did not - nor did he have to - finish the sentence. There was a pause, then he hung up. The process of returning the telephone to its cradle was emphatic enough to accentuate his message.

Doc sat at his desk with the dead receiver in his hand. Mrs. Sidenstricker looked in. She quietly closed the door and returned to her desk. He dragged through the rest of the week hardly interacting with the clinic employees and went through the motions of practicing medicine. At home he picked at his food, slept fitfully and stared into space.

At the next business meeting in Cedar Grove, the administrator stood in front of the room until everyone was seated. Then, he opened the meeting with a statement delivered in the tone of an angry parent.

"The majority of you in this room have been cooperative in the effort management has made to create a system to deliver quality medical care at a reasonable cost. I am sorry to say the same cannot be said for every one." He paused and looked around the room for effect. "We have been lenient up to this time, because we assumed any reasonable individual would eventually recognize the value of teamwork." His expression changed, momentarily projecting disappointment, then he looked over the heads of his audience tingeing the atmosphere with a hint of frustration. Abruptly he returned to the posture of the wronged parent and pounded his palm with a clenched fist. "If any of you believe the practice of tolerance can continue forever, I am here this evening to tell you something. You are sadly mistaken!" There was a hush in the room. It seemed for a moment that no one even breathed. "I think we need to roll all business over to the next meeting and spend the time until then deciding whether we can remain part of this group or not." He stood, zipped his briefcase and swung it off the desk, looked around the room from face to stunned face, and walked out.

Doc got up and left without remembering to get Dr. Hamer's opinion of Shirley's chest X-ray.

The following week Mrs. Sidenstricker informed him the administrator had authorized her to hire a nurse for the back office.

"He said he believes a trained nurse can save money by coordinating the work of the back office staff; in helping him stock supplies, and giving injections and such. You want to know the truth, though, I think the radiologists have been complaining so much about the quality of the X-rays and the surgeons about the follow-up dressing care, that he finally realizes we need someone around here with hospital training."

"Why do you suppose he authorized you to do the selecting instead of dumping someone on us like he has in the past?" Doc asked.

"I think he has been unable to get anyone qualified to move to Wattsville," Mrs. Sidenstricker answered.

Doc did not say anything for a while. Finally, he looked up.

"Don't be in too much of a hurry, Sidenstricker. Let me think about this."

The next day when he saw Mayor Arbogast on the street, a thought occurred to him.

"Say, Bill, isn't that daughter of yours about to finish her nurse's training?"

"Right away," the Mayor answered. "And at the top of her class, too, I might add." He stuck his thumbs in his armpits and expanded his chest.

"Do you think she might be willing to come home to work or is she stuck in the big city?"

"Don't know for sure. I could ask her if you'd like. I been trying to stay out of that because I don't want to influence her decision." He paused and looked away for a moment. "You probably remember how it was with your boys."

A wave of sadness passed over Doc. The Mayor's statement reminded him of how little influence he had in the twin's lives.

"Have her give me a call, will you, Bill?"

"I'll do that, Doc," Bill promised.

Mary Arbogast was waiting in the outer office a few days later when Doc finished his last telephone call. Mrs. Sidenstricker had informed Doc, invited her to have a seat and left for the evening.

"Well, Mary, you're certainly all grown up." Mary smiled. "And you look right smart in your uniform, too."

"Thank you doctor Sizemore. I appreciate your considering me for this job."

"Your daddy tells me you graduated at the top of your class. You must have had a lot of offers."

"Yes, I guess I had a few, but I had my heart set on working for you, doctor Sizemore." She blushed and looked at the floor.

"Well, well. That's mighty nice to hear, Mary. When could you come to work for me?"

"I'll be moving home right after the graduation ceremonies are over next week and I get my cap and pin. A day or two to unpack is all I'll need if that's all right with you."

Doc hummed as he drove home.

Maybe- with her help- I can turn some things around in that office, he thought. He felt better just having some say-so about who was hired, though he knew the administrator had really given the authority to Mrs. Sidenstricker.

"Well, honey!" he exclaimed as he came through the door. "I hired me a nurse this afternoon and I betcha' she's a right good one, too. Mary Arbogast'll put some professionalism in that office." Shirley put her cigarette in the ash tray and kissed him.

"I am so glad, darling. I know it'll help make your work easier. And I always liked Mary, she'll be a good nurse."

"I'm surprised she didn't stay in Charleston. Bill says she had lots of offers," Doc said. "She said a funny thing when we were talking. Said she had her heart set on working for me."

Shirley laughed and kissed him again.

"Darling, don't you know she's had a crush on you since she was a kid? Bill told me the reason she went to nurse training was because she admires you so much." She hugged him and laughed.

"Men are blind, but someone up there must look out for them. She'll work her darnd'est for you, as my daddy used to say."

Doc had been having trouble getting to sleep. He had been lying awake looking at the ceiling and waking in the night with a headache. He had not said anything to Shirley, but she had noticed that he dragged out of the house in the mornings and collapsed into bed in the evenings. The next morning after he hired Mary, Doc got up early.

"You certainly seem refreshed this morning," Shirley said.

"Can't remember when I had such a good night's sleep," Doc answered.

Mary worked out better than he could ever have hoped. She was not in the office two weeks before Doc noticed the difference. She had no trouble dealing with Sturgill and Wampler. She was so competent, and her manner so supportive they fell under her spell immediately. The patients soon recognized their wait was half what it had been. The employees were more cheerful and patients even began to remark that Doc was more like his old self again.

"Mary Arbogast is the best thing that's ever happened to that clinic, honey," Doc said to Shirley one evening. "And she seems to love her job. I don't have to tell her but once," he said. "Half the time I don't even have to tell her at all. I look around and what needs to be done is done without my even knowing when she did it."

"Well, she has made a difference in you," Shirley said.

"She sure has a knack for finding ways to get people to come in instead of depending on me to drive out to their houses. I even heard her calling patients the morning after I had made house calls, telling them they should not have waited 'til night to call. I tell you, she is a jewel." Doc became so excited as he talked, he laughed and pounded his palm softly with his fist. Suddenly, he felt embarrassed. He smiled and kissed Shirley. "She's almost as good a nurse as you, darling."

As he was leaving for the office the next morning Shirley asked if he would stop and pick up some cloth she had ordered.

"Mr. Harper said if he were closed he would leave it on the back porch wrapped up with my name on it," she said.

Other than the clinic, the company store on the main street was the hub of commercial activity. It was a large cement block building with a loading dock out front and a Mail Pouch sign painted on the side in black, blue and yellow. Small light bulbs hanging from the high ceiling inside the building barely dented the gloom. Long flat bolts of cloth, mostly in drab colors, piled high in the front part of the store blocked the light from out of doors. Parked conspicuously along one wall, the big white, refrigerated display case smelled of rancid fat and salt pork. Blood puddled in the edges of the meat trays and streaked the insides of the box. Vegetables and fruits, in season, were displayed on counters in the aisle. Bins of potatoes, onions and apples, underneath the tables, mingled their individual odors of decay into a sweet, musty, almost homey smell. In the back, there was the clean scent from sacks of ground feeds for farm animals and nail kegs filled with different kinds of seeds.

Over on one side near the back door, there was a stack of cardboard boxes with holes in the sides. Constant chirping reminded Mr. Harper to notify the appropriate customers their shipment of baby chicks had arrived. "If you don't pick `em up within two days, dead chicks won't be replaced," he advised his customers to avoid any misunderstanding.

"Got the misses' cloth right back here," he said to Doc that evening. "Don't see you runnin' errands for the wife much, Doc. You have a slow day?"

"Got me a new nurse," Doc answered.

"I heard as much. Mayor Arbogast's girl, heh?" He wiped his hands on his apron and crossed his arms across his chest. "Seems like only yesterday she was coming in here for a penny's worth of licorice. Time sure does fly!"

"Don't it ever?" Doc answered.

On his way home he stopped for gas.

"How's tricks, Doc?" Emery Legg asked.

"Can't complain," Doc answered. "Fill'er up and would you mind checking the tires. Seems like she's steering a little squirrely."

"Yep, this'in up front on the left is pretty low. If she goes down agin', come back and I'll find out where she's leakin'. Might just been a one-time thing. Mighty fine automobile you got there, Doc. I always did like a Plymouth."

Emery Legg's filling station, at the end of the street, also served for automobile repairs. Mr. Legg had purchased his business from Hammond-Newcastle. Much of the repairing was done on the street by the car owner with tools borrowed from the station. Eventually, however, Legg seemed to always get involved whether he intended to or not.

"What'a you think'a that?" Or, "what size wrench should I use for this?" an out-of-work miner would inquire. Next thing Legg knew, he was poking under the hood. Sometimes a car in pieces would rest outside his establishment for several weeks if he did not fix it himself. He was in that garage early in the morning and still there late into the night.

Doc drove down the street past the bus station and waved to a few miners loitering in front of Shorty's. It felt good going home early. He would have time to loaf a bit before supper.

Chapter Thirteen

The Affiliated Mine Workers of America had begun to dominate the landscape the way the coal company had during the previous generation. The miner's lot changed little, except as Bea explained. "He makes more when he works, but he don't work hardly none a'tall. Seems like he's either laid off, or on strike perty near all the time."

The miner continued to live in a company-style house that did not have a foundation. In summer his family was still plagued by varmints crawling through the cracks, and in the winter by the cold and dampness. In addition to a sagging porch and a mangy hound tied up in his muddy front yard, a typical miner had recently added a dysfunctional car with its hood up and a broken refrigerator with the door open. The perpetually hungry hound howled mournfully at night and the odor of the pig pen at the back of the house overwhelmed the dog stench out front. The Hammond-Newcastle Coal Company no longer paid him in scrip, but he continued to owe more than his next three months wages to the company store anyway.

"My man bought a rifle down there 'cause they'd let him have it on time," a miner's wife complained to Doc. "It costs half agin' as much as he could get it fer out of the Montgomery Ward catalog, but he wanted it right now so he could trade it fer drink. And now he's drunk it up and we're in the same predicament we was in when the company printed our money and told us where we could spend it."

She related her story to Doc, because he was the only one in town she could talk to who was not in the same quandary. Doc listened, interrupted as soon as he could, gave her a vitamin B twelve shot and a white box of *black devils*.

"You know I have been critical of old Baumgarten all these years," Doc said to Shirley one evening. "But it's getting so there's not a penny's worth of difference between us."

Shirley reached across the table and put her hand on his arm.

"You know that's not so," she said.

As time passed and he continued to lose more of his influence, Shirley began to worry inordinately about him. One evening as he sat in the living room looking off into space, she held a medical journal in front of him.

"Honey, you don't seem to be reading your journals like you used to. Here's one over three months old, with the wrapper still on it."

"Maybe Tyree B. Cox should read it," he snarled. "He seems to be running everything." Shirley felt it was not the time to press the matter. She discarded the periodical in the trash along with a stack of newspapers.

One night Doc came home late from the clinic and sat with his fork in his hand staring into the plate. His eyes were not focused on anything. Shirley had already eaten, she was on the other side of the table, smoking, watching him.

"What's wrong, darling," she asked after a long silence. Doc reached across the table, took her cigarette and drew the smoke deep into his lungs. He handed it back but she hesitated. She had begun to cough. When she finished, she retrieved her cigarette, inhaled deeply and smiled.

"The administrator delights in humiliating me."

"What do you mean, darling?"

"He never passes an opportunity to refer to the help as the **other** employees so everyone is reminded I am an employee, too. He does it in front of patients as well as the staff. And when he threatens to fire someone, or cut their pay, or adds to their work, he always finds a way to interject, loud enough for everyone to hear, `*You don't need to worry, doctor, you always get your paycheck on time.*' He wants everybody to know I sold them out."

When Doc finished, he looked directly at his wife. His eyes were damp."Oh, darling, I am so sorry." She reached across the table and placed her hand on top of his. "Everyone knows that's not true."

"How can you be so sure? **I don't know it's not true. How could they?**" She was stymied for a moment for how to respond. She knew he was distressed about his loss of control, but she had not fully admitted it went beyond a healthy frustration.

"Has anyone said anything to make you think they believe you sold them out?" she asked. She was fishing for evidence that he was not as depressed as he sounded.

"No. No one has - yet. But, maybe if I had resisted..." Shirley walked around the table. She leaned over his shoulder and hugged him. She gave her cigarette to him and started massaging his shoulders.

"I love you, Dr. Sizemore. I hate to see you so unhappy. Maybe we should leave this place." Doc reached up and patted her arm. He exhaled the smoke from his lungs. Her suggestion scared him. He was accustomed to life in Wattsville and the thought of leaving was too frightening to contemplate.

I came running back here after the carnage I saw in Europe and the inhumanity of those camps. All I wanted was to forget. Wattsville probably saved my sanity. My God, I haven't even been in a hospital since the twins were born, he thought. *What could I do if I left here except go to something worse?*

"I guess I'm just tired, honey. I'll be all right in the morning." She rubbed his back another minute.

"Let's go to bed and I'll give you a real back rub, darling." She pulled him by the armpits like a second urging his reluctant fighter into the ring for the next round.

By the time she came out of the bathroom, Doc was sound asleep.

Chapter Fourteen

Life plodded on in Wattsville. The drug store building was still empty and boarded up.

"Last I heard, the druggist was working over in Rainelle," one of Doc's patients told him. "Don't know what he's doin', though. The drug store over there closed a long time ago."

There was a used clothing and furniture store run by the Salvation Army across the street from the appliance store which had been closed for two years. The union office was upstairs over the combination bus terminal and barber shop, and the gas company was next door.

The school building sat on the only large parcel of level land at the upper end of town beside the creek. It housed all grades from one through twelve and was constructed of cinder blocks painted yellow with metal casement windows. It had a flat roof that had leaked since before the building was occupied. Wet spots accumulated in the hallways, on the edge of the gym floor, in Mrs. Funk's math class and in the principal's office. The janitor put towels and rags down to soak up the moisture - unless the storm were severe, in which case buckets were necessary.

Miss Thornton, the high school English teacher, had formed a committee to appeal to the government for funding to open The Lyric Movie Theater as a regional playhouse. Still closed in spite of her efforts, it had Miners and last season's final game announcement on the marquee with a few missing letters. The big plateglass windows covering the movie poster cases had been gone a long time replaced with plywood that was beginning to buckle and come apart because of rain. Though the government-sponsored playhouse had never materialized, the literary committee did get some surplus lard once and cheese another time. The theater was opened for a few days then, and when the new "surplus commodities acquisition committee," was formed, the Lyric continued to be used as the regular storage and distribution center.

Doc began to see more children with suspicious injuries that could be due to abuse and more women with bruises. That element had always existed in his practice, but he had been able to sit a miner down and talk to him about his temper. Lately he had so little time he began to ignore those signs unless they were pretty severe and, even then, he might only tell the wife to send her man in to see him. That seldom materialized into a visit from the culprit. Once in a while word filtered back that the husband had told his wife to *tell the old so and so to mind his own damn business.*

There seemed to be an escalating number of patients with *the blahs,* more alcohol related problems and more injuries from fights at Shorty's or Nick's.

Chapter Fifteen

The meetings in Cedar Grove took on the character of well-drilled briefings of a military enterprise. Tyree outlined the newest set of rules, "standards," he called them and passed out memoranda. His manner had become more self assured, his speech perfunctory. Often times, Doc couldn't remember a fourth of what was said. He took the hand-outs and passed them on to Mary without more than a cursory glance. Mary had begun to take more and more responsibility for the things that bothered Doc.

For a while, having her to work with had made him feel better, but eventually he recognized that was only because he was denying reality. Mary was just protecting him from the truth. He was no longer running the medical part of the practice any more than he was the business. Every time he interacted with Cox or chafed under his directives, Doc lost some of his motivation. Lately, he had begun to talk less and less to Shirley about what went on at the clinic. When she asked, he often became morose or even defensive.

His participation in the high school football program was the only thing that seemed to give him pleasure any more.

In back of the school, next to the hillside, the football field with its bleachers on either side, hosted the most widely accepted outlet for boisterous passion shared by every faction in the community. Even a few of the coloreds attended the games. (Of course they stood down at the end of the field).

Before Doc came to Wattsville, Doctor Baumgarten had attended the games and took care of the players medical needs. Since Doctor Sizemore's arrival, the coach relied on him to – "keep, my boys patched up so's we can win them games."

During the season, coach Nellis and Doc were about the most popular men in town. Nellis made sure Doc sat on the bench next to him at home games and up front on the school bus to away games over in Webster Springs and Roan County and such when Doc could get away. He and the Doc had become 'thick as thieves,' as the loiterers at Shorty's often remarked.

Coach Nellis, whose wife had left him soon after he arrived in Wattsville, was a one-sport coach in a one-sport town. Some softball was played on the ball diamond, mostly pick-up games, though, and basketball was a "girls' game." His social life, like Doc's, consisted pretty much of work and talking about his work.

Doc had never charged for his services, but the administrator wanted the school to pay a fee to the clinic. He was sure Doc got gifts from parents and town merchants for his "devotion to the boys on the team," and he felt that represented revenue properly due to the clinic.

"I can't prove it, but I know he's getting paid under the table," the administrator confided to his mother. "But that hayseed medical quack can't pull the wool over my eyes much longer. I'm going to put a stop to it and soon," he yapped to her. His mother did not need to comment, her smile confirmed her confidence that her brilliant son would triumph in the end.

When he could stand it no longer, the administrator called Doc into, "my office."

"In the future, I am going to seriously consider changing the circumstances under which you provide medical services for the football games," he announced ambiguously.

Doc knew that Cox had no idea how important high school football was in towns such as Wattsville, and he immediately started a telephone campaign to teach the *prissy bastard* a lesson.

"Sorry Bill, but there is nothing I can do about it," he informed principal Arbogast. "The administrator has a job to do. He is my boss, and he is adamant." Doc, the obviously unwilling victim of a corporate ogre, explained the situation and its likely effect on the football program to all who would listen. "Most likely none of the visiting teams is going to want to play in a town that has no medical care available on the field," he would say. "But the administrator lives in Charleston where it don't matter to him, I guess," he would add as a quiet, but discernable afterthought.

Doc had called coach Holland over in Mount Hope and informed him there would be no medical care on the field for his players. "Yes, that's right, coach, if somebody gets hurt, the courts are likely to hold you responsible." Several parents told Holland they did not want their kids playing Wattsville under those circumstances. Doc knew that a forfeited game, for cause, would knock Wattsville out of the championship and Mount Hope would win the conference by default. The Mount Hope coach knew that, too. At least he did after Doc finished explaining all the circumstances to him.

As the process developed, it became so enjoyable to Doc he had trouble sleeping. He became almost giddy with his anticipation of

Cox's reaction **when the shit hits the fan,** as the refrain reverberated repeatedly through his consciousness.

When the phone rang on the evening of the game, he lit a cigarette, seated himself comfortably, leaned back and crossed his legs before answering.

"What do you mean you want me to be at the games from now on?" Doc's voice registered utter amazement at the sudden switch in the administrator's attitude.

"I never said you couldn't provide care at the games," the administrator sputtered over the telephone.

"Well, I'm sorry if I misunderstood. I thought you said you wanted me to stop and I certainly respect your position as the head man at the clinic and I try to always..."

"Never mind about that."

"Then am I to assume they have agreed to pay the clinic for my services?"

"I just think as a community service, we should do some things free," the administrator pontificated as if he had thought of it himself.

"I don't know. Seems to me you had a point. Besides, the clinic is taking a lot of responsibility and..."

"Goddamn it! Go to the game," the administrator shouted and slammed down the phone. Doc had a warm feeling all over as he replaced the receiver in its cradle.

"You look like the cat that ate the canary," Shirley said as he kissed her goodbye. Humming to himself as he drove toward the football field, he switched on the radio and turned it up louder than usual. Montana Slim's voice filled the automobile's interior. *Tonight they say is cowboy night/get out the old corral and let us take the town by storm/tonight's my night to howl/Tonight's my night to howl/boy/I yippy I yippy Oh!* Doc drummed on the steering wheel in time with the music. He parked the Plymouth in his reserved spot next to the gate and entered the field.

He leaned toward coach Nellis, who was sitting on the bench, and cupped his hand beside his mouth.

"Sorry to hold up the game," he whispered. He could not disguise the triumph in his voice. As they stood for the National Anthem, the coach slapped him on the back.

"I'm kind'a glad for the delay," Nellis whispered. "Them Mount Hope boys look like their getting pretty nervous from the wait. Thought they was goin'ta get off with a de'fault. We let `em know you was on your way soon as we heard. They been sweatin' ever since."

"*Oh say can you see...*" the voices filtered down from the bleachers. Doc and the Coach placed their palms over their hearts. Doc chuckled, when the National Anthem concluded and they re-seated themselves on the bench.

"Now, wonder what made the administrator change his mind?"

"Everbody in town called the union offices," the coach whispered. "Loomis threatened to loose a goon on him after he fired his ass. And he knows Loomis don't talk to hear his head roar. I bet the little snot near shit his pants."

Freddy Harper twisted his ankle and a boy from over in Mount Hope had "his bell rung," as coach Nellis was won't to say. But other than that, Doc sat on the bench with his leg flexed and his hands clasped around his knee and rocked back and forth humming to himself for most of the game.

The next time Doc saw the administrator, he smiled politely and informed him in a loud voice for all to hear, "Should'a been at the game. I think it was the best we played all season." Then he looked around to see who all was listening and continued. "Beat Mount Hope forty-one to nothing."

Then as he passed the administrator in the narrow hallway, "Going to be the conference champions this year. Yes, siree, you should'a been there."

The administrator mumbled something but it was inaudible.

* * *

On a Friday morning a few weeks later, the clinic administrator was going through his correspondence. He had a tendency to let a lot of mail stack up on *"My desk"* before he took care of it.

Important men are like that, he thought. ***"There's always a lot of people wanting an influential person's time and I'd rather attend to business instead of flaunting my power, I always say,"*** he said - every chance he got.

He discarded most of the mail, but one long envelope caught his attention. It was marked "Personal and Confidential" and was from the Democratic National Committee. He opened it and began to read.

"You have been selected, as a prominent member of your community, to meet with the Democratic Candidate for The Presidency of The United States when he visits your area on his campaign tour. Your advice on the important issues of the day will be gratefully appreciated. There will be an opportunity to have your photograph taken with the Candidate at the speaker's table. All those seated at the speaker's table will be invited to generously support the causes so crucial to us all. It is with great pleasure that I anticipate meeting you and introducing you to the Candidate himself. He will be in Wattsville on September 3rd at approximately seven-thirty in the evening." The letter was printed, the last sentence was typed in. It was signed, The State Campaign Chairman, Randolph Jenkins.

Tyree sent a response off confirming his willingness to contribute. He sent no money. He knew enough about politics to get what he wanted first and make his contribution later. The lead men who dropped into Doc's office unannounced on September 2nd, put a considerable amount of pressure on Tyree to write a check then and there, but he held out for the introduction first and then the check.

"The Candidate is a busy man. His time is limited. He will get to all those he can," the clean-cut young advance man complained.

That's what I figure, the administrator thought. *They take me for a country boob. I don't like the rich son-of-a-bitch anyway.*He maintained the benign smile, of one totally convinced. "I understand, I just prefer to make my contribution on the night of his visit," he answered considerately. *If he's too good to have his picture taken with me or to shake my hand, he can get his money from his crooked daddy. I work for my money.* He had seen the deputy sheriff passing out money down at Shorty's, in the parking lot behind Nick's, in his patrol car outside the clinic and in the barber shop. *They seem to all ready have more money than they know what to do with,* he thought.

The Candidate blew into town on his way to someplace important. At the end of the gymnasium, a sheet was thrown over the ping pong table and folding metal chairs were set up in rows on the basketball floor. The candidate, Jenkins, a couple other members of the entourage, mayor Arbogast, coach Nellis, the administrator and Doc huddled around the table. Tyree tried to talk to the Candidate about the status of the gubernatorial elections, but the Candidate kept looking into the crowd, shaking someone's hand, or issuing instructions to one of his assistants.

When the visitors had finished picking at the food served on paper plates, one of the Candidate's helpers instructed Doc and the school principal to move their chairs out of the speaker's line of vision. The Candidate looked over the heads of the sparse crowd, delivered a perfunctory version of his speech, quickly had his picture taken with a few randomly selected attendees and left.

Though he got no encouragement for his political aspirations, Tyree did get his handshake. A man in a straw hat with the Candidate's name on the band, pushed him against the Candidate who turned his head slightly and smiled just as the flash exploded.

As the Candidate's bus left town on its way to Charleston, the Candidate's assistant waved the check in front of the Candidate's face.

"How did that son-of-a-bitch get a place at the head table with a measly contribution like this?"

The next day the picture on the front page of the Washington Papers, showed Tyree and the Candidate smiling directly into the camera, while awkwardly grasping for each other's hands.

The headline read, *"Candidate consults with prominent medical man."* The text went on to say, *"Known affectionately as Doc, to all those whose lives he has touched, this beloved healer gives tirelessly of himself to make his community a better place. The Candidate has made it a priority, to consult extensively with Doctor Earl Sizemore and others like him, to formulate policy that will radically change the face of medical care in our great nation."*

Cox's mother got an ear full of Tyree's sojourn into the inner sanctum of big-time politics.

"The Candidate mentioned the possibility of a nomination to the Governor's race, but I informed him that I am altogether too busy to even consider such a proposal at this time."

The revelation only confirmed what his mother had known all along. She often bragged to her best friend, Thelma Riggs, whom she hated, "All those big-shots depend on my boy. If he didn't keep the books straight they'd be in trouble all the time." Thelma would just smile her little pinched smile, sip her tea, clear her throat elaborately and mention as to how her son was all ready the youngest junior assistant professor at Kanawha College and destined for great things.

"He has started a history of our family," she would reiterate for the umpteenth time and when he writes his book..." Tyree's mother would shut out the rest, she was sick of hearing about the *future prospects of "my son the professor."*

Just wait 'till she hears about this. She won't be so uppity about her mealy mouthed, small-time, professor-son with me anymore, Tyree's mother gloated.

"Now, you mustn't mention that I told you. The Candidate swore me to secrecy. It doesn't look too good when a prominent member of the community turns down an offer like that. Mind you, I'm not saying it was a final offer, that's not the way they work. He was just testing the waters so to speak and probably would have to deny that the offer was ever made. That's the way it works. Those of us on the inside, so to speak, all know that," he added.

It'll be a while before she crows about her scrawny son after she hears about this, Cox's mother thought.

Tyree did not mention that his picture and the sentiment was mis-labeled with Doc Sizemore's name.

The next day, Doc Sizemore treated Mr. Fauss, the high school civics teacher, for a cracked rib he acquired while trying to get into the meeting with a protest sign about the morals of the Candidate. Doctor Baumgarten was visited by two colored boys who were roughed up for being caught hanging around outside the school while the meeting was going on.

"We never did nothin'," Addie Comer said. "We was just hanging around down there 'cause we heard they was buying votes. The deputy said if we was caught tryin' to vote he would see us planted up under that tree above Dogtown Holler."

Doc left the newspaper folded on his desk where the administrator would have to move it next time he was in "*My office.*"

Chapter Sixteen

About noon one day, Doc got a call from Mr. Legg. The mechanic had been working on Dr. Baumgarten's car.

"I been knocking on his door and they's no answer. I talked to him on the telephone yesterday morning. He's expecting me to bring his car back, said he'd be home."

"Did you call the sheriff?" Doc asked.

"No, Doc," he answered. "I just supposed it was more'n likely a problem for a doctor."

"Did you try the door?"

"Yes, I did. It's locked. And I went all around. Doors and windows all locked. The whole place's tight as a drum."

"All right, I'll come over. Wait there. I may need some help." Doc advised Mrs. Sidenstricker to call the sheriff and he headed for Dr. Baumgarten's place.

As Doc arrived on the scene, Mr. Legg had succeeded in prying a window open in the back of the house. He called to Doc to wait out front. "I'll open the front door just as soon as I get in here and come through the house, Doc."

Doc waited listening to the muffled noises of Legg climbing into the kitchen, complaining as he fell over something on the floor. "Doc! Wake up. Doc!" Legg shouted. Then he came running to the front door and fiddled with the lock. Finally, he succeeded in opening the door. "Doc, he's back there in the kitchen."

Doc hurried to the back of the house. Baumgarten was lying on his back on the kitchen floor. He was dusky colored; his skin was cold, his pupils fixed and his mouth was open.

"He's dead'ern a door nail, Doc," Legg whispered.

About the time Doc had satisfied himself Legg was right, Don Chapin arrived.

"You know if he's got any kin?" the deputy asked.

"Not that I know of," Doc answered.

"Me neither," Legg agreed.

"Looks like he had a stroke, though, Don, so I'll be able to sign the death certificate for you."

"Thanks, Doc. That'll save me a heap of paper work." Doc walked back through the house which had served as medical office. As he went, he tried to fathom how one could practice in a place so devoid of equipment. There was a small desk in a nook off the living room and a chair for the patient to sit in. A head mirror lay next to a percussion hammer and a sphygmomanometer on the desk top. A miniature railroad signal with a red and a green light stood in the corner.

"He did all the railroad examinations, Doc," the sheriff said.

"I had forgotten that," Doc said.

A shelf behind the desk contained a case of penicillin for injections and a curtain on a string concealed two more cases of the antibiotic under a sink in the corner.

"I wonder if he used anything else?" Doc asked.

"Not that I know of," the sheriff answered. "Most of his patients over the past few years were just niggers or an occasional white person with a cold who dropped by for a penicillin shot. Done it a couple times myself. Saves the hassle of going up to your clinic and waitin'." He looked a little sheepish. "No offense, Doc."

Doc smiled. He picked up his bag.

"You'll call the mortuary over in Clendenin?"

"Yes siree, Doc. I'll do that right away. I'll do that very thing right away." As Doc opened the front door, the deputy mumbled something else but it was barely audible. It sounded like, "Poor old bastard."

Doc crossed the porch and slowly descended the steps. For some reason he suddenly didn't feel very good. As he drove back to the clinic, he experienced a sense of dread. He had trouble getting his breath, he pulled over and parked by the road. He rolled down the window and inhaled deeply. Initially the cool air felt good, then he felt cold and clammy. His forehead was damp. He touched his face with his fingers, they came away wet. After loosening his collar, he felt better, but when he got back to the clinic, he removed his tie and washed his face and neck with cold water.

Poor old bastard for sure, he thought.

"I think there's no one," he said to Shirley when he got home that evening. "I can't believe it. There he was stone-dead on the floor staring up at the ceiling. He had one hand kinda' stuck out like he was reaching for something." He paused. "Or someone. Can you believe the way we ignored that old man all these years?"

He raised his eyes from his plate and looked at Shirley. She reached over and touched his hand. "A lifetime of service, regardless of the judgments I made about him, and to end up all alone. First I rejected him, then he was ignored by most of his patients.

What a reward." He sat at the table staring into his food. Shirley got up and came over to put her arms around him.

"Most of his patients had left him long before you came here to practice," she said.

"Discovered by the mechanic," Doc whispered. "His car was more important than he was." A tear ran down his cheek, Shirley kissed him and brushed it away.

A search of the doctor's papers showed he had a total of twelve dollars in the bank, forty-two-fifty in his office drawer, a lapsed life insurance policy and a mortgage several months in arrears. The funeral was attended by Doc and Shirley, Mary and Mayor Arbogast, Bea, from the hotel, and if you count driving up to the edge of the cemetery and sitting in his car, deputy sheriff Chapin.

After the service, Shirley and Doc walked back to the car.

"I think that was the saddest funeral I have ever attended," Shirley sighed.

Chapter Seventeen

At the next meeting in Cedar Grove, Dr. Hamer studied the film for a long time. "I have to agree with you, Earl, that spot *is* suspicious." He handed Shirley's X-ray over his shoulder. Doc replaced it in its envelope.

The following week Doc presented the chest film to the visiting radiologist whose exasperation was intensified as much by the black arrow as it was by Doc's persistence.

"How many times do I have to tell you? This is a change in the bronchi due to smoking and living in a coal town."

"But Dr. Hamer down in Cedar Grove agrees it is suspicious."

"And where did he take his radiology residency?" The specialist glanced over his shoulder in Doc's general direction as he spit out the question that was not really a question.

"Dr. Graham in St. Louis has postulated that smoking is the cause of lung cancer and Shirley smokes," Doc insisted.

"Oh, becoming a cancer expert out here in the sticks are we? Sheep have lung cancer Mister Expert. How much do you suppose they smoke?" He handed the X-ray over his shoulder to the obviously dismissed L.M.D., took a long drag on his cigarette and returned it to the ashtray. Doc stood with the film in his hand looking at the busy man's back, then turned and walked down the hall.

Patients began to notice Doc shuffling through the days again, working without enthusiasm.

"Doc don't seem to be hisself," a lady reported to Mary. "I knowed he was kind'a moody there for awhile, but he seemed like he was getting better."

"Something wrong with the Doc?" several others asked.

Mary always gave the same answer.

"He's just tired. He works too hard."

He had trouble sleeping. Shirley would awaken in the night sensing that something was wrong and get up to find Doc looking out the window. He became distant, she would often find him sitting with the paper in front of his face pretending to read, just staring at the print. One night she discovered him on the couch slumped forward, his head in his hands, crying. She tried to get him to talk but he couldn't express his feelings except to say he felt empty.

"Dr. Wescott, please. Dr. Sizemore calling." Doc had decided to get Wescott's opinion about Shirley's X-ray. He couldn't believe that he and Dr. Hamer were both wrong about what they were seeing on that film. The nurse advised him that Dr. Wescott was in surgery but he would return the call as soon as he was available. About two hours later Dr. Wescott called back.

"I'd be happy to take a look at the X-ray, Doctor Sizemore. Send it right away and I'll call you as soon as I get it."

Doc called Mrs. Sidenstricker into his office and asked her to close the door. He handed the large manila envelope across his desk.

"Mrs. Sidenstricker, I want you to mail this to Dr. Wescott right away."

That night Shirley got up. Doc was not in the house. She slipped on her robe and slippers and went out onto the porch. Doc was sitting on the steps barefoot, smoking.

"What's the matter, Earl?" she asked.

"Oh, I guess I'm just feeling sorry for myself," he answered. Then he looked off into the distance. "It's getting so bad I'm having to sneak around to practice medicine."

"What do you mean, 'sneak around'?"

"I just don't trust those specialists they're sending up here. I think the good ones won't work for them. In fact, the best surgeon in Charleston brags that he is at the top of the Union's black list. He says it's a mark of professional competence."

"Where did you hear that?"

"Doctor Hamer told me."

"Let's go inside and talk about this, darling. It's too cold out here and it's too damp for you to be sitting there like that. You'll catch your death." As soon as she finished her warning, though, Shirley started coughing. She bent forward and coughed so hard, she seemed in danger of falling on her face. Doc jumped up and helped her into the house.

"What's the matter, honey? What's wrong?" Her face was pale. There were beads of perspiration on her upper lip. She held her sides in pain and continued to cough uncontrollably. Doc took a handkerchief from his pocket and handed it to her. She started coughing up blood. He helped her to bed and placed towels by her face. She coughed up clots and some bright red, frothy fluid.

Then she vomited. The vomitus looked like coffee grounds. She had evidently been swallowing blood in her sleep. Doc replaced the towels and brought a basin of cool water. He cleaned her face and placed a cool, wet cloth on her forehead. She looked into his eyes and clung fiercely to his forearm. He hoped she could not detect the panic he felt. He smiled, her face softened. She closed her eyes. He kissed her cheek.

My God, how could I have been feeling so sorry for myself and not considering Shirley? he thought.

Doc sat by the bed the rest of the night. In the morning he took her to the clinic for a chest X-ray. The spot in her lung had grown to the size of a small marble. He informed Mary he would not be back to the office for a while and took Shirley home. Mary sent Wampler and Sturgill to stay with Shirley on a rotating basis until Doc could find a locum tenens to take his place at the clinic.

"Well, I am sorry to hear that your wife is sick, but you will have to arrange to get a replacement yourself," the administrator said. "I'm really too busy to just drop everything at a moment's notice to take care of your personal problems. You seem to have trouble learning that some notice is necessary..." His voice trailed off as if he were tired of having this conversation with a recalcitrant child who just refused to learn.

"I have vacation coming," Doc protested. "I may only need a few days. My wife is very sick."

"Be that as it may, if you cannot wait, there's nothing I can do."

Doc called Dr. Jordan to ask if he could take a few days away from his residency to come to Wattsville.

Chapter Eighteen

Fatigue was a constant companion for a resident, but the past week had been especially tough and Jeff's inability to get back to sleep left him spent, even a little depressed. He should have taken a shower but he dozed and procrastinated and dragged out of bed too late to spare the time. He had promised to get to Wattsville by eight.

He left the hospital by the back steps carrying a small bag he had packed the day before. His schedule changes had been on such short notice he had worked two E.R. shifts in a row. He still wore the rumpled scrub suit he had slept in, he was unshaven, his hair was not combed.

The sun barely lightened the sky over the tops of the hills to the east as he crossed the loading dock. He threw his bag in the back seat, started the car and pulled out of the parking lot. When he stopped at a traffic light, he leaned his head on the steering wheel and closed his eyes for just a moment. The next thing he knew, the car lurched forward startling him awake. His foot had slipped off the clutch pedal. Luckily, no other vehicles were coming.

He drove on up MacCorkle and turned onto the road out of town. He maneuvered carefully, early morning frost made Elk River Road's curves and grades precarious. The steady drone of the motor and the warm air from under the dash tempted him to doze. Two or three times he swerved at the last minute to miss an on-coming automobile, or to get the wheels back on the black top after he had let them drift onto the shoulder. He turned the heater off.

The narrow ribbon of macadam wound through low, rounded hills splashed with autumn colors. The hardwoods had changed to spectacular reds and yellows muted by greens not yet affected by the sudden chill. Occasionally a purple leafed paw-paw or a fat evergreen punctuated the colorful mélange.

He stopped at Rose's diner in Clendenin to get a cup of coffee. The hot drink sitting on the dash fogged the windshield. He wiped the inside of the glass with the side of his fist and knocked the cup off its perch with his sleeve. He recovered it in mid-air spilling only a little, but the car drifted onto the shoulder and he whipped it back onto the road. A man in a new Chevy pickup swerved to avoid hitting him, blasted Jeff with his horn and stuck his arm out the window and shook his fist.

The surge of adrenaline energized Jeff. He rolled down the window and continued the journey more alert than before. The paper coffee cup warmed his hand, the liquid his insides. With the window down and his collar turned up, he drove on past hillside shacks, an occasional unpainted farmhouse, barns with signs exhorting him to *Chew Mail Pouch* or to *Get Right With God,* and a few roadside vegetable stands no longer open for business.

Finally, he pulled off the road by a stream running out of an embankment and splashed cold water on his face. He felt refreshed by the chill, but still tired. He sat behind the wheel and rested a few minutes before resuming his journey. When he drove on, he left the window rolled down. Though the sound of the engine was monotonous, the cold air helped him stay awake.

The rest of the trip passed quickly except he almost missed the turn-off. He backed up to maneuver the car onto the dirt. He carefully negotiated the winding unpaved road down the hill, through dense woodland into the little community huddled in the narrow valley. The sun had just started to peek over the ridge. He threaded his way slowly between the church buildings, past the appliance store and the mercantile company to the medical clinic. He parked in the far end of the lot next to several cars all ready sitting side by side.

He straightened his shirt, licked his slightly coated teeth and reached into the back seat for his valise. He rummaged through the hastily packed clothing and found his travel kit. It was an elegant brown color, a present from his folks when he graduated from medical school. He loved the feel of the cool leather.

He squeezed a small ribbon of paste onto the bristles of the brush he extracted from its holder and brushed his teeth. He sucked the excess off the bristles, opened the car door and spit the white foam onto the ground. After replacing the tooth brush in its vented, metal container, he got out and locked the automobile. He straightened his pants, wiped his hair, took a last look in the side mirror and walked to the front of the building, up the steps into the clinic.

It was five to eight, there were all ready several people in the waiting room, either looking at magazines or engaged in muted

conversation. The opaque glass window guarding the business office was closed. Jeff tapped on the pane. The occupants of the
waiting room fidgeted in their seats and eyed him curiously. He
tapped on the glass again.

A voice called from the interior of the building.

"Be right there. The doctor's not here yet!"

"Mrs. Sidenstricker," he leaned closer to the glass and called
softly. "This is Dr. Jordan." The waiting patients had turned silently
in his direction. He thought he noted an air of disappointment in
the room.

"Dr. Jordan!" The soft woman with her pleasant roundness slid
back the partition and looked into his face. "Oh, my goodness gra-
cious!" She shifted her weight away from the glass and straightened
her skirt. "Doctor Jordan!"

"Yes it's me. A bit the worse for being up all night, but if you can
over-look that..."

She did not move. He stood looking through the opening.
"Could I come in and talk to whomever is going to orient me?" He
tried to be as formal as possible to make up for his appearance.

"Oh, oh, excuse me, Dr. Jordan. Oh, yes. Let me unlock the
door." Before she could move, the door opened.

"Good morning, Dr. Jordan." Mary Arbogast held the door
against her side as if she were protecting the entrance, and reached
her hand out to him. "My name is Mary Arbogast. You are..." She
took in his rumpled appearance and smiled, "punctual."

He shook her hand and laughed.

"You are obviously a woman of precisely chosen words. And
very tactful, I might add." Jeff had a feeling he was going to like
this beautiful woman in her starched white uniform and folded
cap. He followed her into the work area where she introduced him
to the other employees.

"This is Mrs. Wampler, Dr. Jordan, and Miss Sturgill."

"Mrs. Sidenstricker and I know each other," he said. "It's nice to see you again, Mrs. Sidenstricker."

"It's nice to see you, too, Doctor Jordan. This is my helper in the business office, Thelma Powell."

"Nice to meet you," Jeff said.

"We did not expect you for another hour or so," Mary Arbogast said. "We might as well get started. Jen and Betty will do all the vitals and register them on the charts. I answer as many of the phone calls for refills and advice as I can, screen the rest for appointments, house calls or call backs, prepare injections, take the X-rays, supervise the pharmacy and help in any way possible. As you go about your work, let me know how I can help you." She offered the advice while the first patients were being readied for their examinations. "I will stick as close as I am able for the next few days. Ask me anything." She paused and looked at him as if she expected questions. She reached out a cup of coffee. "There's sugar on the shelf and cream in the refrigerator. I'm sure this is different from the hospital clinic." She paused again, and when he did not ask any questions she smiled, exposing her beautiful teeth.

"I am certain you'll do a good job, Doctor." With that, she handed a white coat to him, turned and crossed the room toward the pharmacy.

He pulled on the coat, buttoned the middle buttons and thrust his stethoscope into the side pocket. He took the clipboard from Mrs. Wampler, skimmed the chart and went into the examination room.

Later that evening, on his way to make a house call, Jeff stopped to check in at the hotel. He climbed the steps to the large front porch and twisted the butterfly handle on the old fashioned brass bell. A white haired lady who appeared to be in her early sixties answered the door.

"Hello, I'm Beatrice Parker. Everone calls me Bea. You must be the doctor." She had an apron tied at the waist and she was wiping her hands on it. "Come in."

"I'm Jeff Jordan."

"It's nice to meet you Dr. Jordan. If you'll follow me, I'll show you to your room." The floor boards creaked underfoot as they walked down the hall. Heavy carpet muffled the sound.

The modest-sized room had an iron bed and a pressed paper-board chifferobe in place of a closet. The mattress was higher off the floor than usual and rounded on top like a feather tick. It was covered with a pattern quilt with flowers and leaves on it, and a gray wool blanket was folded across the foot of the bed. A cherry wood chair with a needle point seat sat by the window. The cushion was beige with a large yellow rose in the center. A matching dresser, with an oval mirror framed in cherry polished to a high gloss stood against the wall across from the bed. A sink stood, out of place, in the corner, obviously added after the house was built.

A small closet under the stairs to the floor above contained a commode. There was barely space to sit and close the door without hitting one's knees and not quite room enough to stand erect. Wires and pipes were strung alongside the moldings and the light switch was an old fashioned twist-type, mounted by the door facing. Gas light fixtures were still in place and appeared functional - gas mantles intact inside their chimneys looking ready to be lit.

The room smelled of age and damp wall paper.

Bea gave him fresh towels, a bar of soap and one of those skeleton keys that looked as if it would fit half the locks in town.

"What do you like for breakfast, Dr. Jordan?" she asked.

"I'll eat almost anything, especially bacon and eggs over-easy, and I like my coffee strong," he answered.

She smiled and touched the black pedestal phone sitting on an ornate table by the bed. "Everone in town knows the phone number, but just in case, leave it on the wire recorder at the clinic when you finish work in the evening." She started to leave then added before going out the door, "Oh, by the way, it rings in my room, too, so I'll answer when you're not here."

He got back from his house call about eleven, and in the subdued light he could see how the place must have looked in its heyday. The copper roof with its elaborate seams, the widow's walk, the large eagle weather vane and the intricate fretwork under the eaves, the Corinthian columns on the porch and the wrought-iron fence around the front yard verified that the architect had exercised delicate artistic judgment in its construction. Moonlight masked the shabbiness that had corrupted its beauty leaving only the impression of elegant Victorian charm.

Jeff opened the front door gently and tip-toed down the hall. He was sound asleep under heavy quilts, when the phone rang.

"I been coughing for two months. I need to see the doctor." It was a man's voice.

"You come in to the clinic in the morning," Jeff said.

"I cain't afford to miss work," the voice protested. Jeff hung the receiver in its yoke.

Bea tapped at the door. "Time to get up."

"All ready?"

"Yes, all ready." She chuckled.

"I just went to bed."

No answer came from the hall. He slipped into his robe, wrapped the towel around his neck and walked barefoot to the kitchen.

Bea poured dark coffee into a white China mug. He stirred in cream from a pitcher and took the steaming brew to the bath room just down the hall.

The lavatory was about the size of his bedroom and had a large pedestal sink, a commode, a brass stand with large bath towels folded neatly over it and a claw foot bath tub with a circular brass rod holding the shower curtain. A big brass shower head, like the center of a huge sunflower, hung straight down from the ceiling. Jeff stood in the tub and showered with the plastic curtain sticking to his shoulders and buttocks. After shaving, he returned to the bedroom and dressed.

He entered the kitchen and sat at the table. The room smelled of fresh bread, coffee and bacon sizzling in a skillet on the big iron stove. Bea poured him another cup of steaming coffee and brought an oval China plate with fried potatoes, eggs over-easy and bacon, just as he had requested. She held the edge of the plate with a crocheted pot holder.

"Now be careful. That plate is hot," she said.

Lightly toasted homemade bread in a covered basket, salt mixed with pepper in a shallow dish, butter from a wooden mold the shape of a flower, a bottle of ketchup, jam and jelly in open jars, sat on the table.

Bea smiled as she wiped her hands on her apron. "I hope you don't mind eating in the kitchen. You're my only guest and the dining room seems so big and impersonal."

"I prefer it in here. It's a lot more homey, and I appreciate the company." When he finished eating, he stood up and patted his abdomen. "Mrs. Parker, uh, Bea, that was the best breakfast I've had since I can't remember when. I have a feeling you're going to spoil me for the hospital cafeteria."

"Well, that's my job," she said as she cleared away the dishes and wiped the slick table cloth with a clean rag.

Jeff went back to the room, brushed his teeth in the sink in the corner, picked up his coat and stethoscope and drove to the clinic.

Chapter Nineteen

"Yes, it would probably help your cough if you stopped smoking, Mrs. Sizemore," Dr. Westcott agreed. "And I certainly expect you to do that, but we really must remove that lesion and get a biopsy of it."

"When are you thinking about doing that, Doctor?" Shirley asked.

"I would like to admit you to the hospital today and do the surgery tomorrow morning." He turned toward Doc and frowned. "I am sure you are aware, Dr. Sizemore, the ideal thing would be to remove the whole lobe." He paused and turned back to look at Shirley. Doc and Shirley nodded in agreement and he stood up. "Thank you for your confidence. Because of the location, you have a good chance of a cure even if it turns out to be cancer, and the loss of a right middle lobe is easy to compensate for," he said. He shook Doc's hand and before he left the room he paused in front of Shirley and touched her shoulder.

"Follow me, Mrs. Sizemore," the nurse said. "Dr. Sizemore, they need some information from you at the front desk. I'll call you when we get your wife settled."

Doc kissed Shirley. She clung to him longer than was comfortable. That night, Doc stayed in her room on a trundle-bed. He held Shirley's hand. Neither slept very much.

"Dr. Wescott said he thinks he got it all," he reassured her when the report came back with the diagnosis of Bronchogenic Carcinoma.

"I'd feel a lot better if we had got to this only a few months earlier," Dr. Westcott confided to Doc. "There was one little area where it had just begun to break through its capsule. By removing the entire lobe instead of just doing a biopsy, though, we got a wide margin. And, the pleura was clear, so I have every reason to believe we got it all. That one area though..."

"The doctor says I'll be able to go home in a week," Shirley informed Doc two days after the surgery.

Alice Wilson, the Southards and Shirley's mother all came to visit from time to time. The twins came home from Arizona. "You'd think I was sick or something. Actually, I feel just fine except for a little stitch in my side when I cough," Shirley said.

The week passed quickly.

"Thank you, Dr. Wescott," Shirley said. "I will follow your orders and stop smoking."

"That's very important, Shirley. In my opinion, Dr. Graham's work proves without a doubt that smoking causes lung cancer." He looked at Doc and shook his finger. "If you haven't got that message yet, at least do not smoke in her presence."

"I won't," Doc promised.

"You know what the boys said yesterday morning as they were getting ready to leave for Charleston to catch the train?" Shirley asked Doc the following week.

Doc put down his paper. "What did they say, Honey?"

"They said, `Mom, since you quit smoking you smell as good as you look.'" She dropped her hands to her sides and stood in the middle of the kitchen, smiling. Doc stood up. He held his arms wide, she came to him. There were tears in her eyes.

"I love you, Shirley," he whispered. "And the boys are right."

* * *

Doc threw himself back into his work and tried to avoid thinking about that little area of possible breakthrough of the cancer. After a few weeks, and a good report on Shirley's first follow-up examination, it began to lose some of its immediacy.

Her first two follow-up X-rays were clear, but Dr. Wescott pointed out a small area on the third film he would like to biopsy. Sarah Southard took Shirley to the hospital where she was admitted overnight and brought her home to Falls View to recuperate for three days. The biopsy report was not good.

Six months later, tumor disseminated throughout her entire right upper lobe and a skull study revealed early brain infiltrations. She developed a severe cough and started losing weight. Doc called Jeff Jordan and asked if he could interrupt his residency program again for a few weeks to work at the clinic.

* * *

"I will not hear of your taking care of her alone, Earl," Sarah Southard said. "Now, you listen to me. Blanche and I will be there this afternoon so you just put your mind at ease."

Sarah had been visiting intermittently for two months and had been renewing her offer daily to stay with Shirley. She had proposed her solarium as a bright, sunny hospital room, but Shirley was afraid she would be separated from Doc. Now, in the face of Shirley's rapidly deteriorating condition, Sarah insisted on staying in Wattsville to help out.

Ramsay was out of town on business so his assistant brought Sarah and Blanche and a trunk-load of supplies. Blanche, who had worked for the Southards for more than seven years, was an attractive middle age widow not much younger than Sarah herself. She had lived in St. Albans until her husband was transferred to Montgomery by the Forestry Service. When he was killed by the limb of a falling tree, she went to work for Sarah who had previously been a social acquaintance. Though Blanche wore a uniform, the two women were more like friends than servant and mistress.

Alice Watson came over from Clendenin. She stayed with friends in town and came every morning. The three women took care of washing, cleaning, errands, baths, cooking, answering the phone and a thousand other things needing to be done.

Jeff relieved Doc at the clinic and moved back into his room at the hotel. He finished his first day at about nine forty-five and sat down to return phone calls. Several could wait until morning, so he left notes for the crew when they came in. He took care of two over the phone, but one required that he make a house call.

"I just live down past Duck on the left-hand side, Doc. I'll have my boy stand out along the road so's you cain't miss it."

"I know where Duck is," Jeff said.

"Well then, you cain't miss it. Just keep coming down the road like as if you was going to Dogtown, but not that far."

"Just this side of Dogtown then?"

"Dogtown's where our niggers live, so don't go that far. You cain't miss it. If you git to Dogtown, you come too far; they's only niggers living down there in Dogtown." He locked the clinic and drove down toward Duck.

When he returned to the hotel, Bea had retired, his bags were unpacked and his clothes put away.

"You know Dr. Sizemore's wife is not going to live very long, don't you?" Mary asked Jeff after he had been there several days.

"I know she is pretty sick, and he didn't seem to want to talk about it."

"It all happened so suddenly, we are in shock around here. It's just that those of us who have lived around her and Doc..." She touched her cheek to blot a tear, then spread her hands in resignation. She turned and walked away.

Jeff's days and nights were busy taking care of patients with heart disease and respiratory pathology. He began to feel comfortable working with Mary Arbogast, but when he stopped by the house Dr. Sizemore was either busy attending to Shirley or dozing in a chair.

Doc spent every minute by Shirley's bedside or on the front porch with her bundled against the chill watching the sun go down and the stars come out. He talked to her quietly with his arm around her and her head on his chest.

The boys came home and tried to be there without being in the way. They attempted to talk to Doc but he was emotionally drained, and when he was not at Shirley's side he was worn out.

Alice, Sarah and Blanche did most of the cooking and cleaning. Doc never seemed to sleep except in momentary spurts. He was either attending to Shirley or reading to her or watching her sleep. Alice and Sarah worried almost as much about him as they did Shirley. He grew haggard and lost weight. He fell asleep every time he stopped and awakened with a start every few minutes.

He developed a distant look in his eyes and half the time he appeared to be confused.

Doc never allowed Shirley to suffer pain. He gave her enemas so her abdomen was not distended, used frequent catheterization until it became absolutely necessary to leave a Foley in her bladder permanently. He fed her sips and bites and administered I.V.s to keep her energy level as high as possible. He made sure she had morphine any time she needed it. He moved her to the porch when she felt like it and even took her for rides in the car.

Alice and Sarah learned to give her injections. They bathed her, wiped her feverish brow, propped her up in bed and cleaned her when she soiled the sheets.

Ramsay came to Wattsville and took a room in the hotel. The twins spent some of their evenings at dinner there with him. Bea opened the dining room and when Jeff joined the group, it was as pleasant as one could expect under the circumstances.

Shirley wasted away and went into a coma. Sarah sensed that Doc needed to be alone and spent the night with Ramsay at the hotel. Alice stayed the night with friends.

Shirley died quietly at about one a.m. She had not moved or opened her eyes for the previous three days. For more than forty-eight hours, her breathing had accelerated and slowed with intermittent apnea. Doc was holding her hand and dozing in a chair by the bed. He had slumped forward with his head on the side of the bed when something awakened him. He looked up and she had turned her head slightly and opened her eyes. She was staring at him and when he smiled, her emaciated face seemed to relax. She squeezed his hand. Doc leaned forward and kissed her on the lips. There was no response, her mouth was cold, her breathing had ceased.

Sarah was having trouble sleeping. She climbed out of bed and stood at the window looking at the moon. Ramsay got up and put his arm around her. She started to cry. "Oh, Ramsay! I can feel it. She's gone." He held her until her sobbing subsided.

Doc cried until the sun came up. The twins and the Southards took him into the kitchen while the mortician came over from Gauley Bridge and removed Shirley's body. Bernard came when he heard the news.

They buried Shirley in Kaymoor, on a hill overlooking the New River Gorge in a plot next to her father, under a huge oak tree.

Doc and the twins stood on the hillside in the rain. When they lowered her body into the muddy pit, the sun came out through the downpour and thunder echoed through the gorge. Doc had planned to say a few words at the grave-site, but every time he tried to talk he could not force the words over the sobs. He looked at the twins standing bare headed in the rain. Bernard, standing alongside them, looked up. At just that moment, Doc realized his sons were like strangers.

God, how I've neglected them, he thought.

Ramsay held the umbrella in one hand and put his arm around Doc's shoulders. He read from the crumpled paper in Doc's hand. Though some of the words were smudged by the tears and the weather, and Doc's hand trembled perceptibly.

When he finished, Ramsay took the paper from Doc's hand, folded it and placed it in Doc's overcoat pocket. Sarah and Bernard stood beside the twins who cried quietly and rubbed their eyes. Shirley's mother sat in a chair beside Doc and Ramsay, clinging to a large black umbrella, looking confused. Alice touched her cheek with a handkerchief. Ramsay guided Doc back to the waiting limousine.

After the funeral, the Southards had supper in their big dining room for Shirley's mother, the help from the clinic and their husbands, the Arbogasts, Alice, coach Nellis and Miss Thornton, the English teacher, and Shirley's friends from the quilting club and their husbands. The Humphreys came over from Rainelle.

Jeff offered to work another week so Doc and the boys could spend some time together, but after three days of moping around at the Southards, Doc could not stand it any longer.

"No Ramsay, thank you for the invitation, but the boys and I had better be getting back home. Dr. Jordan has stayed over longer than he should have as it is. I know he has been calling and getting special permission from his chief to stay as long as he has all ready."

Doc hardly responded when the twins decided to remain behind with the Southards for a few more days. He drove through the spring countryside to Wattsville automatically, and alone.

Jeff was packed and ready to leave when Doc drove into the parking lot. "Thank you for staying over, Dr. Jordan. Mary tells me you did a good job."

"Thank you, Dr. Sizemore, I'm sorry about Mrs. Sizemore. It must be very difficult for you."

Doc looked at his hands for the longest time before he made eye contact with the younger man. Tears moistened his eyes and a single streak made its way down one cheek.

"Thank you," he whispered. He wiped the tear away with his fingers. Jeff tried to say something more but couldn't. He turned, walked down the hall to the front of the building and stopped. He stood at the door for a long time. He turned and looked at Doc who was still standing in the hallway, then he left.

Chapter Twenty

At the next Grievance Committee meeting, Doc sat in the back of the room while the union representative talked to several people who apparently were registering fresh complaints. When he finished and the last person had returned to his seat, the representative approached the lectern and directed his attention to Doc.

"Now that you are renumerated with a big salary from the union whether you cure anybody or not, and now that you are gittin' regular time off, we suspect that you would give better service to your customers. It is my sa-worn duty to rectify the bad medicine what's been practiced around here by the high and mighty."

"What is it you want me to answer for?" Doc asked.

"There has been a lot of complaints about you not makin' house calls when somebody cain't get a ride over to the clinic. There has been complaints about the pills falling apart and about perscriptions that don't seem to get to a body 'til after she's over what's ailing her. There's complaints about you only takin' two minutes with a person before you shove a box of worthless pills in her hand and scootin' her outa' the office. We are thinkin' of havin' the union lettin' you go and hirin' a real doctor what can do the right thing by us around here. What do you think of that?"

Doc slumped in his chair. He could not believe his ears. He could not think of an intelligent thing to say. He looked around the auditorium at the expectant faces. Countenances, where he had once read genuine affection or at least respect, he saw antipathy.

"Well, as some of you in this room know I have been through a difficult time recently and maybe I have let down a bit. If you will just bear with me a little while, I will see if I can do better." He was ashamed of himself for using his personal life to justify himself to this pack of hounds, but for the moment it was all he could think of.

Other than school and the military, his life had been formed in these mountains. He never seriously considered moving away from Wattsville. He needed time to sort things out and to decide what to do.

After the next meeting in Cedar Grove he collared Dr. Hamer in the parking lot.

"I've been here all my life, too, Earl. I don't know any place else. I have tried to change this system, but it's become obvious to me that I can't. I'm not sure about you, Earl, but I don't look good on a cross. I decided some time ago that I can't save these people from themselves. I just try to preserve as much of my integrity as I can under the circumstances presented to me"

On his way home Doc had to admit Dr. Hamer was right. He would just have to make the best of a bad deal. *When everyone wants someone else to take responsibility for their lives, only someone such as Cox or Loomis would be willing to take on the task,* he thought.

He continued to deliver babies, set broken bones and attend to the ravages of coal mining on the respiratory and cardiac systems of the locals. And, he made a heightened effort to accommodate his customers entreaties. He seemed to be a man who had been through a tough period and rebounded. The white boxes aged and washed away and were replaced only sporadically.

No need to rub the doctor's nose in it any more now that we've got him in his place, he supposed, as he stopped on the bridge and looked at the creek bank.

"Well, I declare if it ain't fine to see the doctor being hisself agin," one lady volunteered.

"Doc ain't half sa hard to git along with these days. `Spose he's got hisself a widder lady someplace we don't know about?" a gritty old barfly snickered and followed the remark with a sly wink. "Might be that rich lady what come so regular before his woman died. You `spose?"

Chapter Twenty One

Life plodded on in Wattsville. The promises the candidate made on his swing through the state had not seemed to translate into a better life for the locals. The general store and the service station were still open but the drug store building was empty and boarded up. Mr. Harper had purchased the store from the company. He initially tried to run his business on trust, but times had changed; so, for the past several months he was not as congenial as he once was, not really stand-offish, more taciturn like and it had become cash only, no credit, no checks and few exceptions.

In order to barely eke out a living at the service station, Emory Legg was in that garage early in the morning and still there late into the night. "He looks tired all the time and his service station ain't what it used to be," more than one customer opined. He was thinking of retiring and he would have, but a service station supported on sales of thirty-nine cents or a gallon and a half or "Jest gimme the amount I got in my hand will cover" wasn't worth much. Doc stopped in for gas and dispensed medical advice in the process, but he had his new Buick serviced in Clendenin.

"I miss that old Plymouth, Doc. They don't make'm like that'en no more," Legg repeated each time Doc drove up in his fancy automobile. The only life Doc had left was his medical practice, an evening once a month when he went to the Medical Hygiene meetings and talked to Dr. Hamer, or a rare weekend now and again when he visited the Southards.

God, how many years has it been since I even did that? he wondered. *I missed my chance to be a husband or a father. Hell, I'm not even a good doctor anymore.*

* * *

He called the administrator as soon as he got the letter from his son.

"I would like to take a full two weeks," he said.

"Well, Dr. Sizemore. Will wonders never cease?" Tyree's voice fairly dripped with sarcasm. "Giving me proper notice at last. This must be something important."

Doc had not taken any time off since Shirley's death when Cox had lectured him about the importance of the *locum tenens'* time.

"My son is getting married out in Arizona," Doc said. *Not something trivial like my wife's dying,* he thought. When memories of Shirley intruded into his thoughts, he tried switching his mind to something else. He couldn't bear to think of her in that muddy pit on that hillside over in Kaymoor. He knew he should have stood up for her. He should have taken her to Dr. Wescott right away, but *I was too busy worrying about myself; feeling sorry for myself.*

"Well, in that case, I am sure it can be arranged."

The wedding would be his first visit with the boys since they came east almost two years previously.

"I'll only be gone two weeks. You keep an eye on the *locum tenens* they send," Doc informed Mary the next day. Then, as an afterthought he said, "Keep an eye on that new handy-man Cox hired, too. There's something funny about him or I miss my guess."

"I'll take care of things, Dr. Sizemore," Mary reassured him.

When the young doctor arrived, she had him wait in the hallway. "Dr. Sizemore!" She leaned in the office doorway and whispered. "The doctor's here!" As Doc looked up from his desk, she turned and indicated the young man standing in the hall.

"Why, Bernard!" Doc exclaimed. "Why it's Bernard Southard or my tired old eyes are deceiving me. I didn't expect *you*." He got up from his chair behind the desk and they shook hands. "Well, you're a sight for sore eyes, son! But why are you here? I expected to see you at the wedding."

"I couldn't get the time off, but my parents will be there. The only reason I'm able to cover for you while you go is this counts as two weeks of my out-patient clinic rotation."

"I didn't know that," Doc said.

"When we work nights while you go to your meetings, that's on our own time. But the hospital has a deal with the union allowing us up to two weeks a year to work as *locum tenens* and count it as part of our internal medicine residency. I traded with another resident so I could work for you."

"Well, son, I'll feel a lot better knowing while I'm gone you are at the helm, so to speak." He put his arm around Bernard and walked down the hall. "Let me see, there's a pediatric clinic Wednesday, the radiologist comes this Tuesday, I think. Mary knows all that stuff, and I left the telephone number where I'll be in Arizona."

"Thanks, Dr. Sizemore. I'll take good care of things for you."

"I know you will, son, I know you will. I'll have a better time knowing you are watching the store."

"My parents have my wedding gift to deliver. Be sure to give the twins my best."

Doc smiled and nodded and opened the door. The cold air rushed in and he thought of something else and closed it. Suddenly he lost what it was he had thought of.

"By the way, Mary Arbogast can answer most everything you need to know. You get a problem, just ask her." With that, he left the building and hurried across the parking lot to his car.

Doc felt good driving along the narrow ribbon of macadam glistening black in the morning dew. A stillness hung in the air and his big comfortable Buick whizzed past the stark winter landscape. Vivaldi's Concerto in B Minor for Four Violins sprung busily from the radio coaxing him to push the speed limit. Roadside vegetable stands squatted back from the highway, with their muddy stopping places in front and "closed for the season" signs hanging from their lean-to porches. "*Chew Mailpouch*" advisories and "*Are you ready for the Resurrection*" admonitions on old barn walls flashed by intermittently.

He turned west on Route 60 along the Kanawha River to Charleston. He parked his car on the esplanade beside the C&O Railroad Depot. The train arrived less than an hour after the porter took his bags.

There was a stop-over for three hours in Cincinnati and an overnight wait in St. Louis. It took three days to get to Flagstaff and his sons were standing on the platform when the big Santa Fe diesel pulled into the station. They shook hands.

Chapter Twenty Two

Mary Arbogast and Bernard chatted while the first patients were being readied for their examinations and she explained the system Cox had designed.

"The lab is the nerve center of the office."

Four boards, two by two by twelve inches each, were fixed parallel on the wall just inside the laboratory door. Slots were cut in the boards at an angle and squares of cardboard with instructions or medications hand-printed on them were kept in receptacles nearby. The medication squares had different doses on each leg of the border and either side of the card. The cards were color coded for each back office employee so the doctor knew where every one of his staff was at all times. The flow of patients in the office was rapid and efficient with the doctor and the help communicating by the positions, colors and instructions on the cards.

"After patients are registered at the front desk, Mrs. Wampler or Jenny Sturgill bring them into examination rooms," Mary said.

"Patients ready to be seen, are indicated by the placement of the cards. When you go to a particular patient, move this card to this slot in the board, so we can tell which room you're in." She demonstrated as she spoke. "When you finish your examination, return to the board, change the card for an instruction or medication card, move your card to the slot for the next patient, then go to that room. Jen or Mrs. Wampler will then take the instruction card or medication card, follow your instructions and send the patient on his way. It usually doesn't take very long. Does that seem clear to you?"

"I think I'll get it sometime before I leave," Bernard answered.

"Jen and Mrs. Wampler will do all the vitals and register them on the charts. I answer most of the phone calls for refills and telephone advice, screen the rest for appointments or call backs, take the X-rays, give most of the injections, supervise the pharmacy and try to make sure you only make really necessary house calls. I will stick as close as I am able for the next few days. Ask me anything. I'm sure this is different from the hospital clinic, but you'll be O.K." She paused, when he did not ask any questions she handed him a white coat. "There's sugar on the shelf, cream in the refrigerator, and coffee in the pot on the hot plate." She pointed to the appliance, then looked him straight in the eye. "Time to see what your made of, Dr. Southard." With that, she turned and crossed the room to the pharmacy.

Mrs. Wampler stood between Bernard and the examination room with a clipboard in her hand. He pulled the white coat over his hospital scrub suit, worked the buttons through the heavily starched button holes and thrust his stethoscope into the side pocket. He took the clipboard, skimmed the chart back to front and went into the little room. There was a chest X-ray on the lighted view box on the wall. He ignored it for the moment. The patient sat, fully dressed, on the end of the table. Bernard looked at the X-ray. It showed an obvious lower lobe pneumonia.

"Wait just a moment," he said to the middle-aged lady and went back into the lab. A bottle of Elixir of Turpin Hydrate sat by the board designated "Doctor." He held up the clipboard to get Miss Sturgill's attention.

"Just wait in there," she instructed the patient she was escorting down the hall, and she came over to where Bernard was standing. "Yes, Dr. Southard. You wanted something?"

"This patient is not even undressed to be examined and her chest X-ray shows pneumonia. I can't examine her if she is not undressed."

"Well, she was undressed but her chest X-ray shows lower lobe pneumonia and Dr. Sizemore always says lower lobe pneumonia requires long acting Bicillin and an expectorant. Mrs. Wampler gave her the Bicillin and the expectorant is right there beside your board." Bernard turned to face Mrs. Wampler, who had walked out of the pharmacy with a chart under her arm.

"Do you mean you have all ready given her a penicillin injection and had her get dressed?"

"Well, yes. Is there anything wrong with that?"

"I might not want her to have a shot. I might have chosen a prescription." Of course he knew the Bicillin injection was the right thing to do, but he felt he should have been the one to say so.

"Prescriptions have to be filled at the drug store in Charleston and are not covered by the Union Welfare Fund, so if you give her a prescription, she will not get it filled. If she sends it to the Union Pharmacy, it will take a week or two to come back. We could give her a few pills here, but she probably won't take them. The Dr. always gives long-acting Bicillin. That way he knows the medicine is in place and working for the full ten days."

"Well, I guess that's OK." Bernard couldn't think of any other objection. He sighed and handed the chart to her. "But in the future, at least let me examine the patient first, if you don't mind." With that, he turned and went into the examination room to take care of the next patient.

The rest of the afternoon Wampler and Sturgill seemed unwilling to take any initiative what-so-ever. They questioned him about every request as if they were afraid they might make a mistake.

Wampler would come into the room and wait until he was through with what he was doing before soliciting his advice, always in the most naive manner.

"You just go on and finish, Dr. Don't let me interrupt you," she might say, and Bernard would have to coax to get the question asked so she would not have to wait while he finished. "I wouldn't want to get this wrong, Dr. Is this just exactly the way you told me to do it?"

At six p.m., the waiting room was still half-full with patients as the help filed out of the building.

"The administrator doesn't like to pay us overtime," Miss Arbogast explained. "We will see you in the morning, Dr."

Bernard thought he detected a smirk play faintly cross her beautiful mouth. He finished up at about nine forty-five and sat down to return the phone calls from the wire recorder hooked to the telephone. Several could wait until morning, so he left notes for the crew when they came in. He took care of two over the phone, but two required that he make house calls.

He stopped, to check in at the hotel on his way out of town and re-introduced himself to Bea. She had an apron tied at the waist and she was wiping her hands on it.

"Come in. I'm Bea," she said. Then she put her hand to her mouth. "Bernard! Bless my soul. It's little Bernard."

"I was afraid you wouldn't remember me," he said.

"Aw, pshaw! How could I ever forget you? And look at you now. All grown up." She paused. "So handsome, and a doctor, too. I can't believe it. I'm so proud!"

"Thank you, Bea. My folks made me promise to give you their regards," he said. "I have some house calls to make so I better put this stuff in the room and be on my way. We'll have plenty of time to talk later."

"I have your room prepared, Dr. Southard. Follow me," she turned with a flourish. She led him down a narrow hallway to a door near the back of the house. The floorboards creaked underfoot. Heavy carpet muffled the sound.

"It's just as I remembered," he said when he entered the room. He left his luggage on the floor and drove down toward Duck. When he returned, Bea had retired; his bags were unpacked and his clothes put away.

The next morning, Bea began the conversation by telling him about changes in the town and some of the inner workings of the clinic. It was not gossip. It was informative and, to a certain extent, it was gentle advice. He got the distinct impression, however, someone from the clinic had spoken to her about his obstructiveness. On his way out the door, he thanked her for the concern, but he was a little upset with the behind his back communication.

He struggled through the morning and continued seeing patients through dinner - alone. The first patient after the nurses returned in the afternoon was a man who needed papers signed before he could go to work as a coal loader in the mine. Bernard asked him to get undressed.

"I'm ok, Doc," he protested. "I don't need no examination. I just need you to fill out these papers. They won't let me go to work 'til the papers are filled out."

"If you want the papers filled out," Bernard said. "I will have to examine you." The patient tentatively sat on the end of the table. Bernard asked him again to undress. He unbuttoned the top button of his shirt. "You will have to take the shirt off," Bernard directed. Reluctantly, he took his shirt off and sat back down with his long underwear still fully buttoned. Bernard asked him to unbutton the underwear and disrobe to the waist. He slowly followed the directions and sat back down on the table, suspenders and long underwear hanging down over the top of his trousers, heavy belt still pulled tight around his waist. Bernard took his blood pressure, listened to his heart and lungs, checked his eyes, ears, nose and throat.

"You don't have to do all that."

Bernard ignored the complaint and asked him to stand so he could check his back. He stomped to the middle of the room and stood with his back toward the young doctor, mumbling. When Bernard asked him to face around and lower his trousers, he refused.

"You ain't sticking your finger in me. You ain't goin'a get me to let some stranger I never seen before stick your finger up me."

"Well, Mr. Spradling, I am not going to complete those papers until I check to see if you have a hernia." Bernard got up from the stool and started for the door.

"OK, but you better make it quick." He loosened the thick belt and opened his fly half way keeping both hands on the top of his trousers. Bernard reached into his clothing as well as he could under the circumstances and put his finger into the left inguinal ring.

"Turn your head to the right and cough."

"What for?"

"So I can check to see if you have a hernia." Spradling cleared his throat and Bernard accepted it, then moved his finger to the right inguinal ring and detected a small bulge.

"Turn your head to the left and cough." Spradling cleared his throat again. "I said for you to cough. Don't clear your throat. Cough." He turned his head to the right directly into Bernard's face and coughed weakly and the bulge became more obvious. Bernard splashed water on his face, picked up the papers and headed for the door. "That's all. You can get dressed and go to the front desk."

"Is somethin' wrong? I passed, didn't I?"

"I doubt it. You have a hernia."

"Is that anything like a rupture?"

"Yes, some people call it that."

"That don't matter. People go to work with 'em all the time."

"I can't believe they would hire you to load coal when they know you all ready have a hernia."

"Well, there's no need to put that down."

"I'm sorry. I know this must be disappointing to you, but I can't ignore something like that."

"I have to turn this in or they won't hire me."

Bernard shrugged his shoulders, left the room and handed the papers to Sturgill.

Later, when he walked out into the hall, he motioned to Mary Arbogast. He could not help thinking how pretty she was as she came toward him. She was starched and efficient, but even the uniform could not hide her allure. When she finished answering his question regarding the formulary, she fixed him with her luminous gray eyes and smiled. She had no lipstick on but her full lips were sensual enough without coloring. He studied her face, examined her mouth, and wondered what it would be like to kiss her.

The rest of the day it poured rain. The water came in sheets, out of the east. As Bernard drove back to the hotel, lightning flashed in huge crackling bursts branching and dancing along the ridges. Thunder roared down the hollows shaking rooftops and rattling windows. His windshield wipers raced back and forth frantically in a losing battle. He parked and ran for the house. He was soaked before he got to the porch. He dripped down the hall and into his room.

Bea knocked and called through the door. "I have a message for you." Bernard opened the door slightly, took the paper with directions to meet a man whose baby was sick. He toweled off as best he could, changed into dry clothing more suitable for inclement conditions and went into the kitchen. Bea handed him a steaming cup of coffee.

"It's a little place up on the ridge," she said.

He finished the coffee, threw his raincoat over his head and ran for the car. His clothes were soaked before he got inside and the heater fogged the windows as he drove out of town.

The heavy forest covering the road up the hill dampened the storm but when he turned onto the highway along the ridge, the wind and rain buffeted the automobile unmercifully. For about two or three miles he fought the narrow, curving blacktop looking for a turnoff before a boy standing by the roadside flagged him down.

"Hi, Doc. You'll have to turn up the hill to get to the house," he yelled over the wind. He climbed in the passenger side and plopped onto the seat. Liquid ran off his hair down around his nose and ears into the top of his jacket. Water dripped out of his sleeve down the front of the car seat when he extended his arm to point the way and oozed out of the tops of his shoes onto the floorboards.

The boy, who could not have been over fifteen, said he had walked two miles to a phone and waited along the road so Bernard would not miss the turnoff. His speech was muffled and indistinct. Bernard understood about half of it.

"Her momma's right certain she's perty sick," he explained. "And I knowed you'd never find yer way les' I showed you. She's afear'd she'll die if we waited `til morning."

The car wandered and skidded for almost a mile up the muddy groove in the hillside, constantly in danger of getting stuck or sliding over an embankment. The road ended abruptly between two houses so close together it barely fit between them.

Bernard left the car in the road and staggered behind the boy to the lower of the two houses. It was a "Jenny Lynn" shanty constructed of wide boards arranged linearly up and down and weather proofed with narrow strips nailed over the cracks. There was no insulation or framing. The structure swayed precariously against the wind and the floor groaned when they stepped inside.

The room was lit by two kerosene lamps sitting on shelves about eye-level.

A bed occupied one end of the room, a wood-stove and a green-painted ice box the other. On the wall behind the bed, a picture of a white wolf on a blue-tinted ridge with a pastel pink sky hung alongside a three quarter view of Jesus' face, well-groomed with curly hair. A mangy black and tan puppy squeezed its head under the ice box to drink from a bowl.

A girl sat on the unmade bed with a bundle of dirty blankets on her lap. She could not have been more than thirteen. In spite of her stringy blond hair and accompanying poor hygiene, she was pretty. The pinched gray face of a baby, almost smothered in the coverings, was quiet, sleeping soundly, sonorous respirations monotonously interspersed the howling wind and rattling windows. Two children and a teen-ager fidgeted at the bedside.

The puppy finished drinking, extricated his head from under the ice box and turned over the bowl. The boy threw a shoe. The dog yelped and ran to the farthest corner of the room with his tail tucked up under his almost hairless belly.

"She just went to sleep, Doc," the young mother whined, looking up at Bernard as he leaned over the infant. "Wouldn't you know? She's been a crying all day long `til just before you got here."

"Unwrap her and let me take a look." Bernard pulled back the covers just a little to start the process. The young father moved one of the kerosene lamps closer to illuminate the baby and the light flickered across his own face. His lip was split upward on the midline and a thick scar pulled the tip of his nose downward flaring his nostrils. He had a harelip and cleft palate which explained his muffled pronunciation.

When the dirty blankets and diaper were removed, the baby began to scream and writhe about, and immediately stuck her fist in her mouth.

"How long since you changed her diaper?" Bernard asked.

"I changed it first thing this morning," the girl answered.

"It's still dry. She must not have voided once all day. What are you feeding her?"

"She's on the tit, Doc, but I cain't get her to take it too good. She don't seem to want to eat none. I got plenty'a milk. She just won't suck my tit." She held her arms apart so he could see two big wet spots on the front of her dress.

"Has she vomited or had diarrhea?"

"No, she ain't puked none a'tall," the father answered.

"Has she had any diarrhea?" Bernard repeated. The couple looked quizzically at each other. "You know number two." They stared at him. "Pooped," he explained.

"No, Doc. She ain't shit none since she's been borned," the mother said. "Except some black stuff right after she come out."

"How old is she?"

"Three days, Doc."

"Well, it looks to me as if she's not getting enough to eat," Bernard said as he finished his examination. "She's hungry and she's getting dehydrated."

They stared at Bernard, then at each other. "Dried up," he explained. "Let me watch you feed her so I'll see if you are doing it right."

The girl looked at her husband. He nodded approval. She bared her swollen breast. Its brownish purple nipple glistened with milk. She started shaking the baby. Bernard instructed her to stop. She put her breast in the little mouth and started shaking again. Bernard put one hand on the baby and the other on the mother's shoulder to hold her still. When she settled down, the baby grabbed the nipple expertly and sucked it into her mouth. Every time the girl started the rocking or jiggling, Bernard stopped her. The baby sucked so fast, she became choked and started coughing. The mother pulled her violently away from her breast and started shaking her. Bernard stopped her again explaining she was just eating a little too fast.

"The coughing will take care of the aspirate, you know - what she gets down the wrong way. No need to worry, she will get better at it and so will you. When she gets caught up, she will stop eating so fast and your milk will regulate to fit her needs. Just do not shake her. When she is finished eating, put her on your shoulder and pat her back gently until she burps." He took the baby and demonstrated.

He asked a few more questions and satisfied himself the baby was not too starved to treat at home. As he turned to leave, the taller of the children started dancing up and down.

"Hi Doc, hi Doctor. You remember me? Remember me?" Bernard studied his face. He could not summon a recollection in the dim, flickering light. The boy did not wait for an answer.

"I'm Billy. I'm Billy Means." For a minute, Bernard still could not remember. Then it came to him.

"Billy, I'll be doggone. Billy, it is you." It had been almost a year since Billy had gone home from the hospital where Bernard had served his internship.

Billy, the last time I saw you, you still had a cast on your arm. I almost didn't recognize you, Billy." The younger kids looked admiringly at Billy. For the moment he was a celebrity. He smiled and shifted from foot to foot. "You sure have grown. I never would have recognized you."

"I'm in junior high school now, Doc."

"Well, congratulations, Billy." Bernard put his hand on the boy's shoulder. He was glad to see the former patient. Billy was in the hospital so long, everyone who worked in pediatrics or surgery got to know him. Everyone who was involved in his care was affected by his unexpected recovery. "You look like you never were in an accident, Billy."

"You took good care "a" me, Doc." He pointed toward the house across the road. "I live in the house up there. These here are my brother and sister, Doc." He pointed to the other two children. "He's my sister's husband." He pointed to the harelip boy. "She's my niece. I'm a uncle, Doc." He touched the baby's head with his open palm.

"Billy, I am so glad to see you, and you're so well. You sure are going to be tall...and an uncle."

He watched the boy change his weight from foot to foot and thought of the broken little body brought into the E.R. not so long ago. It was hard to connect the two. Bernard put his hand on Billy's shoulder and smiled. "I sure am going to tell all the people at the hospital about seeing you, Billy. The doctors and the nurses are going to be happy to hear how well you're doing and being an uncle and all." Billy beamed with pride.

After a pause, Bernard turned. "Didn't you ask your mother about breast feeding?" The girl looked down at her baby.

"Poppy won't let Momma talk to her," Billy volunteered. Bernard looked at the young couple. They looked at the floor. "He'd skin us alive if he knowed we'uz here. He's passed out so we come over to see the baby."

"Sorry," Bernard said. "Well, Billy, you take care of yourself." The husband followed Bernard to the car. The rain had let up.

"Just back her up into the hog pen when I open the gate and you can get her turned around," he instructed.

The hog pen was a fence built around the supports of the house above the road, Billy's house. The front of the house was against the hill and the back was just high enough for one to back a small truck under it. The dirt had been removed to serve as a combination pig pen and automobile turn around. After a few pulls forward and backups, amid squeals from the inhabitants of the pen, and with some advice impossible to understand, Bernard got the car headed back down the road. The odor of hog-churned mud and slop filtered into the auto.

As he drove back down the road, the vision of Billy's face made Bernard melancholy. He had wondered many times how the boy was doing. It was on the very road Bernard was negotiating, the accident had evidently taken place. Billy had ridden his wagon down the hill into the path of an on-coming car.

Bernard drove to the hotel, parked the car and went around to the kitchen. Bea was still up.

"My shoes are caked with mud. I figured I'd better come in this way. I'll leave them on the steps and clean them in the morning. They can't get any wetter."

"Did you have any trouble finding the place?" Bea asked.

"No, your directions were good and the boy waited for me at the turnoff. The baby wasn't sick, though. The mother just didn't know how to feed it. She didn't look to be over thirteen."

"I think she's almost fourteen if she's the one I'm thinkin' of."

"It seems there's some bad blood between the two families," Bernard said. "And their living not ten yards apart. Strange."

"Did you get to meet old man Means?"

"No, Billy said he was passed out."

"From what I hear he's been makin' that little girl sleep with him. Probably angry because she's moved out. Worthless old coot."

"I think I remember hearing about him when Billy was in the hospital. Kept threatening the man who hit Billy. Wasn't his fault and he felt bad enough without being hounded by some shyster lawyer."

"I feel sorry for that boy she's with, bless his heart, hare-lip and all. He's not very smart, but all-in-all he's not a bad sort."

Bernard finished his coffee, took a hot shower, climbed into bed and passed out. It seemed only an instant later he heard a knock on the door. Bea announced it was morning.

"It can't be," he protested.

"I'm afraid it is," she answered. He dressed to go into the kitchen. His shoes sat in the hall, clean, polished and dry.

"Thanks, Bea, but you needn't have done that," he said as he entered the warm kitchen. She smiled and continued with her work. Breakfast was eggs, ham, biscuits and red eye gravy. "That was especially good, Bea," he said, as he left. "I'll see you tonight."

The temperature had dropped precipitously. The wet ground of the parking lot had frozen during the night, and crunched under his feet. He scraped the center of the windshield; but by the time he got to the clinic, he was driving with his head out the window. The waiting room was not as full as usual.

He started his day having a disagreement with a woman over a shot of penicillin for a cold. She insisted that's what penicillin was for; that's the only thing that ever worked; and that's what Doc always gave her. She stomped out of the office leaving the Elixir of Terpin Hydrate he prescribed behind on the counter. Mary Arbogast closed the door she left open and as she walked back past Bernard, she let a hint of a smile play across her face.

I've seen that look before, he thought.

Dinner was interrupted by a house call, to a man supposedly having a heart attack. When Bernard got to the house, a woman standing in the road flagged him down and pointed toward the back of the building. He walked around the side of the house and found a man sitting on his back porch, alone. He looked healthy. He wore a mackinaw coat with the collar up around his ears.

"Who called?" Bernard asked as he walked across the porch.

"My daughter don't come to see me no more," the man complained. He was on the verge of tears. He dabbed delicately at his eyes with a large rag, then blew his nose into it violently. "She don't even care. Nobody cares. I'm just a old man. Nobody gives a shit about a old man a'tall. I done as much as I could. Kids now'a days got no respect." He started to say something more but Bernard held up his hand.

"Where is the man having a heart attack?"

"I'm having a heart attack." He bent forward, grasped the fabric of his coat and started to cry. "They don't give a shit about a old man. They don't give a shit."

"How long have you been having this heart attack?" Bernard asked.

"Seven years. It's been seven years. I been sitting on this porch waiting and having heart attacks and she don't give a shit."

"If this has been going on for seven years, why did you choose today to call the doctor?"

"I cain't stand it no more. Somebody's got to do something." He straightened up, indignant, no longer in pain. "You're a doctor, ain't you? Why don't you do something?"

Bernard felt the man's warm, dry skin, recorded his nice pink color, normal blood pressure and regular, perfectly normal heart sounds. He checked for signs of edema or rales and found none. "I tell you what," Bernard said. "You call the clinic for an appointment and come in. We will talk about this." He returned his stethoscope and sphygmomanometer to the medical bag and started across the porch.

"I don't want no appointment. I don't want no talking. I want something done. I'm having a heart attack. Somebody's got to do something about it. You medical quacks is getting rich off of us people, but you don't want to do nothing for it. You're going to hear from my lawyer about this, you sawbones son-of-a-bitch. I worked in the mines all my life..." His voice trailed away as Bernard walked around the house to the car.

"Ain't ya going to take him to the hospital? Ain't ya going to call a ambulance?" The woman grabbed at Bernard's sleeve as he walked across the front yard.

"He's not having a heart attack. See to it he gets in the house. It's too cold for him to be on that back porch. Get him into the clinic next week for some counseling." Bernard drove away leaving her standing in the middle of the road with her hands on her hips.

He finished the sandwich Bea packed for him on his way back to the clinic. He worked efficiently all afternoon and took care of quite a few patients, mostly with respiratory problems. A man came in for a refill of the codeine tablets he was taking for a broken rib. Ordinarily one of the nurses would put him in an examination room. The Doc would come in carrying the box of pills placed beside the appropriate slot in the laboratory and hand the medicine to the patient. He would make a brief inquiry and leave, but the nurse's slow down had changed all that. The man sat on the end of the examination table, fully dressed, with only his blood pressure recorded in the chart. He protested when Bernard asked him to undress.

"I just come in for my pills, Doc. I know what's wrong. I got a broke rib. I don't need no examination."

"Well, if I'm going to prescribe pain pills, I'll have to examine you. Dr. Sizemore probably knows you, but I have not seen you before, so I need to examine you."

He unbuttoned his shirt, exposing a rib belt.

"Take that off," Bernard instructed. The patient un-strapped the brace. Under the device, his skin was a purple band around his rib cage, a bruise the size and shape of the belt. Bernard checked his liver, it was enlarged, nodular and hard as a rock. He evidently had cancer of the liver and a pathological rib fracture due to the metastasis of the tumor to his bones. It was a simple two minute diagnosis but when he came to the clinic complaining of rib pain, the nurse had taken a rib X-ray and had seen an obvious fracture. She fitted him with a rib belt and placed a box of codeine and the X-ray where Doc had picked them up and taken them to the examination room. The patient, fully clothed, rib belt in place was shown the fracture which the nurse had marked with a wax pencil. He was handed the box of pills and Doc's work was done.

Bernard's examination would have no material affect on the man's life span, but he wondered how much preventable pathology slipped through the administrator's foolproof system. He gave the pills for pain and sat down to explain why the rib fracture had occurred. The patient did not seem to grasp the full significance of what he was being told. He stood up and started for the door, Bernard asked him to come back. "I am not sure you understand what I am telling you."

"Your damn right I don't, and if you want to know the truth, I think you don't know what you're talking about. You don't even know how to read a X-ray. Anybody can see my rib is broke. It's as plain as the nose on your face. You may think your pretty smart, but you don't know the first thing about doctorin'." He took the pills and stomped out of the office.

Bernard finished work earlier than usual and as he entered the waiting room, he saw that it was not empty. Lester Spradling, whose hernia he detected several days before, a woman and four dirty children, stood between him and the doorway.

"The company wouldn't hire me 'cause you told 'em not to, Doc. I want you to see the woman and kids you're starving."

"I never told the coal company to refuse to hire you or anything of the sort. I have nothing to do with their hiring or firing. I can't help it if you have a hernia."

"A what?" The woman looked quizzically at her husband.

He gave her a look that wilted her. "Keep your mouth shut, woman. Ain't you got no sense a'tall? You want everbody knowin' my business?" She shrunk behind him and looked at the floor.

"I'm sorry you don't have a job. Maybe you should have surgery."

"Maybe *You* should have surgery," Lester mocked. "Maybe you should have your ass kicked." He blocked the door.

Bernard pushed past him and crossed the porch without pausing to lock the door. Spradling, with his brood behind, followed Bernard into the parking lot and stood in front of the exit to the bridge. Bernard drove slowly forward until they had to step out of the way.

He had trouble sleeping that night. In the morning, when he drove to the clinic, dawn was just commencing. The town was covered with a blanket of white, ice narrowed the creek to a rivulet meandering around partially submerged rocks, and frozen cataracts and lacy stalactites caught the first glint of daybreak. The camouflaged coal tipple, washery and conveyer shed blended into hillsides shrouded in mist and sprinkled with the snowy skeletons of summer foliage. White gondola cars, piled high with white-topped coal, camped in strings down the middle of the white valley. Wattsville looked like a fairyland.

Bernard called Mary Arbogast into Doc's office and asked if he could get back into the good graces of Wampler and Sturgill.

She only looked at him and smiled, but as the day wore on he was aware things had improved. They worked smoothly and saw a lot of patients. He put the appropriate cards in the appropriate slots on the board. He seconded the shots and parcels of medicines selected by the system.

All day the seeming madhouse operated pretty efficiently because of the leeway entrusted to the help, the routines set up by the

administrator and the simple formulary. The intricate science and
social interaction took only a brief moment before the practitioner
moved on to his next good deed. With Doc gone, the ritual continued without skipping a beat, once the *locum tenens* was whipped
into shape.

The usual coughs, back pains and headaches consumed most
of the day. At the end of clinic hours, he was summoned to the
house of a woman who was "dying." The call came from a neighbor who said the woman's five year old came over to her place and
asked her to call. The child said his mother was dying and that was
all he knew. The neighbor was asked to call because the patient's
phone was out of order. Mary Arbogast shrugged her shoulders as
she gave him the message.

"I have been trying, with some success, to cut down on the
house calls, but..."

Bernard drove up the hollow and turned onto a dirt road leading to one of the auxiliary entrances to the number two mine shaft.
A cable strung between two iron posts marked the end of the road.
He parked and walked up onto the front porch of the dingy brown
bungalow sitting in a clearing just outside the mine entrance. It
was getting dark. A little boy answered the door, a man sat in the
living room in a rocking chair listening to the radio. He did not
look up as Bernard entered the room.

"Don't open that closet, McGee." The woman's voice from the
radio was followed by a prolonged crash of items falling out of the
closet. The man in the rocking chair laughed out loud at McGee's
predicament.

The boy ushered Bernard into a little bedroom in the back of
the house. A plain looking woman lay in bed with her stringy hair
splayed out over the pillow. She had a worn quilt pulled up around
her neck. Her eyes were red from crying. She had a bruise on her

forehead and another under her left eye. Bernard pulled the covers down revealing bruises around her neck. When he touched her shoulder, she pulled away in pain.

"Have you been beaten?" he asked.

She touched her lips with her finger in a gesture for silence. The side of her wrist was swollen and blue.

Bernard examined her and found no evidence of broken bones or internal injuries. He gave her instructions, a package of pain pills, picked up the telephone, without asking permission and called the clinic. When he finished checking in, he pulled a chair up beside the bed and sat down.

"Why did you call the clinic, instead of the deputy sheriff?" His voice was stern.

"If'n the depe'ty come," she sobbed. "He'id take my man to jail and he couldn't work, en we'ud not have nothing to eat." Her quiet sobs shook the bed and her eyes repeatedly darted toward the other room while she answered in a faint whisper.

"Why did you send your child next door and have him lie about the phone and the reason for calling?"

"I knowed you wouldn'ta come." Her voice had become barely audible. The sobs increased. Bernard stood up, put his hands on his hips and looked at the pathetic creature. She continued to sob as he stomped out. He crossed the living room, the man in the rocking chair was still listening to the radio.

"T'aint funny McGee," the woman's voice from the radio provoked several loud guffaws from the man in the rocking chair. Bernard strode out the door, across the porch and down the steps, two at a time.

On the way back to the clinic to check the wire recorder, he stopped at the hotel and ate supper. He shared his frustration about the house call with Bea. "I don't know what she expects me to do and that no-good husband of hers just sat listening to the radio."

"Well, you have to understand. If she didn't tell somebody of authority, he would keep beating her up. Now he'll stop, for a while anyway." Bea cleaned the kitchen as she talked.

"Explain to me why you think she didn't call the sheriff?" Bernard asked.

"Because the sheriff has probably been called so many times he would take her husband to jail and he wouldn't be able to work. They wouldn't have any money, most likely have to pay a fine, they're probably all ready destitute because of his drinking. And besides, if he got arrested, he'd really beat her up when he got out of jail." She cleared the dishes from the table.

"That's almost exactly what she said. It seems like a heck of a way to run one's life." He finished his meal and returned to the clinic to check the wire recorder for messages. After he had checked, he went down the steps and across the parking lot. Lester Spradling was sitting on the hood of his car. As Bernard attempted to walk around the auto, the aggrieved patient slid off his perch and blocked the way.

"You better watch yourself. I'm goin' to git you. You ain't heard the last of me yet." He tried to push Bernard in the chest with his hand. Bernard brushed past shoving him against the next car and got into the automobile. Lester tried to grab the handle. Bernard locked the door. Lester beat on the window with his fists as Bernard drove away.

On his way to the hotel, Bernard stopped at the grocery store to buy a Butterfinger. Lester caught up with him in the aisle. He started yelling at Bernard and shaking his fist. When a store employee tried to intervene Lester pushed him into a stack of cans displayed in the isle. The display came down on top of the grocer.

Spradling followed Bernard to the counter. The clerk extricated himself from the jumble and picked up the phone. "If you don't get out of here, Lester, I'm going to call the deputy sheriff." Lester turned and left the store.

"I'll still call the deputy if you want me to, Doctor."

"No, he probably won't bother me anymore. Thanks, though." Bernard paid for the candy bar and walked rapidly back to his car. Lester waited in the parking lot. He followed Bernard to the hotel and parked across the street. Bernard went in through the kitchen and visited with Bea while she fixed his supper. Before he finished eating, the phone rang and a male voice on the other end inquired, "You the doctor?"

"Yes, I am," Bernard answered.

"Well, get yourself up here to house number thirty seven."

"What?" Bernard was astounded.

"Get yourself up here. Now!"

"I'll tell you something, sir. You need to give me some information. What is going on? What are you calling me about? You know; stuff like that," Bernard said.

"Just never you mind. You're supposed to be the doctor. Get yourself up here right now!"

"I'll tell you what. I'm going to hang up. You decide whether you can talk to me like a human being and figure out what you need me for then call back."

Bernard hung up the phone. He was furious. He had been threatened a few times in the emergency room. He knew people did not like going to the doctor, but the antagonism of this community was more than he had expected. He looked at Bea and shook his head in disbelief. "It seems to me there is a kinda high level of antagonism in Wattsville," he said.

"Well, living in a community such as this does have a tendency to provoke some animosity in its inhabitants from time to time," Bea agreed. "But between a few fights down at one of the beer joints and some shifting around from one church to the other, most of it gets worked off without too much damage."

"Well, I'm about to the end of my rope with this Lester whoever he is and his hernia. If he doesn't let up pretty soon, I'm going to talk to the deputy sheriff about him." He finished supper and sat in the kitchen sipping coffee. Finally, he said, "Am I acting a little surly, Bea?" Bea looked up from her chores and smiled.

A woman knocked at the kitchen door and came in without waiting for Bea's acknowledgment.

"Hi Bea." Then to Bernard, "You the doctor?"

"Yes, I am," he answered.

"My husband is sick. Could you come to see him?"

"Where do you live?"

"Just follow me in the car. I'll show you."

"What's your house number?" he asked.

"I don't remember."

"How long have you lived at the same place?" Bernard persisted.

"I don't remember."

"Do you live in house number thirty seven? Did someone in your family call me a little while ago?"

"That was my son. You've got to over-look that one."

Lady, you may have to overlook him, but I don't, he thought. "If your husband's sick, I'll come see him," he said. He followed her and a younger woman in their car, to a company house about a mile from the hotel.

The snow continued to fall but since the weather had chilled the flakes were fine. His headlights penetrated the wall of white far enough ahead to make driving more comfortable.

While he was getting his medical equipment together from the back seat, the two women went into the house. He walked up the front steps, the dry snow crunching underfoot, crossed the porch and knocked at the door. He waited. The door opened and a man stood filling the doorway with his hairy arms crossed in front of his massive chest. He must have been six feet four if he were an inch and weighed at least two hundred and seventy-five pounds. He had hair on his knuckles, long black hair on his forearms, a full head of unruly black hair, his face was blue-black where he had shaved, and he had hair sticking up out of the neck of his torn white undershirt.

Bernard walked forward a few steps, looked up into the scowl and turned as if to leave. The man quickly got out of the way. Bernard went into the living room that had linoleum on the floor, an unmade-bed against the far wall, a broken-down couch and a rocking chair. He followed the older woman to the bedroom where it was oppressively hot from the heat of a coal stove.

A man, who appeared to be wearing shoes, was in bed with a blanket pulled up around his neck. When Bernard asked what was bothering him he launched into a diatribe.

"Damn doctors. All they want is your money. Won't come when you're sick. All they..."

"What is bothering you medically," Bernard interrupted. "I have no intention of staying here, if all you want is to give me hell. Now tell me are you in pain, have a fever, a cough, or what?" The man's bombast seemed to dissipate itself. He looked sheepish.

"I been coughin'. I got this cough. Ever' time I breath, I cough. I got chest pain. I could cough my lungs up. Doctors won't care..."

"How long have you had this cough?" Bernard interrupted again.

"I been coughing for years. I been coughing all my life. It's them mines. I got black lungs." He put his hand on his chest and hacked up a gob of sputum, rolled it on his tongue and swallowed it.

He sat up on the side of the bed and put his feet on the floor. He was wearing shoes. He leaned forward, grasped the front of his shirt and coughed some more. Mucous rattled in the bases of his lungs. A pack of camels fell out of his shirt pocket. He picked it up took out a cigarette, placed it between his toothless gums and lit it with a Zippo lighter from his pants pocket. The flame was so large he had to squint to protect his eye.

After inhaling deeply, he pointed his orange-tinged fingers at Bernard as if to emphasize his demand and said, "I need some pills."

"Take your shirt off so I can listen to your lungs," Bernard instructed. The patient removed his shirt, his ribs protruded, his Adams apple bobbed up and down, his skinny abdomen sunk in, exposing the bottom of his flared out rib cage. The xiphoid process at the base of his sternum looked as if it were about to punch through his skin. The examination revealed chronic lung disease but no sign of acute infection.

"I noticed you have a Bird machine in the corner. Do you use that to loosen up the secretions in your lungs?"

"Doc has me mixin' water and Vodka in that machine and breathing the smoke. But it causes my ulcers to act up something fierce."

"How many cigarettes do you smoke every day?"

"What difference does that make? I been smoking all my life. It don't matter none. I need some'a them pills the doc always gives me. I'm out. Them white pills."

His wife handed a little white box to Bernard, with Codeine hand written on it, but with no directions.

"These are for pain, these are not for lung disease..." Bernard stopped. He looked at the people standing over him, especially the son; he looked at those bony, yellow stained fingers pointing menacingly. He thought of the man following him around town. He remembered the reaction of the employees to his attempt to make changes at the clinic. He looked back at the box in his hand. ***What the hell's the use,*** he thought. ***It's not worth getting killed over.***

"I'll have to go back to the clinic. Someone come along and I'll give you some more pills."

The two women waited while he went into the pharmacy and came back out into the waiting room with a box of thirty tablets.

The next morning when he left the hotel, the snow was gone, disappeared in an ensuing rain and rising temperature. Wattsville was its normal, muddy, dirty, miserable self again.

Lester was in the parking lot, sitting in his car, smoking. Bernard avoided looking in his direction as he crossed to the clinic.

He worked hard all day trying his best to fit into the system. There was real pathology passing through the clinic and he felt a good portion of what he did was helpful. Just before quitting time Mary Arbogast informed him he had been summoned to the grievance committee meeting that evening.

"What is the grievance committee?" he asked.

"Someone has made a complaint against you."

"To whom?"

"To the union."

"I don't care about the union. I don't work for the union."

"Yes, you do. This clinic is over ninety-five percent paid for by the union welfare fund. You may think Doc pays you, but he doesn't. Medical Hygiene, Inc. gets its money from the union. You should go to the meeting." She touched his tightly crossed arms with her finger tip to emphasize the point, and walked away.

He took his time getting to the high school after he finished up at the clinic and walked into the auditorium after the meeting was in progress. The seats were arraigned in theater style, each row higher than the one in front. On the stage a small man sat behind a table talking to someone in the audience. He shifted his cigarette to the side of his mouth when Bernard entered and acknowledged Bernard's arrival with a pause in his conversation and a nod. Lester Spradling sat at the side of the room glowering directly at Bernard. Bernard could not resist glancing in his direction from time to time. His stare never wavered.

The little man on the stage informed Bernard a woman had complained he refused to treat her for a cold. Bernard asked for a reminder of who she was.

"It don't matter none who she is. Why wouldn't you treat her?"

"I can't answer. I don't remember refusing to treat anyone. If you will not tell me whose complaints I'm supposed to be answering for, I'm going to leave. I've got better things to do." He started to rise out of the chair.

"She had a cold and you wouldn't give her a shot of penicillin. You must remember her." Bernard sat back down.

"Well, I'm not sure. But if it's the woman I think it is, I didn't refuse to treat her. We just disagreed as to how she should be treated."

"She said you wouldn't give her any medicine for her cold."

"I offered cough medicine. She refused it and walked out of the office without it."

"She didn't want no cough medicine. Doc always gives her penicillin shots."

"We had a disagreement about that."

"She told you the doctor always gives her penicillin shots. What's to disagree about?"

"I thought she might be mistaken. Doctors don't usually give penicillin for colds. I assumed she was mistaken."

"She told you she was not mis-taken," he overemphasized. "Doc always gave her penicillin."

"What do you expect me to do about it?"

"She wants a penicillin shot."

"What kind?"

"What do you mean, what kind?"

"What kind of penicillin?"

"Penicillin, penicillin. What kind of penicillin is they? Penicillin! What's the matter with you? She just wants a shot of penicillin." His face turned red. He began to shout.

"Not only what kind, but how much?"

"What are you, a smart-aleck? You expect me to know what kind? You're the doctor! You're supposed to know what kind!"

"Right. I am the doctor," he said quietly. Then he got up and left.

The next day Arbogast told him the man with the heart attack and Lester Spradling were also at the meeting to complain about him; and a woman who was mad because he tricked her.

"Someone said I tricked..." he did not finish the question. Half-way through the sentence he remembered: he had been called to the woman's house because she could not hear, or get out of bed, or walk. He suspected she was feigning illness so he said, "I think you have something wrong with your kidneys. I need a urine specimen to help me find out. So I need you to go in the bed room and pee in this bottle." She not only heard the instructions, she got up and went into the other room to void. Bernard instructed her family to bring her to the office and left without treating her or waiting for her to come back with her urine.

"Doc will have to answer to the administrator when he returns. Have you ever considered that the administrator may refuse to pay you." Mary wagged her finger back and forth in front of her face. "He is not a man to view such behavior with forbearance, you know. Especially if he gets fined."

"What do you mean, fined?" Bernard had never heard of such a thing.

"The union can fine him if Doc doesn't perform according to their wishes. Didn't you know that?"

"I had no idea. I really didn't intend to walk out. The little pipsqueak just made me angry." Mary turned and walked away.

At noon Bernard went on a house call to see a man who could not breathe. He was sitting up in bed gasping for air. His ankles were swollen and his lungs bubbled when he exhaled. His heart rate was at least a hundred and eighty beats per minute. Bernard opened the window to let in cold damp air. He gave the man a mercuhydrin shot, put tourniquets on three of his limbs, gave him a shot of digitalis and drained off a pint of blood. His condition improved rapidly. When his heart slowed, its irregularity became apparent. He had atrial fibrillation.

"How long has your heart been irregular?" Bernard asked. The patient cupped his hand behind one ear.

"What say?"

"How long has your heart been beating that way?"

"About twenty years." The man shouted.

"What do you take for it?"

"What say?" He cupped his hand again. "What'd he say?" He looked at the woman standing at the bedside, who could have been his wife or his daughter. She held one finger up to quiet him and addressed Bernard directly.

"He takes digitalis for his heart; has for twenty years. He ran out about ten days ago. His breathing has got worse all week. Today he got so bad he couldn't hardly breathe at all."

"Why did he run out of digitalis?" Bernard asked.

"We sent the order in, but it never come back," she explained.

"You sent what order into where?"

"We sent the Doc's prescription into the union. They was supposed to send the medicine back. We been waiting now going on to three weeks."

"Well, send someone over to the clinic to pick up enough digital is to tide him over until you get it from the union. I'll have directions written on the box. He will need to take extra tablets for a few days so he can get caught up, or his dropsy will come right back." The woman saw him out and thanked him for coming.

On the way back to the clinic, Bernard puzzled over the explanation.

As he drove across the bridge to the parking lot his attention was drawn to the creek banks. The incline leading down to the water was littered with little white boxes. He had seen them the first day and had intended to ask about them but he forgot. After he parked the car, he climbed down the slippery bank. Every box he rattled contained a full load of medicine. He scrambled up the bank with some difficulty and went back to work. That evening as they finished, he pulled Mary aside and asked about the digitalis.

"It happens all the time," she said. "The union pays for the medicines people on miner's welfare take. We can give a few pills or a couple ounces of common medicines for acute problems, but drugs prescribed for chronic conditions have to be sent from the mail-order pharmacy run by the union. It is not really uncommon for them to lose a prescription or mail it to the wrong address, and if it is for something they don't have in stock..., well."

"Can a patient call and find out what happened to the order?"

"If they like hearing a busy signal, or talking to someone who has no idea what's going on, or who lays the phone down and forgets it."

"Can't they look in their records to see what happened to the order?"

"They don't seem to keep much in the way of records. Or if they do, they can't seem to find them when they're needed."

"Why couldn't the patient go to the drug store and spring for twenty five cents worth of digitalis to hold over until he could solve the problem; get another prescription or something?" Bernard asked.

"We haven't had a pharmacy in town for several years now. The nearest one is Charleston," she said. "Besides, he's supposed to get it free. He was promised. It's due him. He worked in the mines. It's his right. I guess you've heard all the reasons by now."

"Yes, I guess I have. While we're talking about it. I picked up some of the boxes beside the creek..." Arbogast's laugh interrupted his question.

"I wondered when you'd get to those."

"Why would people throw away the medicine the doctor prescribes for them?"

"Half of them don't come here for medicine. They come to socialize. They come because it's their due, or because they were promised free medical care and they're going to see to it they get what's coming to them. You know: all the same reasons."

"Why don't they at least take it home and throw it away?" Bernard asked. "Isn't that kind of a slap in the doctor's face?"

"It's their statement, their defiance. Deep down they know there's very little value in something for nothing. They know there's something wrong with a system that treats them as if they are children. They know they should be managing their own lives. They have no place else to protest and no other way to do it."

"What do you mean?"

"They used to be Mountaineers. They had grit. Now they're recipients. They know there's something wrong with that. They know the Dover's powders and Brown's mixture they get from Doc and the commodities they get from welfare are not worth the cost. The humiliation, the loss of dignity they suffer standing in line for free lard or waiting in a crowded waiting room for free medical care makes them angry. They identify Doc with the system. But they're not really mad at him. They're just mad. Those little white boxes are symbols of more than I can tell you in one evening." She spread her arms, palms-up in a gesture of futility. "Dr. Sizemore has so little time..."

"Why does he do it? Why doesn't he practice better medicine? I know he knows the difference. You've got to admit most of that stuff he prescribes is fifty years behind the times."

"Don't be too harsh on him. When he came here, he tried to be good a doctor. He was, too. You should know better than anybody. They beat him down and when he protested, the union threatened to replace him. He just does his best to help alleviate pain and distress, but there's nothing he can do to make Wattsville into something it isn't. He knows when they're demanding pills for their feeling of powerlessness. You have to admit, every one of those boxes has something harmless in it. He just goes along with their needs as he sees them. It's not his fault there's a living in what he does, and the threat of ruin if he tries to do better." She patted Bernard's arm and waved good bye as she headed for the door, effectively ending the conversation.

Bernard did not have to go out that night. Lying in bed, thinking about the conversation, kept him awake for a long time. The next morning the rain stopped. It was Sunday and he lounged in bed until almost nine o'clock when Bea announced breakfast was ready. He ate leisurely. After he finished he drove to the clinic to see what was going on.

A man in soiled white pants and shirt was sweeping the floor and cleaning the counters. Bernard had seen the man coming and going from time to time but never seemed to get around to finding out who he was.

"Hi, Dr. Southard," he said and put out his hand. It turned out he was the janitor and handy man. His name was Luke. He was soft and he needed a shave. He slightly exaggerated his movements as he emptied wastebaskets and generally straightened the office.

While Bernard was taking care of patients, Luke pitched in without being asked and answered the phone. Bernard overheard his talking to the callers, recording messages. Between calls, he brought patients into the rooms, took their blood pressures, temperatures, pulses and recorded complaints, making Bernard's task much easier.

"You sure were a big help, Luke. Where did you get your medical training?" Bernard asked.

"In Chicago. I'm a licensed nurse in Illinois. Not a registered nurse, but qualified to work in old folk's homes, mental or rehabilitation facilities, doctor's offices, and as a nurse's assistant in the hospital."

"Why are you working as a janitor?"

"There aren't any jobs for men in nursing in West Virginia," he said. "No one will hire me." He was not complaining, just stating what he believed to be true.

"Why don't you move?"

"This is my home. Besides, eventually they'll need me here. When I get a chance, I'll get past the prejudice. I am a good nurse."

"I'll confirm that," Bernard agreed. He thought about Luke's explanation and remembered a Negro orderly at Memorial in

Charleston, whose name was Roosevelt, (or was it Washington?), he sure knew a lot about medicine. One night while cleaning the E.R., he saw Bernard trying to bandage a finger. He swept around and around the surgery room until the nurse left, then asked if he could help. He checked to be sure the nurse was not coming back and showed Bernard how to roll, twist and anchor the dressing. It worked great. Since then Bernard had taught several other doctors how to do it. He told Luke the story.

"I'll bet he's an orderly because he's a man," Luke said.

"And because he's a Negro," Bernard added. "When I get back to the hospital, I'm going to ask."

"Go on home Doctor. I'll lock up," Luke said with a smile.

"Thanks, Luke. Thanks for your help today. I'll see you tomorrow." Bernard waved as he closed the door and crossed the porch. As he walked down the steps to the parking lot, a car came up the road and turned across the bridge. A large man got out and walked toward the clinic. A woman struggled out from the passenger side and followed about fifteen or twenty feet behind. They brushed past Bernard and entered the building. The woman had trouble getting up the steps. The man disappeared inside before she got to the porch. Bernard watched her labor up the stairs. He couldn't tell whether she was in pain or having trouble breathing. He closed the car door and headed back into the office.

"She's having trouble breathing," Luke said when Bernard came into the room.

Bernard examined her and determined she was having an emotional attack. She gasped for air, her hands shook, her mouth and tongue were numb. She had no feeling in her hands. Her fingers curled tightly into her palms. She was sobbing uncontrollably.

"What happened?" Bernard asked. She cried louder and tried to answer between sobs but couldn't get the words out.

"She cain't breathe, Doc," her husband answered. "I don't have no idea what happened. It started all of a sudden. We was just driving into town and all at once, she couldn't get her wind." He shrugged his shoulders.

Bernard questioned him further and found they were coming home from vacation when it happened. The holiday had gone well. They had a good time and were just getting into Wattsville when she suddenly clutched her chest, gasped for air and started to cry. She began to shake and could not talk. He drove straight to the clinic without even going home first.

"We still got our bags in the car," he said.

Bernard gave her a Phenobarbital tablet, a sip of water and turned off the lights in the examination room. He motioned for her husband to follow him. He left the door partially open and went into the waiting room, the man following reluctantly. They could hear her sobbing softly. They sat in the waiting room and Bernard asked about their vacation.

"This was our first vacation since we got married. My momma watched the kids and we drove down to Myrtle Beach." Off season it was cheap and not crowded. They had several sunny days on the beach. They went to restaurants; they even went to a supper theater where the waiters were singers. They had a wonderful time. They had been married eight years and had three children. He worked in the mine. She was a housewife. They were both born in the county and went to high school together. He said they had a good marriage.

Bernard listened to the story; then left the confused husband sitting in the waiting room and went back to the examination room. The woman was more relaxed and a little sleepy. Her eyes were swollen and her nose was red, but she was breathing slowly and her fingers had straightened out. Bernard sat down and put his hand on her forearm.

"How old were you when you got married?" he asked gently.

"Sixteen," she answered.

"Did you finish high school?"

"No."

"Why did you drop out?"

"To get married."

"How old was your husband?"

"Eighteen."

"Did he finish high school?"

"No, he had one more year, but he didn't finish. He couldn't play football no more, so he quit."

"Why couldn't he play anymore? Was he hurt?"

"No, he was only allowed to play four years. He played all his football, he just didn't finish school. I was a cheerleader. We was going together for two years before I got so we had to get married." She looked him straight in the eye, seemingly to be sure he understood the significance of that.

As she continued talking, her color came back. She became animated. She laughed. She had been popular and pretty; he was a football star. Now he was a coal miner and a slob. She was overweight and chronically tired. She endured her life. She complained. She went to the clinic and got pills. She ate too much. She put up with her kids. She lost her sex drive. She let her husband have sex, then lay awake listening to his snoring. She tolerated her life Then came the vacation.

Even off-season, Myrtle Beach gave her a glimpse of the world outside the hills. She had been to Charleston. She even flew in a plane once to visit her Grandmother when she was twelve, but the vacation to the beach was different. It showed her, as an adult, that she was stuck. When their car approached Wattsville town limits on the way home, she developed a heavy feeling in her chest.

She could not breathe. She felt as if she were going to die. Her heart hurt, she felt a heavy weight of oppression. She could not see. She blacked out. She was afraid if she went home, she would die. She wanted to turn around and run away as fast as she could. She was afraid she was losing her mind.

"I was scared I'd do something bad if I went home. Maybe even to the kids." She became calm as she talked. "I know there's nothing you can do, but it helps just to have you listen. Nobody ever listens to me. Sometimes I get tired of being a waitress to my four kids. He's like a fourth kid, you know?" She nodded her head toward the waiting room.

"Do you have anyone you can talk to?" Bernard asked.

"Not about how I feel. My momma says, `That's a woman's lot.' My sisters remind me he don't hit me or run around on me none. The kids is too little and you cain't talk to the preacher about anything personal or it's likely to come out in his sermon. And the Doc's too busy. Maybe they's right. Maybe I just don't know how to be happy..."

Bernard held her hand. He advised her she was not crazy and agreed it must be difficult to live in a coal town. He told her even though he liked his work and the people he worked with, he found the conditions kind of harsh in Wattsville.

"I think I understand a little of how you must feel," he said. "You should try to open up a little more with someone you can trust, preferably a friend. I'll bet there are women near your age or someone you went to school with who feel the same as you. If you ask how someone close to you feels and then listen, I'll bet you'll find out your not the only one who feels the way you do. When you start out with a complaint like you have with your sisters, though, they think they have to try to make you feel better.

That's why they try to say something positive instead of under-standing your feelings."

He also recommended she tell her husband some need she had and see if he could respond. They talked the better part of an hour. He made some other safe recommendations and it was obvi-ous she was ready to go home. She hugged Bernard at the door, right in front of her husband who looked sheepish. Bernard was afraid he'd be angry and was a little uncomfortable until the wor-ried look on the big man's face turned to a smile. She grabbed her husband's arm and they walked out of the clinic together. She held onto his arm and there was spring in her step. She dragged him around to her side of the car and waited while he opened the door. He closed the door, glanced back at the clinic, scratched his head, walked around to the driver's side, got in and drove away. She scooted over close to him as he turned the car onto the main road.

Luke smiled. "That was nice, Doc."

"Well, thanks Luke. It felt pretty good to me, too!"

They left the clinic and when Bernard drove into the hotel parking lot, he thought he caught a glimpse of someone running across the road in the dark. The hotel sat on a level piece of land between the road and the creek. The railroad on the opposite bank turned away from the creek and headed across the valley to-ward the coal tipple. Across the highway, the densely wooded hill rose sharply to a rock cliff. He scanned the hillside for movement. *I guess I'm getting paranoid,* he thought. He went into the hotel by the kitchen door.

Lil fixed supper and after he finished eating, he went to bed. He was not fully asleep when the phone rang and a woman asked him to come back to the clinic.

"My little girl has got a powerful fever and she's pukin' a right smart, also. I'm worried sick about her."

"What's your name," Bernard asked.

"Fillagrew," she said after a short hesitation.

"Filla' what," he asked.

"Fillagrew," she answered.

"OK, I'll meet you at the clinic in twenty minutes, Mrs. Fillagrew. If that's agreeable with you."

"That's agreeable," she answered.

He dressed warmly, splashed cold water on his face and left through the kitchen door. He was still on the porch when he saw a flash which drew his attention to the cliff on the hillside. It was followed immediately by a sharp crack and something whizzed by his head close to his ear. The sensation as it hummed through the air was as much energy as noise. At first, he thought it was an insect, then the flash-crack happened again. They came so close together, he did not have time to think. The second volley shattered the window of his car on the passenger side. A third eruption was followed by a splash of dirt in the parking lot. He instinctively ducked his head.

My God, somebody's shooting at me! he thought. He turned and ran back into the house just as another retort came from the hillside. As he entered the kitchen, he felt a sting, then a burning sensation in his right buttock. The burning traveled down his leg to the outside of his ankle. Something hit the big iron stove, with a thud. He slammed the door shut and ran for the phone. He fumbled with the little telephone book. He could not find the sheriff's number. Bea padded bare foot down the hall pulling on her Indian blanket robe as she came.

"What in heaven's name's going on?" she asked as she tied the cord around her waist.

"I'm trying to find the sheriff's number. Someone's shooting at me."

"You just sit yourself. I'll call the deputy sheriff." She took the phone out of his hand. Bernard turned to walk across the room to sit.

"Oh my God, you've been shot!" Bea screamed.

He looked down at his leg. He was trailing blood on the linoleum. Then, for the first time, he became aware of the warm wet sensation in his pants. He reached inside his trousers in back, pulled his hand out and looked at it. It was covered with blood.

"You go ahead. Call the police. I'll go in the bathroom and clean myself up." He grabbed a towel and his robe and went down the hall to the bath. He undressed and looked at his back-side in the mirror. A spot on the back of his buttock looked about like a cigarette burn, but the wound on the side was spurting blood and it was flowing down his leg. He pressed the towel hard against the wound. There was no pain. He held the towel tightly against his side and finished disrobing. He climbed into the tub and turned on the water. He showered. Blood ran down the curtain, across the tub and into the drain. It let up as he stood there in the water, but did not stop.

Blood oozed from what appeared to be an exit wound. It was a ragged stellate tear with its edges puffed out away from the surrounding skin. The bleeding diminished to a trickle. He picked a small piece of metal off a blob of fat near the edge of the injury. It was a piece of copper. He pressed the towel hard against the tissue defect, dried with another towel and slipped the robe over his shoulders.

"You all right in there?" Bea called through the door.

"Yes, I'm O.K.," he answered.

"Deputy sheriff Chapin's here. Best you come out when you can."

Bernard waddled down the hall holding pressure against the wound. The deputy sheriff, a big, soft, formless man in an ill-fitting uniform, smirked when he saw where Bernard had been shot. He covered the smile with his hand and leaned against the kitchen counter. He looked down at the floor to hide the grin when he lowered his hand to take the coffee Bea offered.

"I'd better get dressed. I'll be back in a minute," Bernard said. As he retreated down the hall with the huge towel pressed against his backside he heard a muffled giggle behind him.

The deputy took down the information, put the piece of copper and the misshapen slug Bea had found on the kitchen floor into his pants-pocket and sipped his coffee.

"I'll need to talk to you, if I find out anything, but if you cain't identify who it was you saw, I doubt there's anything we can do." He closed his notebook, put the coffee cup on the drainboard, touched the bill of his cap toward Bea and left.

Bea confirmed that the name the woman gave was probably false. "There's nobody around here by the name, Fillagrew, I know of and I been here all my life." The deputy sheriff had said nothing when he wrote the name on the form he filled out. The woman never called back.

Bernard may have dozed a little that night. He mostly sweated, tossed and turned and stewed. It was obvious no one would be arrested. The deputy's investigation had been casual. He treated the evidence as if it were litter. He never mentioned getting out and looking through the woods before the weather could obscure any traces of the sniper. He probably did not intend to even investigate the call. The elements of a proper inquiry ran around in Bernard's brain into the morning hours. Finally, when sleep continued to elude him, he got up and wrote down his thoughts.

The next day he was so sore he could hardly walk. The drive to the clinic was especially uncomfortable because of the hard car seat and the broken window. He found a hemorrhoid ring in the Doc's office and carried it around to sit on.

About two thirds of the people he encountered offered condolences and the others snickered, or made crude, humorless remarks. At noon, he called the deputy and told him he had been awake all night thinking and had some ideas he would like to share about the investigation.

"In the first place," Bernard said. "I'll bet a ..."

"I know you're from the city and I realize you're a smart young feller with a lot of book learning, and I know you think we don't know much up here in the woods. All the same, I'd appreciate it if you'd leave this case to me." And he hung up.

"That son-of-a-bitch," Bernard said out loud to himself. He spent the rest of the day trying to focus on his duties, but he had trouble concentrating. He worked quietly, interacting less than usual with the patients and the staff.

A woman, at least a hundred pounds overweight came in for a cortisone injection into her knee. Her chart indicated she had numerous previous injections for osteoarthritis of her knees. She should lose weight and do muscle strengthening to diminish the pain and, if necessary, take aspirin.

Bernard knew she would develop Charcot joints if she continued to get cortisone shots to reduce the pain. The knees would become floppy and unstable and she would become a cripple.

He looked at her dull, round features. Her lusterless eyes returned his gaze. He started to say something in explanation but he hesitated, then began preparing her leg for the shot.

"Ouch! Oh! That hurts, Doc. Don't do all that fool scrubbin'." She pushed his hand away. "Do you have to be so rough?" Bernard's hand trembled as he tried to give the shot into her deteriorating joint. Mary Arbogast picked up a gauze sponge and pretended to wipe the skin near the injection site. She subtly steadied his hand at the same time.

"Thanks, Mary," he said later. "I think getting shot has shaken me up even more than I suspected."

She did not answer. She just put her hand on his arm and smiled. His day proceeded in the same vein. It was as if he had lost his confidence. Mary spent her afternoon at his side, assisting.

She smiled at him as they finished the last case, a burn. She had helped him with the debridement. The man had burns over his entire face and both hands. His story was he took the radiator cap off a steaming auto. Mary said that probably his still had blown up again.

"He's not much of a moonshiner." She laughed. "He got himself pretty good this time."

"That was rough," Bernard agreed. "I think we got him cleaned up fairly well though, don't you?"

"Yes, you did a good job," she said. "I don't think he's going to scar much at all."

"You were a big help. You're a good nurse," he said. He was tired, but he felt better. For much of the afternoon and the entire time he and Arbogast worked together over the moonshiner's burns, he had completely forgot his own wound.

"Why, thank you, Dr. Southard. I think you're a good doctor, too. And your rubber cushion makes you look so distinguished."

Bernard laughed. "God bless this place. I'm sure going to have some memories when I leave here."

"I hope all your memories will not be bad ones." Her voice was sad. "There's a lot to learn in a place like this you can use in the future."

"Like what?"

He had not intended to sound so cynical. He had worked with Mary long enough to respect her. He wanted to hear what she had to say.

"I'm sorry, I didn't mean to say that in that way. I know I have a lot to learn," he said.

She didn't speak for the longest time. "Are you sure?" she finally asked.

"I think so."

"Well, communities like this are hard on everyone who lives in them. The people of Wattsville get the kind of medical care they have the capacity for," she said. She looked down at her lap and fiddled with her fingers, then she looked at Bernard. "I know you don't approve of everything Dr. Sizemore does, neither do I. But this place has taken a lot away from him. He's done a lot more good for Wattsville than it has for him."

"I'm sure he has. Has my disapproval been that obvious?"

"Yes, it has. Someday you will be the old doctor someplace. Think about it."

"I will." He smiled. "What else?"

"Are you sure?"

"I think so."

"Do you remember the time you went up the hollow supposedly to make a house call and you refused to give the people a ride back to town?"

"Well, yes. They lied to get me up there, just so they could get a ride to town. I was pretty upset. I hate being used like that."

"Why didn't you say so? They could respect that, but you lied and said you were not going back to town. The only place the road goes is back to town. You humiliated them. They know their lives are not right. They are only one generation removed from pioneers.

They don't know how things went so wrong for them, but they feel impotent to do anything about it. The only thing they have left is their pride. Probably it's a false pride, but it's all they have."

He was stunned. ***Have I forgotten everything Dr. Sleeth taught me?*** he wondered.

"The old man who thought he was having a heart attack, the woman feigning paralysis; they were crying out for understanding. Maybe they wanted sympathy, maybe they didn't merit that, but at the very least they deserved not to be humiliated. Just a little understanding would have been enough. And the man with the broken rib. Doc knew that telling him about his cancer would not do him any good." She paused. "I'm telling you this because I think you're willing to listen. I saw it in you. I talked to Luke. I've seen you when you came back from seeing someone who was really sick. And you're perceptive. None of the other *locum tenens* doctors ever asked me about the boxes on the creek bank. You could fit into this or any other community you wanted to."

He sensed the pain behind the sadness in her face.

"You love this place, don't you?" he said. Her expression softened.

"Wherever you decide to go, be sure you can live with the pressures, though." She looked off into the distance. "Dr. Sizemore was a good man and the things that have happened here took away his dreams." She touched Bernard's shoulder with her hand and looked into his eyes, "I remember you when you came here to visit the twins." Then she turned and left.

That night the phone awakened him and when he answered there was silence on the other end. He repeated his hello several times and finally hung up. A few minutes went by, it rang again. He picked up the receiver and held it to his ear without saying anything. He could hear breathing.

"This is Fillagrew," the voice said in a halting manner.

"I see," Bernard answered.

"I didn't mean to shoot you, Doc."

"Oh? Seemed like it to me."

"I was just trying to scare you." His voice was halting at first but it had become calm. "You got to jumpin' around so much, you got me kinda' discombobulated."

"Well, I was pretty discombobulated myself."

"I'm sorry, Doc. I hope you don't think we're the kind that shoots people what don't deserve it. I was powerful mixed up."

"I'll be OK, I guess," Bernard admitted. Somehow he felt sorry for the person on the other end of the line. There was a short silence...

"I thought maybe you'd feel better know'n people in these hills ain't like that."

"Thank you, Lester," Bernard said and hung up the phone without waiting for a response.

The next evening when he got to the rooming house, Bea gave him a note with a phone number and no comment. He dialed the number. Mary Arbogast answered.

"How would you like a home-cooked meal, Dr.?" she asked.

"Bea's a wonderful cook, but a change would do me good," Bernard answered. She gave him directions to her house not far away. He informed Bea he would be eating out.

He cleaned up and drove to Mary's house across the creek against the hillside in the upper end of town. The little bungalow was painted brown like all the others, had stairs leading up to a front porch and a neat patch of grass surrounded by an unpainted picket fence. The rain, which had been heavy all day, was beginning to be a cloudburst.

Mary opened the door as he reached the top of the stairs. He hung his raincoat in the hall and left his wet shoes on the mat just inside the door.

"My roommate is away for the weekend. She's visiting her boyfriend at the University. I thought since we are both alone, we could have supper together." She smiled and shrugged her shoulders. "I love to cook and it's nice to have someone to fix for."

"I was pleased you called," he said.

"Have a seat," she said. "I've a bottle of wine open in the kitchen.

"Mind if I follow you? Maybe I can help."

"Not at all," she answered. "But supper's all ready prepared."

He sat at the dining room table while she checked the oven. She placed hot rolls in a basket and covered them with a cloth. She lifted the lid from a pot and smelled the steam that wafted into the air. She turned and looked at Bernard. He was enjoying watching her. He smiled. Her face and neck pinked slightly. She placed the rolls on top of the oven.

The cooking smells were tantalizing. She used herbs that reminded him of the smell of exotic restaurants in New York or Washington, D.C. After an initial hesitation, their conversation came easily, they talked of everything except the clinic.

"Are you really that skinny little kid who used to stare at the twins and me when I visited Wattsville?"

"One and the same," she answered. "Did you know I had a crush on you?"

"Well..."

"No, you didn't," she teased. "You didn't even know I existed."

He was embarrassed. She glanced at him over her shoulder as she worked. She was having a good time at his expense. He sipped his wine and smiled. He was having a good time, too.

He had been there less than an hour, when the front door burst open and a young woman strode into the kitchen. Her hair, the fur collar of her coat, her shoulders, even her long eyelashes were dusted with fine droplets of water. She was outrageously beautiful, and upset. Without waiting to be introduced, she thrust out her hand.

"I'm Laura, Mary's roommate." Bernard stood up but she retracted her hand and turned to Mary.

"The damn roads are blocked, the bridge on the main road's under water. I couldn't even get to Clendenin. It's raining so hard you can't see your hand in front of your face. Sure smells good. I'm starved." She poured a glass of wine and left the room. Mary worked for a while without commenting. She stirred and seasoned and checked her oven, then looked at Bernard and smiled.

"So you get to meet Laura." She did not seem upset. "I can stretch the meal for three, without much trouble."

About twenty minutes passed, Laura returned with no makeup and her hair wet. She was wearing pale green silk pajamas with an open dressing gown hanging loosely from her shoulders. Every line of her body, every movement, hinted that she wore no under garments. She had a towel around her neck. She poured another drink and disappeared again.

"I'm starving," she called from the other room.

When Mary had set the table, Laura returned. They ate by candle light. A beautiful woman and an absolute goddess competing for his attention excited Bernard physically, and did nothing to diminish his appetite. Laura was upset about the roads and her interrupted plans, but implied mainly she was starved for masculine affection. Every movement, every glance hinted at seduction. They talked about nothing very important through dinner and as they finished, the phone rang.

"It's for you, Doctor," Mary said as she handed the receiver to him. The man on the other end was a preacher.

One of his parishioners, who had been going to a doctor in Clendenin, was about to have a baby and there was no way they could get there. He would have to bring her to the clinic in his pickup.

"How long do you think it will take for you to get here?" Bernard asked.

"About an hour," he thought. "She lives on the ridge above the highway. Roads up on this hill are a quagmire tonight."

"How close are her pains?" Bernard asked.

"About six or seven minutes apart according to her mother. And pretty hard," the preacher added.

"Is this her first?" Bernard asked.

"Yes. It's her first," the preacher answered.

"OK, I will meet you." Bernard hung up the phone. "I have time to help with the dishes before I leave," he said.

"No, you don't. We will do the dishes," Mary said. "You're our guest." She was adamant. "I'll make you a cup of coffee for the road. Just sit yourself. There's plenty of time for Laura and me to do the dishes after you've gone."

When he finished the coffee and figured he had better be on his way, he thanked Mary for the supper, waved in Laura's direction and started for the door.

"I'll see you out." It was Laura. She followed him through the living room.

Mary called, "Goodbye," from the back of the house.

At the door Bernard turned, Laura was against him, instantly. She caressed him with her body. He was right. There was nothing between her skin and the pajamas. She kissed him with her lips parted, her tongue thrust itself into his mouth. It lingered for a moment. She ran her hand down the front of his chest and abdomen. Gently her fingers wandered over his pubis and caressed the inside of his thigh. She retracted her tongue and with their lips still engaged, "Come back," she breathed into his mouth. "I'll be up." Then she left. It took a minute for him to get his breath. He could hear conversation in the kitchen. He closed the door as quietly as he could.

His hands trembled as he drove to the clinic and parked the car. He fumbled with the keys, finally got the door open and turned on the lights.

The preacher, a young girl and an older woman stomped their feet to rid themselves of the mud as they came into the waiting room. The girl was in pain. She bent over, held her breath and grunted. The grunt ended in a muffled, suppressed little scream. She straightened and followed Bernard into the office. The older woman came along behind. The preacher touched Bernard's shoulder and whispered.

"I'll wait here. Call me if there's anything I can do, Doc."

Bernard did not succeed in getting the girl totally undressed before the next pain hit. Everything stopped until it was over. As she lay on the table, he covered her with a sheet and blanket. He put her feet up in stirrups and examined her pelvis. The baby's head was already crowning so he delivered a little boy almost as soon as he sat down and placed a towel across his lap. He clamped and cut the cord, tied it and removed the clamp as he handed the baby to the older woman. She took it with no change in expression, wrapped it in a blanket and, without showing it to the mother, she walked to a chair and sat. Bernard delivered the placenta, gave a shot of pitocin in the girl's buttock and took her feet out of the stirrups. As soon as he extended the table she rolled on to her side and gazed across the room at her baby. The older woman held him up for better viewing. Then she stood up and tucked him inside her coat.

"We best be going or we'll never git home," she said. "Thank you, kindly, Doctor. We're much obliged." The girl dressed and followed her to the waiting room.

Before they left, the preacher whispered to Bernard that he could only get them within about a mile of their house. They would have to walk the rest of the way.

"Is that going to hurt her any, Doctor?" he asked in a voice calculated only for Bernard to hear.

"I'm not sure. I don't guess so," Bernard answered.

The young girl, bundled up against the rain, wearing her galoshes buckled as high as she could, looked forlornly at Bernard and whispered "bye" as she left the clinic. Without another word, the two women headed for the preacher's vehicle. As they crossed the dark parking lot, the preacher, head down against the driving rain, waved without looking back.

Bernard cleaned up the mess, put the sheets and towels in the laundry, the instruments in soapy water to soak, and headed back to Mary's house.

He walked up onto the porch, raised his hand to knock on the door, then he hesitated. He raised his knuckles again, but still he did not knock. He walked to the living room window. Laura was dozing on the couch, her feet pulled up under her revealing the roundness of her thigh and buttock. Her breasts moved seductively as she breathed. Bernard watched her for a few minutes. She yawned and turned on the couch to get more comfortable. The fire was blazing in the hearth; its light accentuated her beauty as it danced over her face.

He turned and walked across the porch, down the steps and climbed into his car. He sat there for a moment before starting the engine. He drove back to the hotel.

The next day he thanked Mary Arbogast for the hospitality. She responded graciously. There was no hint she was disappointed in the way the evening ended.

As the days went by, the routine became more familiar.

"I enjoy working with you, Miss Arbogast," he said one evening after finishing with the last patient.

"Why, thank you, Doctor." She smiled. "By the way, could I interest you in supper?"

"Do you mean tonight?" he asked. He had begun to fear she would not invite him again.

"Yes. Laura is out of town for a few days, I could sure use some company."

"I'd love it. Can I bring anything? Wine or anything?"

"No, just yourself." As she opened the door to leave, she turned and smiled. "And your whoopee cushin."

Mary fixed Southern fried chicken and followed the meal with the best custard pie with graham cracker crust Bernard could ever remember eating. He had two pieces. "How did you know this is my favorite?"

"I have a spy in Bea's place." She laughed as she replenished his coffee. She motioned for him to follow her into the living room. A log was burning in the fireplace. She sat on the couch and patted the cushion next to her. She looked up at him. In the firelight her eyes were opalescent.

He sat down and put his arm around her. He kissed her and she responded gently. They slipped to the floor and stretched out on the warm rug. She lay on her back, put her hands on the back of his head and pulled his face against her breasts. She wore a silk blouse with no brassier. He put one hand around her waist, the other under her head and kissed her neck. Her mouth opened and he moved so he could kiss it. Her tongue searched for his tongue, her hands caressed their way around his arms to his chest, down the front of his abdomen to his fly. She unzipped his pants. He slid his hand up her back under her blouse. Her skin was smooth and warm. He opened the blouse and kissed her breast. She slipped her panties off and they made love.

"You'd better go," she pouted later, as if she did not really mean it. "You'll be leaving Wattsville soon and I'll still live here."

"I'll go, but I don't want to." He smiled at her with her chin between his fingers.

The next morning, he could not wait to get to the clinic. It was delicious watching Mary go about her duties. She acted the same, but she was different. She had been beautiful, now she was more than that. She took his breath away. She left for dinner before he could speak to her privately and at the end of the day he missed her again. He went by her house, there was no answer to his knock.

At the hotel, Bea fixed his supper. He ate in silence and went to his room. He called her number twice, the second time she answered.

"Yes, I would like to see you. Come over. It's still early. I wasn't planning to go to bed for a while." She seemed receptive when she answered the door. "I'm glad to see you," she said. "I was afraid you wouldn't want to see me again."

"Why would you think that?" he asked.

"I was pretty eager last night. I wondered whether you would respect me in the morning." She laughed.

He put his arms around her and kissed her.

"Would you like some coffee?" she asked.

"Yes."

They sat on the couch. The firelight played over her face. Her eyes were moist.

"You're sad."

"Yes, I suppose I am. You reminded me I have missed a lot by staying here." She paused, looked into the fire as if she were framing her next statement, then looked at Bernard. "And I don't mean the sex. Having you here has meant a lot of different things to me. Especially since Dr. Sizemore's life has taken such a turn."

"You really care for him, don't you?"

"He's been a wonderful man. His life here has not been easy."

Bernard could not think of anything to say. Mary seemed so pensive. He held her hands and looked into her eyes for a long time.

"Can I see you again? Charleston's not far away."

"I don't know." She kissed him. "Last night can never happen again. I cannot explain, but I'm not like that." Then, she changed the subject. "I enjoyed working with you, Dr. Southard."

* * *

Doc came back the next day. "Well, Bernard," he said. "I hear you did pretty good. I understand I only have two or three grievances to clear up, the staff hasn't all quit and the building's still standing. For the time you've been here, I consider myself pretty lucky."

"I appreciate that, Dr. Sizemore," Bernard said. "I think I learned a thing or two."

"Now, that's refreshing." Doc laughed. "For a man's only been shot once, you must be a quick learner." He put his hand across Bernard's back. "You think about a place to practice some day, I could use some help."

"Thank you, Dr. Sizemore. I'll think about it." He said goodbye to the staff. Mary kissed him then turned and walked quickly out of the building. He said goodbye to Luke and wished him well. Later at the hotel he hugged Bea and kissed her cheek.

"I'll miss you," she called as he carried his luggage to the car. "Oh, I almost forgot. Deputy sheriff Chapin phoned. He arrested Lester Spradling. He wants you to come by and sign the complaint."

Bernard climbed gingerly into his wounded automobile, started her up and drove part way across the parking lot. He stuck his head out the window and waved. "Call him for me will you, Bea? Tell him to forget it. I'll get my window fixed, my rump will heal. I think I learned enough to compensate me for that." She smiled and absent-mindedly wiped her hands on her apron.

He drove slowly out of town and up the winding road, the wind was still pretty cold, but he did not mind. He needed to be alert, he had a long drive ahead and a lot to think about.

The trip back to Charleston was over too quickly. He did not want to see anyone for a while so he parked on Summers Street and went to a movie at the Kearse. He was glad the theater was almost empty. He had trouble concentrating on the cowboys and Indians in the first feature and the F.B.I. agents surrounding the farmhouse and riddling it with bullets in the second. The compromises he discovered Dr. Sizemore had made and the pressures he experienced from conditions in Wattsville troubled him. Back in his own world, he felt depressed.

And then there was Mary Arbogast!

* * *

"Mary," Doc said one Monday morning a few weeks after he returned from Arizona. "Was that Dr. Southard I saw driving out of town Sunday afternoon?"

"Why, yes it was, Dr. Sizemore." Her face colored just a hint of a shade darker.

"I must'a been out when he stopped at the house," Doc snickered. "Guess that's why I didn't see him." He looked at Mary with a knowing smile. She turned and walked into the lab area. The back of her neck reddened slightly.

Mary met Bernard in Fall's View at the Greystone Inn. He was seated by the window watching the doorway when she arrived. He crossed the room and they embraced.

"Do you think your parents will approve of me?" Mary whispered after they were seated.

"They will love you almost as much as I do," Bernard answered. He placed his hand over hers on the table. The waiter shifted his weight from foot to foot and toyed with the menus. The restaurant was crowded. Several couples glanced in their direction, nodded and smiled.

"Do you know everyone?" she asked, as he acknowledged waves from diner after diner and the waiters called him by name.

"They're just using me as an excuse to get a good look at you," he teased. The setting sun reflected off the falls and the green hills faded to gray, the candle in the middle of the table cast its soft light on Mary's face.

"You suddenly look so serious, Bernard. Is there something wrong?" she asked.

"Oh, no," he answered. "You are just so beautiful..." Mary smiled.

After supper, they drove up the hill to introduce Mary to his parents.

Chapter Twenty Three

"Yessir, you heard the truth, Doc. I'm going to retire. Sold the place to a man name of Chargin. He's a boxing promoter in Charleston, I think. He'll be taking over end of the month." Shorty had a daughter in Florida and he told Doc he was moving in with her. "Got a trailer out in back of her place. Her divorce'll be final in a month. It'll help her out, me being there. Ever since Mabel died, I been kinda' lonely, myself. You know how that is, Doc."

"Maybe you'll find yourself a wealthy widow-lady down there, Shorty. They're all over the place in Florida." Doc laughed and patted the little bartender's back.

"I cain't say I'd know how to meet a wealthy lady, Doc," Shorty said.

"Got all the money in the world widow-ladies. Those big-city fellas work themselves to death and their rich widows go down there to Floridia looking for another man. Don't try to understand it, that's just the way it is. Beach'es in Florida full of `em. Lonely widows from New York, got lots a money. Take up shuffelboard. They'll be all over you. Lap a' luxury, Shorty. Yessir lap a' luxury, widows got it all." Shorty looked at the floor as if to shut out any competing thoughts and smiled to himself.

Three days after Shorty's departure, Doc walked into the bar and there in the back of the room sat the new bartender. "Well I'll be a monkey's uncle if it ain't Noey Kelly, as I live and breathe."

Noey was talking to a customer but he stopped his conversation and looked up to see who was responsible for the commotion. The lack of recognition was obvious and Doc stopped in his tracks about ten feet away from the confounded Kelly.

"Earl Sizemore," Doc announced.

"Earl?" Noey asked. He scratched his head trying to remember.

"You remember - Earl. I was in high school when you and Red Pattison started the Wattsville Brawlers Boxing Club."

"Earl Sizemore. I'll be damned. Earl Sizemore. I heard you went to college or something. Or was it the Army? How the Hell you been?" He didn't get up but he patted his abdomen as if to point out Doc's lack of conditioning. "Not fightin' any these days, eh?"

"No. " Doc laughed, going along with the charade. "How about you?"

"Havin' some trouble gettin matches. No body wants to fight anymore. They got it all tied up. Cain't get a match. Ranked number two and cain't get a match."

"I heard Chargin bought this place. That true?" Doc knew Noey had not been ranked number two in three decades. His license had been revoked because of the vicious beatings he had taken and that was at least twenty years ago.

"We're partners. He put up the money. I do the work. Ain't that the shits? What'a you doin' these days?"

"I'm a doctor," Doc answered. "Here in Wattsville."

"You a horse doctor or a people doctor?"

"A people doctor, though some are horses asses I reckon."

"Well, have a beer on me, Dr. Earl Sizemore and while you're drinkin' it, maybe you can tell me why my pecker won't get stiff no more like it use'ta get."

"That's a hard question, if you know what I mean." Doc said.

* * *

Noey Kelly got drunk one night a few weeks later and fell down the stairs leading from his living quarters over the bar. Doc had been cleaning up after delivering a baby when he heard the banging out in front.

"Hold your horses. I'll be right there," he called as he came down the hall.

Several of Kelly's late-night customers stood in front of the clinic with Noey on a make-shift stretcher. "Bring him into the exam room and put him on the table." The men hoisted their burden up onto the exam table and heaved a collective sigh of relief. "What happened, Noey?" Doc asked.

"I can whip that son-of-a-bitch," he said. His face was pasty, his skin damp, his speech slurred. He struggled to set up.

"Hold his shoulders," Doc instructed the bystanders as the leg flopped over the side of the table. "Noey! Hold still. It looks like you broke your leg. I gotta' put a cast on it."

"Ain't nobody putting no cast on nuthing," Noey yelled as he fought the restraint. His effort soon wore him out though, and he fell back exhausted, mumbling incoherently.

Noey's shirt fell open revealing the huge surgical scar on his abdomen. "Holy shit! Look at that scar," Earl Braxton exclaimed. "Wonder what caused that, Doc?"

Doc's memory went back to that night the Wattsville Brawlers disbanded in a hail of gunfire and he had dived under the ring to avoid a stray bullet.

Noey had toppled over the ropes onto the floor bleeding from a hole in his abdomen.

Doc remembered crawling out from under the ring after Buck Mace took the gun out of Irene's hand. She hadn't even resisted. She just stood over her fallen lover looking down into his distorted face. Irene and Noey had been living together, she was eight months pregnant when she found out Noey had been running around on her. She came into the gym and shot him while he was sparring with Junior Jarret. The baby was born while Irene was in jail and Noey was still in the hospital. Complications from that gunshot wound kept Noey from being Champion of the World.

Doc split the pants leg to reveal the injury. The femur stuck out through the skin of Noey's thigh. Noey complained half-heartedly and went to sleep as Doc applied wet dressings over the exposed bone.

Doc did not answer Earl Braxton's question. He called the mine office and arranged for the ambulance to take Noey to the emergency room in Charleston.

The day after his return to Wattsville, Noey began to complain of pain under the cast and Doc gave him pain pills. Two days later pus began leaking out from under the foot of the cast. Doc went up the stairs to Noey's bedroom and detected the putrid odor of gangrene as soon as he opened the door. Noey was in bed with the blankets pulled up around his neck. His body shook with the chills and his bedroom reeked of decaying tissue. Noey screamed the entire time it took Doc to split the cast. By the time the procedure was complete, Noey had fainted from the agony.

Doc started him on double doses of Chloramphenicol and Bicillin. After four days he was better and within three weeks Doc stopped the Chloramphenicol, but the drainage continued so he administered injections of Bicillin at twice monthly intervals.

"Noey, I think that leg is going to be all right after all. Could'a lost it if we hadn't got right on it, though," Doc said one evening when he went to the apartment over the bar.

"I think I can come into the office for the dressing changes, Doc," Noey said. "I'm gettin' around pretty good on these crutches you lent me and I ain't had no fever in some time now."

"I don't mind stopping by for a friend," Doc answered. *No use having him come to the clinic and stirring up Cox,* Doc thought. He had not been charging Noey.

"I surely do appreciate the personal care, Doc, and it's mighty white of you to forget the charge like you done. All them shots would've set me back a pretty penny."

Noey's femur healed with a crook in it and he walked with a decided limp. The twice monthly Bicillin injections seemed to finally control the infection but his leg drained for the better part of a year before the fistula closed.

"Just use that cane and favor your leg, Noey. You're a lucky man we didn't have to amputate," Doc said. Doc couldn't pay for another beer in Kelly's place after that, though he continued to make a gesture toward his pocket each time he was served.

"Put your money away, Doc. That beer's on the house," Noey announced each time Doc came in. "Your money's no good in here. I cain't thank you enough, Doc. A fighter's got to have two good legs."

"I heard Mr. Kelly broke his leg. I saw him walking with a cane and he said that if you ever run for office, you've got his vote for sure," Mary Arbogast said. She seemed puzzled that he had not been into the clinic.

"Hey, wait a minute," Doc enthusiastically changed the subject. "Is that what I think it is?"

"Yes, it is," Mary answered. She held her hand out with her finger hyperextended so Doc could see the ring. She blushed ever so slightly and her face seemed to light up.

"Dr. Southard is a mighty lucky young man, Mary." He paused and for a moment it seemed as if he were somewhere else. Then his body shuddered and he looked at Mary. "Since Shirley..." he whispered. It was as if as he stood there he had experienced Shirley's presence.

Mary said, "Thank you, Dr. Sizemore," but she was certain he did not hear. She left him standing there, still seemingly transfixed.

Later, she told Bernard, Doc appeared to have left his body. "I felt so sorry for him, but," she paused, "there was just nothing to say. I felt as though I were intruding."

Chapter Twenty Four

Doc pulled into the parking lot, a group of men were loitering in front of the steps of the clinic. He did not recognize some of them and the ones he did recognize, he had not seen in years. "Hi Doc," a well dressed man of forty pushed through the crowd and extended his hand.

"Hi Charlie. Haven't seen you in a month of Sundays. Where you been keeping yourself?" Charlie's parents and his married sister were Doc's patients. They had often reminded Doc of Charlie's whereabouts and his activities, but for the life of him Doc couldn't remember much of the information just at that moment.

"Working over in Dayton," Charlie answered.

"What'cha doing over there, Charlie?"

"Working in a hospital, Doc. Doing maintenance work. I'm kinda' jack-a-all-trades. Anything breaks down, I fix it."

"How long you been doing that, Charlie?"

"Oh, better part'a six years now, I reckon."

"Do you miss the mines?"

"Not on your life, Doc! Not a minute of it."

"What is all this, Charlie?"

"We're going to set up a picket line here in front of the clinic, Doc," Charlie said. He motioned with his hand just where the line would be drawn.

"Well, that's going to block the whole parking lot, Charlie. What you picketing the clinic for anyhow?"

"We been cut off from the welfare," a man in the crowd volunteered.

"What's that got to do with the clinic? I haven't seen any of you in here in God knows how long. If you want medical care, you got to come ask for it. What in God's name has got into you?"

"You don't understand, Doc. It ain't got nothing to do with you." Charlie turned his back and started directing the formation of the picket line. Doc walked up the steps, baffled by what he saw. There was one woman in the waiting room where there would normally have been twenty.

Doc looked at her sitting on the wooden bench. "Mornin', Abigail."

"Hi, Doctor Sizemore," she answered. Doc went on down the hall to his office. Mary Arbogast stuck her head in the doorway.

"What do you think of the army?" she asked.

"Come on in, Mary. Looks like we're going to have a light day. What the hell's going on?" She came in and stood in front of Doc's desk. "Do you have any idea what this is about?" he asked.

"Those are people who used to live here and work in the mines before they moved away," Mary explained. "Most of them have jobs in Cleveland or Akron or Cincinnati or someplace. My brother will be out there after a while. He's been working in Pittsburgh for five years."

"Sit," Doc ordered. "What does he say? Your brother, I mean."

Mary settled herself in the chair next to the desk and continued her explanation. "Well, it only costs a dollar a month to carry your miner's card if you're laid off, so all these men continued to do that. Some of them haven't worked in the mines in fifteen years, but they get free medical care for their entire families with that card. The working miners are sharing the royalty they get on every ton of coal with men who haven't been miners in years."

"Why in God's name did the union negotiators include them anyway?" Doc asked.

"To pad their rolls, to give them more negotiating power. The more people in their union the more weight they thought they could throw around." Mary could not hide the cynical tone in her voice. "But it backfired. The fund is going broke. They are about to lose their hospitals and the pharmacy. So they cut off free medical care to anyone who has not worked in the mines in the past twelve months. The Catholic Church has all ready made an offer on the hospitals."

"God bless America, Apple pie and the trade union movement," Doc exclaimed. "Now I've seen everything. Union workers picketing their own union." He scratched his head and shook it back and forth. "Now you got to admit it, Mary. This is funny."

Mary got up and turned to leave the room. She looked over her shoulder at Doc who still had the perplexed expression on his face. "Kinda like the dog that caught his tail," she said.

The number of picketers dwindled as their vacations played out. Miners crossed the picket lines, the union paid no attention to the grievances and the governor turned a deaf ear. The families who had legitimate claim to continued medical coverage were treated as ruthlessly as the opportunists.

"I got black lung, Doc. I cain't work a`tall and they's cutting me off first a' the month. I cain't tell what they `spect me to do," one emaciated miner complained.

Over the next few months, Doc realized the disabled "chronic lungers" were being dropped as fast as the administrator could justify doing so. Tyree warned Doc there may have to be a dollar charged for an office visit and some kind of a charge for medicines.

"If we don't economize every way we can, we may have to cut your salary," he announced at the end of his visit to the clinic one day. "I've been going through the files and there's lots of these people who come in here regularly who aren't even sick."

"You should not be going through those files," Doc said. "Those are confidential."

"We pay you to work in the best interest of the welfare fund," Tyree answered. "After all, in the long run that's what's in the best interest of the patients who really need medical care. And we have an obligation to oversee the medical activities paid for by the fund."

"But, those are the patient's most private communications with their physician. That's supposed to be private."

"Oh, come now, Doctor. When you became an employee of this organization you knew where your obligation was. You certainly took your check every month." He seemed especially harried and short tempered. He was feeling the pinch of Loomis' scrutiny.

Loomis worried about his empire for the first time since he had ram-rodded the closed shop down the coal operator's throats. He would like nothing better than to find a scapegoat for his managerial inadequacy. There was no one on earth he would rather sacrifice than "..that twerp Tyree B. for bullshit, Cox," as he referred to the administrator. The only problem Loomis had was he feared

Cox might have squirreled away something with which to protect himself.

"He acts mighty snotty lately," Loomis reported to the board. "I need somebody to find out what he knows."

In truth, union interference and the royalty on each ton of coal was pricing the fuel out of the market, and non-union "truck mines" were beginning to take more and more of the local business. In addition, surface mining was beginning to flourish in the west, far from the reaches of the Affiliated Miner's Union.

* * *

"You talk to him, Mary," Ramsay pleaded. "God knows he will not listen to me."

"I'm sorry, Mr. Southard. Bernard has to make up his own mind about where he practices medicine," Mary answered.

"His mother says the same thing." Ramsay laughed. "I guess I'm just going to have to shut up about this." He looked at Sarah. She shook her finger knowingly.

"I've tried to tell him not to push Bernard," she said to Mary. "I know you both will make the right decision when the time comes." Mary smiled and looked at Bernard.

Bernard looked out the window.

The next time Bernard visited Mary, he talked to Doc about the possibility of his coming to Wattsville.

"If I'm going to keep the best nurse in West Virginia," Doc teased. "I guess I better take you in to be my partner. Couldn't get along without Mary, you know."

"Then you'll talk to the administrator?" Bernard asked.

"I'm pleased, Bernard. With your help maybe we can whip this place back into shape." He looked at his desk then at the young doctor sitting across from him. "I sort of let things get out of hand..." His voice trailed off. He was mumbling. "I used to be a doctor," he almost whispered - staring at Bernard but not seeing him. Bernard felt uncomfortable, as if he had been eavesdropping.

Bernard stood up and waited. It seemed like a long time before a shiver ran through Doc's body and he awakened. "Oh, excuse me, Bernard. I'll bet you want to go see Mary." He looked out the window.

"I'll talk to the administrator, first thing."

Bernard drove slowly to Mary's house. He couldn't shake the sadness. "What's the matter, darling?" Mary asked when she opened the door. "You look as if you've seen a ghost." He put his arms around her.

* * *

"Well, Bernard, you've got to make your mind up soon," Jeff Jordan said. "Your residency will be over in a month and you can't possibly find a better offer."

"I know, Jeff," Bernard answered. "You and Dan have really been generous and I do appreciate it." He paused. "But..."

"But what? You're not still thinking about going up to Wattsville are you?"

"Well, I've sort'a had my heart set on it all these years. And..."

"And?" Jeff's expression became more serious. "And, if half of what I hear about the changes in that practice are true, you'd be smart to just put that notion out of your mind before you do something stupid."

"I suspect you may be right. But..."

"But?"

"Well, he was once a good doctor. Maybe a great doctor," Bernard said.

"Hell, son, that's the point. The first time I worked up there, you couldn't find a better physician. But, from what I hear..." He didn't finish the sentence he just shook his head and looked at Bernard, kind of in disgust.

"You have no way of knowing it, but I probably wouldn't be alive now if it weren't for him, and if I were, my life wouldn't be worth living," Bernard said.

"That doesn't oblige you to throw that life away trying to save him. You know, Bernard, a doctor can't work for an organization that tells him what to prescribe and who to prescribe it for."

"A doctor works for his patient regardless of where his paycheck comes from," Bernard said. "In medical school they said..."

"Do you still believe your med school professors knew anything about practicing medicine in the real world?" Jeff interrupted. "Don't kid yourself. It makes a difference where your paycheck comes from. In our practice we will not even take a check from the insurance company."

"Why not?"

"Because we don't work for the insurance company. We work for the patient," Jeff answered. "When the man from the insurance company told me that they would send the check directly to me so the patient could not cash it and not pay the bill, I said no thanks. Dr. Sizemore was an excellent doctor, and from what I've heard he was a good man. He just forgot who he was working for."

"I appreciate the advice, Jeff, and I'll let you and Dan know very soon; if you'll just be patient with me a little longer."

"Has this got something to do with that gorgeous nurse of his?" Jeff asked.

"She kinda feels obligated," Bernard answered.

"OK, son," Jeff acquiesced. He placed his arm over Bernard's shoulder and they walked down the hall toward the cafeteria.

"But don't keep us waiting forever. You'll not get a better opportunity than this."

Jeff bid so long and went to lunch. Bernard went out the back door of the hospital and drove to Wattsville.

"Well, well, I'm mighty glad to see you, Bernard! I've talked to the administrator. He'll be here in a little while to discuss that matter with you." Doc seated himself and waved his hand toward the chair by his desk. "I'm ready for some help around here. There's enough work for two; that's for sure."

Bernard smiled, thanked Doc for setting up the meeting and while Doc left to see a patient, he wandered into the lab and talked to Mary Arbogast. He touched her hand and Mrs. Sidenstricker looked up from her desk and smiled.

Cox breezed in, an hour after the time he had promised to meet Bernard and walked straight into Doc's office without speaking to anyone. "Send the young man in," he called to Mary before he seated himself.

Doc followed Bernard into the office, but Tyree dismissed him almost contemptuously with a wave of his hand. "We will not be needing you in our meeting, Dr. Sizemore. I'm sure you have work to do." He stood up and motioned for Bernard to sit, then re-seated himself behind the desk. "Do you want the girl to bring you coffee or anything, young man?" he asked.

"No, thank you," Bernard answered.

"Nurse," he commanded Arbogast. "I'll have a little less cream if you don't mind. You always seem to get too much in my coffee. And be sure it's hot," he called after her as she walked down the hall toward the coffee pot. After he had sipped of the pale, lukewarm contents of the cup she placed on his desk and mumbled something about no one around there ever being able to get anything right, he directed Bernard to close the door. When Bernard stood to follow the direction, Mary looked over her shoulder and winked.

"I'll get right to the subject, young man. How did you find out we were planning to replace Dr. Sizemore? I thought only Loomis and myself knew of our plans."

"I didn't..."

"Oh, come now don't deny you're here for his job."

"I came here to discuss a partnership with Dr. Sizemore. He informed me you would meet me for that purpose."

"Well, young man, I happen to know you have worked in this clinic several times over the past few years, and unless you have had your eyes closed and your brain turned off, you must be aware the formerly illustrious Dr. Sizemore has made himself obsolete. We have been considering a change for some time. Of course it would not be possible for us to continue the same rate of pay, as the coal industry has taken a down-turn, but given the problems resulting from language barriers in some of the clinics we have all ready converted..." He paused and rubbed his chin. "We would be able to make a small concession to avoid replacing him with a foreigner."

Bernard was flabbergasted, he sat stony-faced. He felt empty. Later, as he drove through the beautiful summer afternoon toward Fall's View, he tried to remember how the meeting had been terminated. He parked on the hill overlooking Kanawha Falls and watched the sun go down before he went into the house.

"Well, Bernard, have you decided to accept the offer from Dr. Jordan and Dr. Newbil?" Ramsay asked.

"Yes, I have, Father," he answered. There was more than a tinge of sadness in his voice. Ramsay suspected its source.

* * *

"Regardless of what your recollection is, if you'll just look at the contract you'll see Hygiene Inc. has acquired possession of the property free and clear. That includes the fixtures and equipment; so be forewarned against trying to take anything out of here without my permission."

Tyree B. Cox was emphatic with his instructions before Doc was allowed back into his office to get his personal effects. The locks had been changed, Mary Arbogast had been fired, "Let go," was the way the administrator had put it. She moved to Charleston to work at the Memorial Hospital. A young doctor from Manila was brought in to work in the clinic three days a week. He would work the other three in Prince.

"Wouldn't catch my woman in there," some of the miners vowed. "No self-respectin' woman'd let a black furrin'er examine her even if she were diein'." So business dropped off for a time, but a change in prejudices soon turned out to be easier than paying for one's own pills.

Even though the "Filipino" was only available three days a week and the specialists had long ago quit coming to Wattsville, the drop in business was not enough to resurrect the welfare fund. Additional cut-backs followed in the form of co-payments for medicines and inevitably in further reduction of the services.

The administrator watched Luke interpreting for Dr. Marcous one day and noticed the patients seemed to trust him more than the physician. He made arraignments to send Luke for a four month course in diagnostics and installed him as the Physician's assistant. That was six months previously and it worked out so well that the "Filipino" was assigned to cover three clinics two days a week each and male nurses were hired to fill in the gaps.

"He seems kinda prissy to me, too, but at least he's a American and a body can understand what he's talkin' about," some of the patients explained when they chose to see Luke rather than the doctor.

At the state conference in Charleston, Loomis announced the changes were "part of the necessary cut-backs in the wake of financial reverses suffered by the union welfare fund." The next day he fired Cox and within a week, Randolph Jenkins, who had just been elected representative to the U.S. Congress, announced an investigation into "reports of mismanagement" of the union welfare fund.

"We will not tolerate the mis-use of monies designated for the betterment of the citizens of our fair state," he pontificated. "In order to get to the bottom of the mis-management of this troubled financial empire, I have appointed John J. Loomis to head-up a citizen's committee. He has the full support of my good offices and the subpoena power of the U.S.Congress. No stone will be left un-turned..." And on and on the voice of sure justice droned. Two months later, the Gazette headlines reported in huge letters, "Clinic Administrator Indicted!"

* * *

Mary Arbogast married Bernard and started working part-time in the back office of Newbil, Jordan, and Southard, Internal Medicine Associates. Eventually, she and Bernard had two children. Bernard stayed in touch with the twins but he and Mary only visited Doc twice after Bernard's meeting with the administrator.

"It's just too depressing to see what has happened to him," he told Ramsay.

* * *

The linen closet off the living room would serve quite well as storage for supplies and by moving the couch over against the wall there was plenty of room for a desk and chair. Doc hadn't used that part of the house in years anyway and it was just off the foyer so patients wouldn't have to traipse through the rest of the house to get there. He planned to see people for whatever they could pay because he knew they would choose him over some foreigner they couldn't even understand.

"I'm sorry, Doc, but the union won't cover my medicines `less I go to the clinic," he was informed by his former patients. Or, "My records is over at the clinic and they won't let me have them to take to another doctor." Or, overheard when someone pretended he didn't know Doc was around, "Time he was let go. Just a old quack far as I'm concerned. I wouldn't trust him far as I could th'ow him."

And, there were not enough colord's left in town to make much of a practice.

After a while Doc stopped visiting Kelly's or the store and he didn't even get out of his car anymore when he went over to Mr. Legg's service station. Legg was getting feeble but he would toddle out and "fill `er up" for cash.

Doc spent a lot of time sitting in the living room in a smoking jacket Ramsay Southerd had sent him from China, dropping ashes on his chest, wiping them down the front of his shirt. He had started drinking and his hand shook so much he had trouble giving the occasional penicillin shot he was consulted for when someone found the clinic too inconvenient.

One day Doc dozed off in his chair and awakened with a start. He had saliva draining out the corner of his mouth and down to the curve of his chin. He wiped it away with his sleeve. He was momentarily confused as to whether he was dreaming or not. ***No,***

I was not dreaming, he decided. *I'd better get going or she'll deliver without me.*

Now where did I put that bag? He rummaged around in the closet, found the worn leather medical bag and got his hat and coat off the rack in the foyer.

Good thing I got that new car. That old Ford would never make it up the hill to Birdie's house. He looked at the automobile parked in the drive. *I could have sworn I parked the new Plymouth out here. Spose I left it over at Legg's?* He stood there for a few more minutes trying to remember what it was he was thinking about.

Then, he went back into the house.

END!

5472256R0

Made in the USA
Charleston, SC
20 June 2010